Praise for *Hov*

Jet Mykles' *Leashed: Two for One Deal*

"*Leashed: Two for One Deal* has such a BLISTERING hot plot that I couldn't put the book down, even for a moment. The pace never slows, remaining consistently fast paced, while the action, both in and out of bed, left me glued to the pages. I'll be going back to read this one again."

—Francesca Haynes, *Just Erotic Romance Reviews*

Raine Weaver's *Wolfe's Gate*

"*Wolfe's Gate* by Raine Weaver takes an old fairytale and reweaves it into an exciting escapade. Ms. Weaver's characters are forceful and passionate, even the secondary ones. It is no wonder, then, that her love scenes leave scorch marks and tension runs high as mystery mounts."

—Keely Skillman, *ECataRomance.com*

Jeigh Lynn's *All Hallow's Moon*

"*All Hallow's Moon* is a very sweet and endearing read. The characters are all likeable and such a joy to read about. Ms Lynn has created a story that is filled with good humor, deep and abiding love, and content, affable characters that easily make you smile."

—Marina, *Cupid's Library Reviews*

LooseId®

ISBN 1-59632-333-7
ISBN 13: 978-1-59632-333-9
HOWL
Copyright © 2006 by Loose Id, LLC
Cover Art by April Martinez

Publisher acknowledges the authors and copyright holders of the individual works, as follows:
LEASHED: TWO FOR ONE DEAL
Copyright © October 2005 by Jet Mykles
WOLFE'S GATE
Copyright © October 2005 by Raine Weaver
ALL HALLOW'S MOON
Copyright © October 2005 by Jeigh Lynn

Printed in the U.S.A. by
Lightning Source, Inc.
1246 Heil Quaker Blvd
La Vergne TN 37086
www.lightningsource.com

Contents

LEASHED:
TWO FOR ONE DEAL

Jet Mykles

Dedication

This one's for the members of my Yahoo Group, for their undying support. Also, for my editor, Raven, who told me to write about boys and more boys!

Prologue

I toyed with the talisman. At the moment, it was just a trinket. A burned twig, a feather, a written note, and a piece of string tying it all together. No one who didn't know what it was would even look at it twice. I twirled it over the bowl, deciding whether to do this.

I had to do this. Roland wasn't going to let up. At some point, he was going to catch me when my guard was down, or he was going to become more powerful and just take me. It was only a matter of time.

But the spell could prevent that. Cast it and let protection come to me.

Sighing, I dropped the talisman into the shallow pool of blood—my blood—at the bottom of the earthen bowl. Woodenly, I spoke the words to release the spell. With a quiet, inaudible rush, the talisman absorbed my blood, glowed briefly, and with a flash of intangible flame, the bowl was empty.

Let all hell break loose!

Chapter One

"Meg!"

"What?"

"Where are you?"

"Down here."

I heard Gwen stomping toward me and wondered if she stepped heavily on purpose. I mean really, she was all of five feet tall and probably weighed eighty pounds. How did she make such a noise?

She rounded the end of the bookcase, batting aside a dangling paper jack o' lantern to find me kneeling on the floor. I was considerably taller than five foot—I was five foot ten, actually—and kneeling to put books away on the bottom shelf was not a comfortable position for me. I glanced up and groaned. Not because of the fact that my legs from the knees down had gone numb, but because of what she held in her hand.

"You've been going through the trash again."

She waved the embossed envelope at me. "And it's a damn good thing I did! Do you know who this is from?"

"Yes."

"And you threw it *away?*"

I met her determined blue-eyed stare with my own brown-eyed one. "Yes."

She gaped, struck dumb, amazingly enough. It didn't happen often. I took the opportunity to use the sturdy bookcase and the cold floor to push-pull myself to my feet.

Gwen finally found her voice. "You're going to turn down an invitation to Shannon Cavanagh's Halloween party?"

"Yes."

"Why?"

I sighed, reaching up to put my disheveled ponytail back in place. Long strands of my straight black hair had managed to work their way free during the last hour that I'd been working. Or had I pulled them free? "She doesn't really want me there, Gwen."

She shoved the black-and-gold invitation toward my face. "This proves otherwise."

I pushed the invitation aside, not even looking at it. "She sent it as a courtesy to a witch in her territory."

"She didn't send *me* one."

I tried not to flinch. There were good reasons Gwen didn't get one, but she never wanted to hear them. "You don't have the pedigree that I do."

Luckily, that explanation almost always worked, even if it made her grimace. "Yeah, well." She opened the invitation, eyeing the gold-on-black script. Very high class. Very Shannon.

"It says you could bring a guest. You could bring me. Introduce me."

"No." I picked up the box I'd emptied of books and turned to walk away.

"Aw, c'mon, Meg."

"No."

"She might be able to help you."

I froze. "Absolutely not!"

Like one of those little terrier dogs that keeps nipping at your heels, Gwen followed me. "Have you asked her?"

I shoved aside a paper skeleton dangling from the wall near the front counter. "Why would I do a fool thing like that?"

She trailed me past the front counter into the back room before she grabbed my arm to stop me. The look she gave me was less annoyed than worried, a strange look on that round little face that usually showed defiance.

"Meg, I'm serious. Roland's going to come after you. You need help. And the guardian spell hasn't worked. It's been two weeks."

I took a deep breath, tossing the empty box into a corner. "I know that, Gwen."

"So—" She waved the invitation at me again. "—maybe it's time to look somewhere else."

"Not Shannon, Gwen. She wouldn't help me."

"Why not?"

I grumbled. "Just let it go. Trust me. Shannon would be about as helpful as my mother."

"And I still don't understand why you don't call her. She's your *mother*."

I shook my head and lifted another box of books. "I don't know how to explain it to you any better than I already have, Gwen." She and I had only known each other two years, but we had one of those solid relationships that just seemed to work. It was refreshing for me, since very few of my relationships ever really worked.

When I turned, she stood in the doorway, another invitation in her hand. That one made my blood run cold. It was white, with tasteful black lettering, elegant and understated. Gwen held it up with a sympathetic grimace.

"I found this one, too."

I pushed past her with the box, headed toward the front of the shop. "You've got to stay out of the trash."

"Meg, he'll come for you. You know that."

"Yes. I know."

"Halloween is tomorrow night."

"I know that, too."

"What are you going to do?"

I stopped at the end of one of the few bookcases in the far front corner of the shop, well away from the computer nooks and the front door. "I don't know," I whispered, trying to keep despair from resurfacing. I *hated* feeling helpless, and this whole situation did nothing but. "I'll call my sister tonight. Maybe Talia can…" I stopped, frowning.

"What is it, Meg?" Gwen stepped toward me, concerned.

I shook my head, propping the box on my left hip to free my right hand. Something like invisible ants marched up under my skin. What *was* that? I flexed my hand, but the tingling in my fingers didn't stop. Actually, it wasn't just my hand; it was my entire arm.

"Oh, shit!"

I whirled to face the door. The box clattered to the floor, forgotten in favor of the spell that I gathered in my palm. To a non–magic-user, it looked like I held nothing. But anyone with even a glimmering of the Gift or any training in the magical arts would see a whirling ball of yellow-white.

The bell over the shop's door jangled as it opened. I was at a bad angle to the front door, so I couldn't immediately see the person. I had to wait until whoever it was stepped in fully before I could see who had set off my metaphysical radar.

He was young. That was my first impression. Probably legal, but just barely. My second impression was that he was gorgeous! Tall and slim and built like a baseball rookie. Lean and muscular. He wore a faded denim jacket and matching jeans with a worn black Aerosmith T-shirt. A mess of light brown hair hung haphazardly almost to his shoulders, and the bluest eyes you ever saw scanned the shop from within the face of a teen idol. It took all of three seconds for that gaze to land on me, and the blue eyes changed. The color remained, but they were no longer human eyes at all. Canine.

A werewolf.

Gwen gasped. I grabbed her arm to pull her behind me and held the spell ready. I didn't let loose. He didn't jump at me, just shared a stare. After a breath, he smiled.

Mmm, yummy! This was my protection?

I started to smile back, but he was pushed farther into the shop by the arrival of another. A bit taller than the first, this man barged into the shop with his eyes fixed on me. Like he already knew I was there. I barely got an impression of angry green eyes set into a face capped with silky black hair before he lunged, snarling.

The spell left my hand before my thought to release it happened. It hit his chest square, and I barked the word of power to activate it. He screamed, an entirely feline scream of rage that had our two customers ducking for cover.

I didn't have time to wonder at his appearance. The first man echoed the attack of the second, and because the spell wasn't ready, he actually reached me before I released another into his chest. He howled, tackling me as he fell.

It was done in a space of heartbeats. Both men lay stunned and moaning on the floor of the shop. I half-sat, half-lay beneath the wolfman. The wire rack behind me teetered, then fell, paperbacks toppling to the floor.

"Holy shit!" Have I mentioned Gwen is a wonder with words?

I didn't glance at her, though, too fascinated by my handiwork. The yellow-white energy spread through the auras of both men, alive as it crawled over their twitching bodies. It sank through their skin, their muscles, their bones, and I *felt* it. Not like it was happening to me, but like the spell was an extension of the hair on my arms, burrowing into their bodies. Then, as though it were being sucked up, the leashing spell coalesced into bands about their necks.

Unseen to any but me, another band snugged about the base of their cocks.

I groaned as the spell settled.

They were mine.

Chapter Two

"Why did you attack me?" I demanded of the green-eyed wonder.

Oh, what a wonder he was! If I'd thought the wolf was gorgeous, the cat was beyond belief. He was movie-star gorgeous. If James Bond looked like this guy, then I could easily see why women fell at his feet. Or, rather, into his bed. His features were sculpted with a smooth, touchable curve to them. His emerald-green eyes were hooded and sultry, with long, thick lashes. His black hair fell heavily across the right side of his face. The mouth set within a square, stubbly jaw was simply made to drive a woman to distraction with soft, suckable lips. The rest of him wasn't bad, either. His muscled torso was displayed nicely by a tight white T-shirt. Worn black jeans shaped lovingly over thick thighs and calves.

He sat up, met my stare, and growled. There was no doubt he was a shifter. Only shifters could be leashed. He had a feline look to him. Although I could be wrong. Not all shifters' builds matched their inner beasts.

My leashing spell pulsed about his throat, invisible to any but me and even fading to me as the spell settled. Soon, I'd have to concentrate to see it. But, until then, it was a clear indication of his murderous thoughts. "I won't be leashed."

I glanced up, but Gwen had already left my side to hustle our customers out and flip the closed sign. The two were regulars and knew I was a witch, but there was no sense in endangering them.

"I've got news for you, buddy," I told my new guest. "You are."

He bared his teeth, overlong canines evident. In less than the blink of an eye, his green irises expanded and his pupils slitted. I glanced down, and sure enough, his fingers had elongated to claws.

Trying to hide my nerves, I glanced down at the wolfman. He was just now pushing himself from his sprawl across my legs. He didn't seem nearly as bothered as his friend. If they were friends. They'd come in so fast, I couldn't tell. Wolfy just sat back, his fully human gaze darting from me to the cat.

"Look," I said, eyes back on the cat. "I didn't want to leash you. If you hadn't jumped me, we could have discussed this calmly."

The claws evaporated back to normal human fingers, but the slit eyes remained. "That's rich. Calm discussion with a witch." His voice was dark chocolate sauce, rich and decadent.

I scowled. "I resent that."

"Yes. You would."

"Listen, buddy, I didn't want to do this in the first place—"

"Then let us go."

"I can't. I need help."

"You could have asked."

"And you would have come?"

He snarled. The sound nothing at all like a human could make.

"Yeah. I didn't think so."

Something inside me trembled at a daunting realization. The guardian spell that I'd cast was supposed to call to a shifter. It talked to something deep inside them that was attracted or compatible with the witch. No one quite knew the specifics, but everyone knew the attraction was there. Unfortunately, it didn't mean that the shifter would *like* the witch. Often, it was a matter of dominance and submission. A dance as old as time between witches and their familiars. Personally, I hated the thought, but desperate times called for desperate measures.

But I digress. I trembled because something within me called to *him!* Called to *both* of them. Extremely few witches can attract and hold two beasts. I would not have pegged me as one of them, despite my lineage.

"Look. Let's talk this out."

He sneered. "Talk? Aren't you just going to give the command for us to jump?"

"How high?" We both looked at Wolfy, who was grinning like his beast. Oh, good Goddess, he was adorable! The lopsided grin alone was enough to heat my blood to a simmer.

I smiled. Kitty growled.

"Oh, c'mon, Mike. We're here now. She leashed us." Wolfy shrugged. "What choice do we have but to talk?"

"Thank you!" I glared briefly at Kitty—Mike?—then extended my hand with an accompanying smile toward Wolfy. "I'm Meg."

He took my hand. "Rudy."

He didn't let go. Instead, we smiled at each other for too long a moment. Then, with the grace of the shifter he was, he rolled to his feet. My hand still in his, he used it to haul me to my own feet.

"It's nice to meet you Rudy. Mike," said Gwen, bustling up to my side as she shamelessly eyed the men. "I'm Gwen." She looked ridiculously small beside Rudy. He topped my height by at least three or four inches.

"The name is *Michael*," came the correction. "Rudy is the only one I let get away with that."

I gently pulled my hand from Rudy's, trying to seem casual about it. Touching him was terribly distracting, and I couldn't take my eyes off Michael because I didn't trust him. Yeah, that's why I couldn't take my eyes off him. If you believe that…

"So you *do* know each other?" I asked.

Rudy smirked. "Yep. We're a pair. Can't have one without the other."

Lucky me!

"Oh, for fuck's sake," Michael growled, rising effortlessly. He stomped his booted feet to settle his jeans. His hair fell in a glossy black sheet just past his shoulders, some of it hanging over the right side of his face. I itched to brush it away.

"Why don't we all go in the back and get more acquainted?" Gwen suggested, slipping her arm into Rudy's.

Rudy grinned at her, opened his mouth to speak.

"And you are?" Michael asked before I could extricate her.

"She's my friend."

"She's not a very powerful witch."

Gwen shot him a glare. "Wanna see what I can do with my little bit of power, kitty cat?"

He met the glare with his own. "Wanna see how fast a jaguar is, little girl?"

"Stop it!" I put emphasis to my words by shoving Gwen away from Rudy and thinking a tug on Michael's leash. It was the equivalent of yanking on a dog's chain, and it made him growl—again—but it also shut him up and backed him a step away from Gwen. "This has all started out badly, and I really need for this to go right. I'm running out of time."

I rounded on Gwen as she opened her mouth to say something. "You stay here and open back up. The last thing we need is for the shop to close down. We need to make next month's rent." I turned and pointed to the men. "Did you come in a car?" Both nodded. "Fine. You can give me a ride home. We'll talk there."

Chapter Three

Normally, I don't let strange men drive me home. But, in this case, I literally had a leash around their windpipes and a garrote around their balls, and they knew it. As far as hurting me went, that was out. The leash spell was as old as the relationship between witches and shifters, and witches had refined it and passed it on over the centuries. Physical harm to me was their pain. They could survive my death, but it wouldn't be a pleasant experience, even if I died quickly. The backlash of my soul severing from my body would implode the spell. It had been known to remove heads and cocks. Only shifters with the help of other witches had ever survived it intact.

Michael pulled out of the local fast-food drive-thru, leaving Rudy to rummage through the six bags of food.

"Okay." Michael glanced at me in the rearview mirror as he stopped at a light. "Talk."

I crossed my arms over my chest. "Bossy, aren't you?"

"You have no idea," Rudy muttered, handing me a bag. Yes, a single bag. The other five were for them.

I spread out in the leather backseat of the black Jaguar, enjoying the luxury. It didn't seem that Michael, at least, was dirt poor. That was something.

"If I'm expected to die for something—for some*one*—I want to know about it as soon as possible." Again those green eyes speared mine in the reflection. "Am I expected to die?"

I flinched. "I hope not."

Michael accepted a double-burger from Rudy. "Then out with it."

I sighed, munching on fries. "There's another witch that wants me."

"Wants you?" Rudy asked, turned sideways in his seat so he could watch me as he, pardon the expression, wolfed down his food.

"Wants me. He's forming a coven and thinks I'll make a great addition."

Rudy shrugged. "So? Don't witches form covens all the time?"

"Let's just say that Roland isn't real big into sharing responsibilities."

"Ah," said Michael. "Wants the coven and all the control?"

I grimaced. "That and more. Roland gives new meaning to the word dominance."

"A burgeoning grand wizard. What's his name?"

"Roland Parks."

"I've never heard of him."

"Would you have?"

"Michael knows a lot of people. Witches and shifters especially."

"What do you do, Michael?"

"I'm a private eye. I make it my duty to keep tabs on the magically inclined."

I blinked. Whoa. I may have hit the veritable jackpot. "I haven't seen you around."

"We're new in town," Rudy chipped in. "Just arrived earlier this week."

Which explained why it'd taken two weeks for my spell to work. The conundrum, of course, was had they moved because of my spell, or did I cast my spell at just the right time? No, I hate puzzles like that, so that's as far as I'd think about it.

"Roland's been low-key. He studied in Europe and the Middle East for most of his life. He doesn't come from any of the families or branches that I've heard of, and he doesn't make himself known as a witch. I didn't even know when we were first dating."

"You dated?"

"Past tense. We met a few months ago. He's a good-looking guy and can be charming when he wants to be." I shrugged. "Dating's a crapshoot, right?"

"Did he know you were a witch?"

"I didn't think so then, but now I'm pretty sure he did."

Michael nodded, gesturing for another burger, which Rudy readily handed to him. "Go on."

I shrugged. "That's it. We dated a few times. Nothing too serious. Then he took me to his house one night, and that's when I found out he was a witch. He told me then that he wanted to form a coven, and he wanted me to be the first member." I sighed. "By then, I was already ready to break it off with him. He was way too much into controlling my life. He always chose where we went, and he'd started to tell me what to wear and how to behave. Nothing too major, but it added up. Then he pretty much showed his true colors when he showed me the rooms he had ready for me in his house."

"Rooms?" Rudy asked.

"Roland's got buckets of money. He's into real estate, I think. He's got one of those showplace houses on the hill, y'know? He'd put aside rooms for me and wanted to move me in."

"Nice of him." Rudy grimaced.

"Wasn't it, though?"

"How did you get away?"

"One on one, I'm a match for him, magically speaking. I don't think he expected that, especially since I don't advertise what I am. But since I turned him down, he's managed to lure at least three witches into his coven. He's also got a leashed shifter now. The odds are stacking up against me."

"You sure he's still after you?" Michael asked.

I thought of the invitation. "Oh, yeah."

"You sure it's just three witches he's got with him?"

"No, I can't be sure how many."

"If he's got the others, why does he still want you?" Rudy asked.

I glanced away. "I'm the one that got away, I guess." I didn't look back to see if they bought it.

"So you needed help."

I glanced up to meet Michael's gaze in the rearview mirror. "Yeah."

"Why didn't you call Shannon?"

I frowned. "Shannon and I aren't on the greatest of terms."

"A coven forming with a dominant grand wizard would be something of interest to the grand dame of the Southwest."

I sucked up some of my cola. "Yeah, well, she's not inclined to believe a word I say." I glanced up at the signs. "Get off at the next exit and go right."

"Why wouldn't she believe you?"

"History."

"Listen, I know she's a huge bitch, but she's not stupid or blind."

"You know her?"

"I know of her."

"Yeah, well, she doesn't like me. Turn left at the light."

"Why?"

"She just doesn't."

He stared at me in the mirror as he waited for the light to change. The silence lasted a bit longer after he turned, until finally he asked, "What did you do?"

"It was a long time ago. Right, up ahead."

"What did you do?"

"I was young and stupid."

"What did you do?"

"Listen, you're not my father…!"

"What did you do?"

"You're a fucking broken record."

"And you're evading the question."

"Hold on. This part gets tricky."

I leaned forward and helped him navigate the twisty roads that snaked through the trees and valleys on the way to my house.

"Nice area," Rudy commented once.

We arrived at my little blue house in due time, turning into the dirt driveway and winding up the tree-covered hill. Witches need space. We live in houses surrounded by nature. Witches need trees and bushes and insects. Witches need at least a modicum of open air, and we need a connection to the earth. We can work and spend time in cities, but a witch forced to live in the city confines is a witch either without her power or slowly dying.

I directed Michael to park in the shade behind the house, then led them in through the kitchen door. I glanced back and saw the look on both of their faces that told me they felt my shield. A thought and a mutter from me, and the shield touched their leashes. There. They were a part of my shield, as was fitting for my leashed protection. They could enter and exit freely.

It was more trust than I'd ever given anyone within a few hours of knowing them. But then, I'd never leashed anyone before. It was an unfair one-way street. I knew I could trust them, but they had to wait to see if they could trust me.

Judging from the way Michael watched me, I didn't think I'd earned his trust yet.

He dropped his empty fast-food bags and drink cup onto the counter, then faced me, arms crossed. "What did you do?"

I scowled, dropping my own bags on the kitchen table, then stalking across the linoleum to the living room.

"We have a right to know," he said, following.

"I know, I know. But it's embarrassing." I sank down onto my deep, comfy sofa, sulking mightily.

Rudy laid his denim jacket over the back of the matching comfy chair and sank into it, carefully out of the line of fire between me and Michael. He crossed his arms over his chest, drawing my attention to the black tribal tattoos that ringed his biceps.

"I'd really rather not repeat my question, Meg." Michael stood in the kitchen door, huge and daunting like the angel he was named after.

"I'm the witch. I thought I was in charge."

The glower on his face made me wish I hadn't said it. "We're the ones who get to stand between you and this Roland person. We've a right to know why you can't get help anywhere else."

"Okay, okay!" I muttered a curse. "I opened a gate into Shannon's private rooms and stole her scrying bowl!"

Michael didn't move, eyes locked on me.

"I gave it back," I continued, "and I didn't tell anyone. But word got out. Obviously, it didn't make her look too good. She's not inclined to talk much to me anymore."

Rudy fidgeted, glancing from me to Michael. "Why'd you do it?"

Although I spoke to Rudy, my eyes were on Michael's carefully blank face. "Like I said, I was young and stupid. I did it just to prove to her that I could."

"Wait a sec, you said her *private* rooms? Weren't they shielded?"

I nodded.

Rudy whistled. "Whoa."

"That takes a lot of power," Michael said, stepping slowly into the room.

Still watching him, I nodded. What was he thinking? "Yes, it does."

"That was ten years ago." Shit! He'd heard about it. "You said you were young. How young?"

"Sixteen."

Rudy leaned forward, as excited as a kid watching the last inning of the World Series when his team was winning. "You broke into a grand dame's shielded rooms at *sixteen?!*"

"She wasn't grand dame then."

"Yeah, but still..." He turned to Michael. "Holy shit, Mike!"

Michael cuffed him upside the head without even looking. Those green eyes never left mine. "What's your surname?"

I got the impression I was just confirming for him. If he knew the incident, he probably had a pretty good idea who I was. "Grey."

"And your mother is...?"

"Tara Grey." Like there was any other who could be my mother.

Michael exploded into a long string of curses that made both Rudy and me jump. At least, I'm pretty sure they were all curses. Some of them were in other languages, and I wasn't much good at them. A fact that never failed to annoy the hell out of my tutors.

"Tara-fucking-Grey! I've been leashed by the wicked witch of the world's daughter!"

I sat very still. I didn't take offense at the moniker. He wasn't far from the mark.

Even Rudy's eyes had gone big. "You're the daughter of the grand dame of the Northeast?"

"One of them."

"How many does she have?"

"Seven!" Michael answered for me. "Any traditional grand dame has seven daughters. Especially in *that* lineage." He turned on me again. "Which one are you?"

"Six."

"Not the seventh?"

"No."

"Well, that's something, anyway."

"Why?" Rudy asked.

Michael was muttering as he paced my rug, so I answered for him. "The seventh daughter of the seventh daughter of the seventh daughter, etcetera, has extra power. The women in my family have managed an unbroken line since the 1200s." I smiled ruefully. "You should meet Ruella."

"She's number seven?"

"Yep."

I jumped when Michael pulled the coffee table back from the couch, giving him enough room to sit on the heavy wood table, facing me. Some of his anger seemed to have leeched away, but his concentration on my face was fierce. "Does this Roland Parks know who you are?"

"I never told him directly, but I think he knows by now."

He nodded. "That would explain why he wants you so badly."

"That was kind of my thought."

"With your background, you should have been able to spell him away. Why haven't you?"

I squirmed. "Well, see, there's the thing. I'm not a very good witch."

"Huh?" That was Rudy, who was still leaning forward in the chair.

I blew an exasperated breath through my lips. "I was a horrible student. I don't like to read spellbooks. They bore the hell out of me. And I don't have the best memory for tons of spells. I'm a fast learner, but only tend to remember just what I need to for the spell I'm doing at the moment. I usually forget them afterward."

Surprisingly, Michael smiled. Well, almost. The corners of that gorgeous mouth twitched up a bit. "An instinctive? In the Grey line?"

"Yeah. My mother's not too happy about it, either."

Michael subsided, studying me thoughtfully, so Rudy took up the questioning. "Why didn't you just go back to the east? Wouldn't your mother protect you?"

I frowned. "Being part of my mother's coven is only slightly less repulsive than being under Roland. Besides, she doesn't trust me around, either."

Michael's eyebrow quirked up.

"Your mom's that bad?" Rudy asked.

I smiled tiredly toward him. "My mother's not entirely *bad*. I do love her. But she doesn't tend to remember that there are other people in the world besides her. I like my freedom. Her answer to my problem would be to make me a part of her coven. That is *not* an option, as far as I'm concerned."

Michael leaned forward, elbows on his thighs, hands dangling between his knees. Startled, I fell back into the couch, instinctively putting a little distance between us. I bit the inside of my lip, trying really hard not to ogle all that carved muscle on his arms, defined by the tight fit of his T-shirt. But it was hard. He was so close, I could *smell* him, for Goddess's sake. Fresh earth and thick, musky male. He made my mouth water.

"What are you doing in California?"

"Huh?"

"What are you doing in California?" If he noticed my distraction, he didn't show it.

"I like it here."

He scowled. Waited.

"Okay, it's as far away from my mother as I can go and still be in the United States."

"Why California? If Shannon doesn't like you…"

"None of the grand dames or wizards like me. But I know Shannon."

"There's Hawaii and Alaska," Rudy pointed out helpfully. "They're farther way than California."

"Neither of them appeals to me."

"Why do you have to stay in the States?"

I couldn't look away from Michael, even though I was answering Rudy. My fingers dug into the worn upholstery of the couch as he steadily studied my face. What did he see? "I don't have to, but I like the States. Besides, I'm really bad with languages."

"I thought all witches were good with languages," Rudy said.

"Yeah, well, like I said, I'm not a very good witch."

"Just a very powerful one," Michael said softly. Those green eyes gleamed at me from behind thick black lashes. "Are you more powerful than her?"

"Who?"

"Your mother."

I stared back for an equally silent moment. "We don't know."

He nodded, and I heard the silent "aha" as pieces clicked into place for him. "Did she send you away?"

"Sort of."

"Because she's afraid you'll take over."

I shrugged, doing my best to follow the conversation. His closeness was extremely distracting. "That's Ruella's job. She can have it. I told them all that." I carefully, without drawing attention to the move, straightened my leg so that the outside of my thigh wasn't resting on the inside of his.

"They don't believe you."

"No." He didn't seem to notice my move.

"Does Shannon think you're here to take over? Is that why she doesn't trust you?"

I sighed, clutching my hands in my lap. "I've done everything I can to assure her that I'm not, but I doubt she believes me."

We were all silent with our thoughts. Michael sat up, gaze pointed toward my bookshelf, but I doubted my paperback collection was his focus. Rudy sank back in his chair, brimming with expectation. I stayed very still and watched Michael. He was quite obviously the leader of the two, and he knew way

more about the situation than I could have hoped. I felt ⌐
confident that, with him on my side, I could stave off Roland.

Of course, with him at my side, I'd love to do a bunch of
other things. Afternoon sunlight streamed through the sheers
on the window behind the couch, touching off mahogany
highlights in his hair. It may have been fancy, but I'm pretty
sure that I could see the ghost of the rosettes that would
decorate his hide when he changed to a jaguar.

Jaguar. Sleek, silent, deadly. Top of the food chain in the
rainforests of South America, if I remembered my high school
studies correctly. Studying his profile, I could almost see the
beast in the rounded tip of his nose and the curve of his jaw.
Certainly those striking eyes were the mark of a beast. My heart
stuttered as I drank in the line of his neck, watched the
thumping of his pulse. Dropping my gaze down to the wide
expanse of his chest and the bunching of the muscles of his
arms, I wondered what those muscles felt like. I wanted to
squeeze them, to see if they were as hard as they looked.

Dropping my gaze to my lap, I indulged myself with a
fantasy, imagining him in his other form. Was he a yellow
jaguar, or black? Was he as thick and muscular in the other
form? He would have the same green eyes, the one thing about a
shifter that didn't change even if the pupil shape altered. Would
his fur be soft and smooth, or glossy and thick? And what about
Rudy? Tall and lanky as he was, I'd bet he was one of those slim
wolves. All compact power ready to be released like a spring
lock. Was his pelt the same sunny brown as his hair? I'd actually
touched wolves before, shifters even. I'd felt the coarse outer
layer of fur and burrowed my fingers in to discover the soft,
downy hair beneath.

...ie! Unbelievable! Two dangerous predators, ...by human intellect, and they were there to ...a heady feeling. A rush of power. Not to ...that either one of them could give me masturbation material for weeks on end, just wondering what it would be like to...

"Stop that," Michael growled.

I snapped open my eyes, not having realized I'd closed them. "Stop what?"

"You're playing with my leash." He glanced at Rudy. "With both of our leashes."

I glanced at Rudy to see him sprawled back on the comfy chair, a hot grin on his lips and his eyes at half mast. Glancing down—I couldn't help it—I saw a discernable bulge in his jeans.

Blushing, I focused on my hands in my lap. "Sorry. I didn't know you could feel it, too."

"You really didn't know?"

I glared at Michael. "I've never leashed anyone before."

"But you've been around those who have."

"And I think I told you that I'm a horrible student. I never thought that I'd cast the spell, so I never really paid much attention."

"Why wouldn't you cast it?"

"I don't like the idea of owning anyone." I tried to convey the truth with my eyes, willing him to believe me. "I really wouldn't have called you if I wasn't desperate for help."

Like the burgeoning dawn, a smile grew on his face, and it was devastating to my poor little heart. I think my breasts actually swelled, and I know something inside my belly burst and leaked out between my thighs. He startled me by switching from the coffee table to the couch beside me. I couldn't help the small cry that escaped my lips as I shrank back from him. He faced me, one knee folded before him and the other bent over the side. He leaned in, sliding his arm over the back of the couch to take a lock of my hair between his fingers. "What you were doing felt like a caress. Like you were running your hands through my fur, but more." His voice had gone all low and husky, and his eyes hooded even further. The combination did terrible things to my heart rate. "What did you feel?"

"It doesn't matter. I'm sorry. I won't do it again."

I jumped, yelping slightly, when Rudy bounded from the chair and dropped to his knees before me. Boldly, he pressed his belly to my knees, leaning into me like a dog might. "Don't say that. I liked it." He batted his eyes ridiculously at me. "Do it again."

I giggled. Couldn't help but laugh at the puppy at my feet. I sank my fingers into the waves at his temple, and he leaned into the caress, closing his eyes and smiling. I gave in to the temptation to scratch, and he hummed happily, letting his tongue loll a little to the side, I think to make me giggle. Which I did. When my giggle subsided, he opened his eyes. They'd gone all half-lidded and slumberous. His hands slid up the outside of my thighs. "Do it again."

I took a deep breath. The cute wolf was fanning the flames that the sexy cat had started somewhere in my womb. I knew that shifters could smell sexual arousal, and mine was going to soak my couch soon if I didn't stop this. I gently straightened the hair I'd mussed around his ear. "Listen, maybe you should go back to sit in your chair."

"Awww." Instead, he sank down in my lap, chest on my thighs, nose practically in my belly button. Abruptly, he switched his grip on my thighs so he could pull them apart. He inhaled deeply. "You don't really want me way over there, do you?"

I pushed his shoulders to stop him from pressing in between my legs. Didn't work. "C'mon, Rudy. Time to stop."

"Don't wanna," he muttered into my navel. My T-shirt didn't seem to be a barrier for his nuzzling. I grabbed his hair with both hands to stop him from getting to my breasts.

He opened his eyes to meet my gaze. Big blue eyes touched off something deep in my chest. "I don't know you," I told him sternly.

"Don't you?" I glanced at Michael, who was watching us with...*interest?* Was *that* what I saw in that hooded gaze? "You called to us."

"I didn't call to you directly. I called to..." I trailed off, at a loss to explain it.

"To something within us that attracts us to you."

"Us?"

Michael smiled. So unfair! A girl couldn't possibly defend herself from that.

To prove the point, Rudy somehow managed to escape my hold on his hair, and his hot, wet mouth closed over my nipple. I gasped. Did I even have a T-shirt and bra on?

"Wait..." I breathed, but Rudy wasn't listening. His arms circled my waist to pull me closer, his teeth and tongue busy making my nipple love him.

This kind of stuff didn't happen to me. I'm not that kind of girl. I guess I'm attractive enough. A bit too tall, if you ask me, but I kept myself in good enough shape that there was only a little fat on me. I do have nice cocoa skin, thanks to my very dark-skinned father and my pale-skinned mother. My hair is long and straight, a silky black that I wish had more curl to it. I could turn a few heads if I tried.

Sex had stopped being an issue for me a few years ago, when I'd decided that I just didn't like it much. Roland had been the first man I'd dated in three years, and we never got to the sex part before he showed his true colors.

This was a different story altogether. Rudy fed hungrily at my breast, nipping, snarling, moaning happily. I tugged at his hair, but that only seemed to goad him on.

I should use the leash. I should stop this. I remember thinking that very clearly. I still wasn't even sure if Rudy was *legal!* I think I even started to gather the magic. But then Michael slid between me and the back of the couch. And where *had* his T-shirt gone?!

Never had I had the pleasure of being sandwiched between two gorgeous male bodies. Never had I melted into a puddle of goo while one feasted on my breast and the other reached inside my shirt to undo my bra. Nearly perfectly synchronized, Michael drew my shirt and bra up to my chin and Rudy left, then returned to, my nipple, still humming.

"Okay, guys, stop," I moaned, my tone mismatched with my words. "You don't have to do this."

"Oh, yes, we do," Michael murmured. He nudged my head to the side with his nose and drew back my hair, exposing my neck for a long, wet slide of his tongue. "That's what good little pets do."

I squirmed, hating his word choice. "I don't... You're not pets."

Rudy actually whined. "Please," he spoke against my breast. "I *want* to be your pet."

I stared at him, then gasped when Michael bit my neck. "It's part of the leashing."

His hands slid up to fondle my breasts as Rudy leaned back to concentrate on removing my jeans.

"No, it's not," I protested, fighting feebly. Rudy batted my hands aside.

"But it is," Michael purred. Literally purred. I'd heard that big cats don't actually purr. Whether or not that's true, shapeshifters *do* purr. His chest beneath my back actually vibrated. It was a yummy feeling, like a hard, sexy, buzzy mat. "Your pain is our pain. Your pleasure is our pleasure."

I froze. Aghast. "Huh?"

"Never learned that part, huh?" He tweaked my nipple, making me groan. "If you let it, the leash can work for pleasure, too."

Rudy pulled off my jeans, taking my plain cotton panties with them.

I panicked. "Wait, guys! I wasn't planning on having sex. I haven't…"

Rudy ignored me. Eyes hungry, he dove in, and I lost the power of speech. My back bowed, the back of my skull tucking into the curve of Michael's neck. Chuckling, he trapped me with his arms, making me helpless as Rudy's tongue slid inside me. Over me. Through me. Goddess!

"Open up," Michael coaxed. "Let us feel it with you."

My hips became a separate animal, rolling and pumping to get closer to Rudy. "I don't—" Rudy guided my thighs onto his shoulders, "I can't… Don't know how. Uuummm!" Rudy cradled my ass with big, strong hands, angling me so he could suck my clit into his mouth.

"All right," Michael said, plucking at my nipples. "We'll work on that."

"Guys, wait! I...oh! Oh, yeah. Oh, more! Oh, Goddess!"

They both held me as I came hard into Rudy's sucking mouth. He moaned, covering my sex and drinking deep enough to spark another, smaller spasm through my body.

"Oh, yeah," Rudy groaned, releasing me to lean back and start releasing the button of his jeans.

Michael kissed my ear, nibbled my lobe as I watched anxiously for Rudy to release his cock.

Which is when they heard the car.

Chapter Four

They both froze, heads snapping to face the front hall. Head muzzy from two lovely orgasms, it took me a second to realize it. Then I froze. "What?"

Rudy slid back to all fours, of a sudden far more animal even if he still had human form. He sniffed, then shook his head. "Nothing yet." Gracefully, he rose to his feet, eyes on the window as he carefully avoided showing himself in it.

"What is it?"

"There's a car outside," Michael told me. Gently, he pushed me from his lap. "Stay down." When I was clear, he twisted to face the window behind the couch. Crouched low, he very carefully didn't disturb the sheers. The gauzy curtains were probably just enough to disguise his presence at the window.

Rudy stood at the side of the window, positioned so that my heavy burgundy curtains hid him as he peered out. "Meg, you know anyone with a blue Pontiac Sunfire?"

I shook my head, pulling my shirt and bra down to their appropriate positions. I crept back onto the couch, crawling over Michael's broad back to peer out over his shoulder. "Shit. The big one is Brent McMillian. He's Roland's shifter."

"Leashed?"

"Yeah."

"The others?" Rudy's calm was unnerving, given his puppy behavior before. His eyes remained trained on the people getting out of the car, every bit as intent as Michael's stare.

"Brent's pack? I don't know."

"Any of them leashed?"

"I don't know."

The group of four stopped just off of my porch, just out of shield range. Brent cupped his hands to his mouth. "Hey, little witch! Come out and talk."

"He can't get through the shield," I said.

"There are ways to break shields. He could carry something from Roland."

I looked at the back of Michael's head. Damn! He knew more about magic than I did. Who *was* this guy?

"Think they know we're here?" Rudy murmured.

"Meg, can sound travel through your shield?"

"Usually."

"What is Brent?"

"He's a wolf."

"Then he knows someone's here," Rudy confirmed. "We came through the back, so he might not have caught our scent, but he'll have heard murmuring. What do you want to do?" He never took his eyes off the group outside.

Michael sat back. As I was practically riding his back, he took me with him. I slid off an amazing collection of muscle, bunched under smooth, satin skin, to stand beside the couch. He turned to study me for a moment.

"Little witch!" Brent called from outside. "Come out and talk."

Michael flicked his glance to Rudy. "Go out with her."

Rudy turned into the room. "Just me?"

Michael looked at me. "It's not common to have two of us. It would be nice to let them know she's protected, just not *how much* protection."

I licked my lips. Sounded good to me.

Rudy whipped his T-shirt off, exposing a sparsely furred chest. "What's that for?" I croaked.

He grinned. The intensity of moments before vanished. "Just to get you to look at me."

I gaped. Michael chuckled. Brent yelled again.

"Fucking shifters," I cursed, stomping toward the front door.

"Meg?"

I whirled. "What?"

Michael held up my jeans. "You may want these."

Making up curses as I went, I yanked the jeans from his hand and put them on as I headed back to the door.

"No panties. I approve," Rudy laughed softly, reaching out to steady me before I fell. He also grabbed at my ass.

I slapped his hand. "Bad dog!" Which only made him laugh.

I yanked open the front door and had the pleasure of seeing Brent's satisfied grin falter at the sight of the werewolf at my back. "What do you want, Brent?" I growled. After all, he'd interrupted something pretty special. A girl was allowed to be grumpy for that.

Brent's yellow eyes rounded to canine, locked on Rudy. The two of them sized each other up while the rest of Brent's pack stiffened behind him. Brent was one of those guys who was just big. I was still surprised he was a wolf and not a bear. He wasn't fat by any means, just really thick. From the cropped brown hair atop his square head to the heavy soles of his workboots, he was one solid muscle. Rudy might be taller, but Brent outsized him.

Not that it seemed to bother Rudy. He stood ready just behind my left shoulder, his hands relaxed, his shoulders set. His blue eyes—still human—met Brent's amber ones with a steady, challenging gaze.

"Who's this?" Brent demanded of me.

"A friend."

"What's he doing here?"

"This is your business how?"

Brent narrowed his eyes, nostrils flaring as he sniffed. I knew enough about shifters to realize that he'd know Rudy was leashed. "Aw, Meg. Why'd you have to go and call for help? That'll only make Roland mad."

"But, Brent, honey, I *live* to make Roland mad."

His smile was not at all pleasant. "That's not smart."

"Yeah, well, my mommy raised an idiot. Go figure."

The other shifters with Brent started to pace behind him, like a milling pack of dogs. Oh, wait, they *were* a milling pack of dogs.

Brent sighed, outwardly calm except for the eyes that he kept trained on Rudy. "You think this cub's going to protect you?"

Behind my left shoulder, Rudy growled. I think the sound shook the floorboards beneath my feet. Damn!

"Yeah, I think so."

"There's only one of him."

"Well, then there's me, moron."

His smile grew. "Then there's you." The eyes finally turned to me. Yippee. Rudy could have them back. "I've got a gift for you."

"I don't want it."

"You don't know what it is."

"Is it from Roland?"

"Yes."

"I don't want it."

"Too bad."

He lobbed something at me, small and round, about the size of a baseball. No, I didn't try and catch it. I shot a blast of energy at it. Uncouth of me. Other witches had more elegant methods of handling such situations. I'm not very elegant. Short blasts of energy often work quite nicely, I've found. But, it seems, that's what I was supposed to do. The little thing actually *caught* the energy and *pulled* at me. The damned thing pulled at my energy! It hit the house shield and pulled at that, too.

Rudy snarled. In the blink of an eye, he was gone, and a huge, light brown wolf launched off the porch. I stumbled back toward the open door, trying to get my bearings and wrench my magic back from the innocuous ball that now lay on the ground just off the porch.

A werewolf lunged through where my shield should have stopped him. His—definitely his—body was naked and covered with fur, but he stood upright on two burly legs. Black claws tipped the fingers that extended, preparing to slash at me. I tried to attack with a blast of energy, but whatever it was that had my magic, had it fast. I fell back through the open space of my front doorway, collapsing on my back. The dark gray werewolf scrambled up the porch steps toward me, followed closely by another in full wolf form.

A feline scream caught us all by surprise. Flat on my back, I was in an excellent position to see the gleaming black chest and belly of the black jaguar that sailed over me and into the body of the werewolf. The half-human-shaped beast yelped, tumbling back into his companion with an armload of massive, clawing cat bearing him to the ground.

I struggled to sit, still desperately trying to gather my magic. Deciding that all I could do was try and get my magic back—I certainly wasn't much help without it—I searched the ground for the ball, spying it where I'd seen it before in the short grass just off the porch. I pushed to my knees and scrambled for it.

A wolf caught it up in his jaws before I could get there. He glanced up, the ball held in his teeth, and I recognized Brent's yellow eyes. I could have sworn he grinned at me.

Before I could do more than cry out, he spun on his hind legs and sprinted away. His companions broke away from Rudy and Michael and fled as well, all of them bleeding, one of them badly.

The wolf and the jaguar that were my protection let them go, standing sentinel to either side of my porch steps. The four wolves shifted back to naked human down at the bottom of my driveway and piled into the car.

"That ball he threw at me," I said, finding my voice. "It drained my magic. He took it."

Michael swung his big head to me, green eyes wide in surprise. Then he growled, spun, and shot off down the driveway. Rudy was two lunges behind him.

They were too late. The Sunfire's tires squealed, kicking up dirt as Brent and his pack took off.

Chapter Five

Michael skidded to a stop, averting his head as dirt and gravel rained on him and Rudy. As the car retreated, the big cat sat staring after it, his tail jerking. The wolf darted in front of him after the car, but stopped at a coughing snarl from Michael. Rudy whined a question. Michael shook his head.

Michael stood, all elegant feline grace, and loped back toward the house, Rudy at his side. I had plenty of time to admire then as they came. Sunlight shone blue-white on Michael's glossy black fur, sliding off his hide like water as his thick, powerful body stretched and bunched as he ran. Rudy's light brown pelt caught the gold of the sun, and the lighter ruff about his neck nearly gleamed in a golden halo around his head.

When he reached the bottom of the porch stairs, Michael shifted back. It's not like in the movies where they like to dramatize the change to make it look long and painful. It's not messy. It's magic. And it's fast. One second there was a black jaguar, the next there was a flash of something that wasn't quite light, and then there was a man. A naked man. Michael's clothes would be lying in a pile somewhere within the house. Rudy's jeans lay on the porch beside me. Assorted clothing from Brent's pack lay scattered across my yard. When they change, somewhere in the split-seconds between shapes, a shifter's body becomes incorporeal. At that time, anything they're wearing or carrying falls to the ground. It was better than the ripping and tearing of clothes that happened in the movies.

So when Michael and Rudy shifted back, I got my first good look at them nude. Oh, my Goddess! All of my feminine parts screamed at me to lie back and spread my legs and let them finish what they'd started before Brent and company so rudely interrupted. Michael's honed body was covered with a light dusting of pure black hair that gathered in a curly nest at the base of a thick cock. Rudy's slim frame proved to be finely muscled. Body hair was sparse, but did gather around a nice, long cock.

And they'd had me sandwiched between them!

I scrambled to my feet as they mounted the stairs, completely unable to hide the fact that I'd been looking my fill. Rudy caught my arm before I fell as Michael brushed past me. I stared up into Rudy's grinning face, amazed when he planted a sweet kiss on my open lips. "All that you expected?"

"Quit playing," Michael barked from inside the house. "Get in here, both of you."

Rudy kissed me again, then pushed me gently through the doorway. He turned to scoop up his jeans, and I just couldn't help dawdling so I could ogle his ass. Fine, curved perfection. If I were to judge by the look he gave me when he straightened, he'd known I would look.

I yelped when Michael grabbed my arm, spinning me around to face inside the house. "Pack a bag," he ordered, pushing me toward the hall. "We're taking you to our place."

I stumbled, catching myself against the wall beside the kitchen. "What?"

He had his jeans in his hands and pulled them on. Button fly. No underwear. Whimper. "You're not safe here. They'll probably regroup and come back later tonight. You're *not* going to be here."

Reality set in, pushing aside the lust inspired by acres of beautiful muscles and golden skin. I sank against the wall, hands behind my butt, and stared at the wall across from me. "It's ok, Michael; you don't have to do this."

Rudy froze in the midst of putting his jeans back on.

Michael, who now sat on the edge of my coffee table, paused with one boot in hand. He growled. Damn, that was sexy! I'd miss it. "What?"

I sighed, running a hand through my hair, pulling a hank of it down over my shoulder to play with. "I felt the leashes dim with the rest of my magic. Just like the shield." I scrunched up my lips. "I'm sure you can break free now. Go ahead, with my blessing."

"What'll you do?" Rudy asked, buttoning his jeans. Shame, that. "From what you've told us, Roland's not going to stop."

"I know. I guess I'll have to call one of my sisters."

I could almost hear Michael grinding his teeth. Imperiously, he pointed toward my bedroom. "Get your ass in there and pack a bag. You're coming with us."

I grimaced. "Thank you, but no. I know you don't want to be leashed, and frankly, I didn't really want to hold the leash. I was just looking for some help. I'll just ask my sisters or some— Ack!"

Michael grabbed my arm and propelled me toward the bedroom. "Perhaps you didn't hear me. I didn't *ask*."

I frowned at him. "Who the fuck do you think you are?"

"Your protection." He actually swatted my ass! "Scoot." He turned to point at Rudy. "Go with her and see that she packs. I'll bring the car around front."

Chuckling, Rudy advanced on me. Gently, he propelled me down the hall. "There's no arguing with him when he's like this. Or, well, *ever*." The smile dimmed a bit, his gaze honest. "But he means what he says. We'll protect you."

I shook my head. "But it puts you in danger for no reason."

"I have a perfect reason," Michael interrupted, planting himself at the end of the hall. His boots were now on, and he tugged his T-shirt down over that mighty chest. I wanted to sob. "It's my job to keep track of witches. I'm a bit put out that I found out not only about one but *two* that I didn't know were in the vicinity."

"But I…"

"*So*—" He spoke louder to shut me up, not that he wasn't loud enough already. "—you will come with me so I can find out more about him. *And*, if he's as bad as you say and as I suspect after our little altercation out there, you will help me to track him down and stop him."

My heart sank a bit. Okay, it made sense. It did. I'd already gotten the idea that he was a witch-tracker of some sort, although I hadn't really heard of such a thing. Witches tried to keep track of shifters, so why shouldn't shifters try to keep track of witches? Especially the unleashed ones. But it kind of hurt that he didn't want me around for *other* reasons. Of course, that was ridiculous.

I took a deep breath and nodded. He waited until I'd turned around before delivering the telling blow in a deep, velvety voice. "Not to mention the fact that Rudy and I have yet to fuck you silly."

My knees actually buckled. How embarrassing. Rudy had to slip his arm around my waist to keep me from melting into a puddle on my hardwood floor. He laughed, the bastard. "Oh, *that* worked."

Muttering obscenities, I carefully pushed from Rudy and turned to the bedroom. I went straight to the closet and pulled out a duffel bag.

"How long do I plan on being gone?" I asked, hearing Rudy behind me.

"Pack for a week. We'll come back and get more if necessary."

"A week?"

Rudy waved a lazy hand and wandered into my bathroom. "It'll probably be longer than that. I think it'll take us a good, long time to fuck you silly. I *hope* so, at least."

Hot lust sizzled in my groin, and I nearly felt what it was like to swoon. How disgusting! I dropped my duffel bag onto the bed and went to the dresser. "Are you ever serious?"

"Hardly ever," he answered from the bathroom.

I mulled that over as I collected T-shirts, sweaters, and jeans. As jovial as he usually acted, I'd seen Rudy in action. He was quite the fighter, ample protection all on his own, despite his young age. Paired with Michael, I don't think I could have been safer. Mother would be so proud.

Rudy returned and dumped a small pile of toiletries on the bed beside my bag. He turned to the closet. "You have one of those little travel bags?"

I chuckled, causing him to glance over his shoulder. His bare shoulder, I might add. And, my, what a wonderful view of a long, tapered back! "What?"

"Rather domestic, aren't you?"

He smiled. "I make a very good pet." The heat in his eyes fried my brain. "Bag?"

"On the floor."

While he retrieved it, I tried to mesh my noggin back together. He also brought the witch's costume that hung from an upper cabinet's handle. "I like this," he said, waggling his eyebrows. "A witch going as a witch?"

I shrugged. "I appreciate irony."

He chuckled. "Halloween party?"

I thought of the two invitations. Mentally shook my head. "No. Just work. The plaza around my shop will be a huge street party, though. It's fun."

He rolled the dress—quite well, I might add—and tucked it into my duffel bag. "I take it those go with it?" He nodded toward the witch's hat and broom. The costume and the trappings were all bogus, of course. I'd never seen a witch fly on a broom, and outside of costume parties and Halloween nonsense, we never wore such hats. But most of us with a sense of humor owned such a costume.

"Yep." I got the shoes and stockings for the costume; then, without thinking, I retrieved bras and undies and shoved them all in the bag.

"Aw, nothing frilly and lacy?"

I'm quite sure I blushed. I could *feel* it. The look of delight on his impish face confirmed it. "I don't have anything frilly and lacy. No one to wear it for."

He caught my wrist and tugged me off balance, tumbling me onto the bed. Immediately, he pounced. "Until today."

I braced my hands on his shoulders, trying to keep him away. "Are you sure you're a wolf and not a kitten?"

"He's more of a puppy, really," said Michael from the doorway.

Rudy, undeterred by either Michael's presence or my hands, swooped down and took my mouth with his. He grasped my wrists and pinned them to the bed beside my ears. I lost myself in the satin glide of his lips on mine, of the tongue that slid within, then tangled with mine. Puppy he might be, but, Goddess, he could kiss! I dimly heard movement around us. When Rudy released me finally, I was bemused to see that Michael had finished packing for me.

"Let's go," he said, shouldering my bag.

Rudy rolled off me, and I scrambled up. I had the costume's broom and hat in my hand when I heard my nightstand drawer open.

"Aha!" Rudy crowed.

I dove, but Michael caught me around the waist. I watched, helpless, as Rudy pulled out both of my vibrators. "Two!"

I sagged, mortified.

"Bring 'em," Michael said, dark delight lacing his voice.

Chapter Six

Rudy pelted me with questions about the area as we drove to their place. His enthusiasm was infectious. I'd only lived in Southern California for three years, but I'd already become jaded. As they were newly arrived from Missouri—which, he assured me, was *the* most boring place on earth—he wanted to know *everything*. I couldn't get a word in edgewise except to answer his questions. Michael was silent for most of the trip. I caught him casting speculative glances at me, but he'd never keep the eye contact long.

I'm not sure what I expected of a bachelor pad shared by this twosome. Whatever it was, it wasn't this. They had quite a nice house, set on the edge of a forested area about forty-five minutes from my place. It turned out to be a five-bedroom, two-and-a-half-bathroom ranch house, with one of the bedrooms serving as an office. There was also a covered deck that surrounded the house on three sides. The fourth side contained an open carport that sheltered two covered cars and a dusty Cherokee.

I trailed them into the house. The furnishings were sparse, but nice, and the house had the just-moved-in look, complete with boxes lining some of the walls and empty bookcases.

Michael turned in to one room, the office, and Rudy led me further down the hall.

"Here's our room," he said, pointing to the left, then turned in to a room directly across the hall. "And here's the guest room."

The white walls were blank, but some framed nature photographs were propped up against one wall, presumably ready to hang. The indigo blinds were open to the waning light of day. A blue-swathed, queen-sized bed received my bag.

Rudy caught me up in his arms. "Although, you won't be sleeping here."

Wait. What had he said? *Our room?* A dozen little mannerisms, tiny things Rudy and Michael had said and done, all clicked into place. I pushed at his chest, making him look at me. He paused at the puzzled look on my face. "You and Michael are a couple."

He smiled. "Yes. Is that a problem?"

The easy confirmation staggered me, rounded my eyes. "Well, no, but…"

He leaned in to rub the tip of my nose with the tip of his. "But what do we want with you?"

"Yeah."

"Mmm, three's company."

I let him kiss me, but I don't think I gave as good as I got. I was far too shocked. Too thrown off. Too damn aroused! Two guys together didn't bother me, but I'd never really wanted to *see* two guys together before. Not like most men want to see two women together. But the thought of Michael and Rudy locked in a naked, sweaty clinch had me squirming.

Rudy pressed me against the erection straining his jeans, plundering my mouth. He walked me back toward the bed, but stopped halfway there.

"That bed's not as comfortable as ours," he muttered against my lips, bending quickly to pick me up.

"Wait."

"No."

We met Michael—shirtless, shoeless, and looking scrumptious—in the hallway. He shook his head, a small grin on his face aimed at Rudy. "You have a one-track mind."

"You know it," Rudy confirmed, laughing as he carried me into the master bedroom. "And, by the way, your goo-goo eyes at me gave our secret away. She knows we're together."

"My goo-goo eyes? What the hell are you talking about?"

Rudy dropped me gently on the thick mattress of a bed that had to be bigger than a California king, with a top that was every bit of four feet off the newly carpeted floor. It had one of those huge bookcase headboards—mostly empty—and a sturdy footboard of the same dark mahogany wood. No cover, no top-sheets, just a hunter-green fitted sheet on the mattress.

"Yeah," Rudy continued, facing him. "I've told you time and time again that you just can't conceal your love for me."

Michael grunted, hands at his pants. "Ridiculous canine."

"Lovesick kitty."

They both shucked their jeans, one grumbling and one chuckling. I sat, bewildered, gazing at two fine specimens of malehood. My mouth went dry. They were a study in contrasts. Michael was thickly muscled and dark, Rudy sleekly toned and light. Michael had an unshaved, almost unkempt look, while Rudy had a smooth, young face and his hair was the only shaggy thing about him. Green eyes to blue eyes. Brooding grin to blinding smile. Thick, heavy cock to long, sleek cock.

Rudy stepped into Michael, slipping an arm about his waist and sliding the other hand down his chest. His hand ended wrapped around Michael's growing erection. Giving it a familiar stroke, he leaned in to brush Michael's lips with his. Impish, he turned to me. "Pretty, isn't he?"

I was still, breathless, mesmerized by the sight of them. Muttering, Michael grabbed a handful of Rudy's hair and turned him back for a more thorough kiss. Clearly a meeting of mouths that had touched countless times before. Rudy melted, even though he was the one with a handful of cock. Their lips meshed together, tongues peeking out as they played with each other. Rudy broke the kiss to suck in air, and Michael shoved him toward the bed.

I started, hardly remembering that I was really there and not just watching some beautiful movie. But they remembered I was there. They came at me, crawling onto the overlarge mattress from either side.

"You guys don't have to do this," I stammered, edging back toward the mirrored center of the headboard. I yelped when Michael caught my ankle and tugged me roughly toward him.

Rudy crawled behind me and pulled at my shirt. "Oh, we *want* to."

"What for? You've got each other. And I know you can break the leashes."

Michael attacked my jeans, a man intent on a mission. "And neither one of us has a juicy pussy that I've yet to taste."

Rudy dropped me on my back, hovering over me. "See, the pussy likes pussy."

"But..."

"The puppy likes pussy, too," he said, tugging my bra off. "And sweet, luscious titties."

He cupped my breasts, plucking my nipples with each thumb and forefinger. Michael got my jeans off and forcibly spread my legs. No playing around, he plunged in and licked me from ass to clit in one, rough swipe. We groaned together. My back arched, putting my breasts right where Rudy wanted them. He bent in and sucked one of my nipples, hard. I dropped my back to the bed, and he followed, devouring my breasts. They both ate at me, and a meal had never been happier to be consumed. My body tried to writhe, but they held me still, one pair of hands firmly on the inside of my thighs, holding them apart, and another set of hands plumping my breasts into a hot, hungry mouth.

Did it get any better than this?!

I dragged in a breath, and the scent of hot, musky male penetrated my brain. I opened my eyes. My cheek was pressed against one of Rudy's thighs. I tilted my head back a bit, and yep! There it was. His turgid cock was hard, nearly pressed against his muscled belly. Hungry, I reached for it, wrapping my hand around soft skin and hard muscle. He groaned around my nipples. I tugged, and he got the hint. Somehow he managed to bend nearly double, inching his hips closer to my head so that I could finally suckle the head of his cock.

He released my nipple with a popping sound. "Oh, Goddess, that feels good!"

He straightened up, inching forward so I could take in more of him, which I did gladly. I'm not a deep-throater, but I can suck like nobody's business, which I proved on him. He kept his fingers plucking at my breasts, but most of his attention centered on what I was doing with my mouth.

Meanwhile, I was having a bit of a problem concentrating solely on either the cock in my mouth or the tongue and lips at my pussy. Good Goddess, the kitty was good at that! His mouth covered my sex, his agile tongue alternately diving into my channel and batting at my clit. I squirmed and bucked, but he held me still with strong hands on the inside of my thighs, pushing me closer and closer to orgasm. He sucked hard and pulled away from my cunt with a loud pop. Then he fell back to just suck my erect clit into his mouth, holding it with his teeth and lashing it mercilessly with his tongue. I lost it. Inhaling a scream, I pulled deeply on Rudy's cock, making him yell and shake and very nearly come. He yanked out of my mouth forcibly before that happened, and I was left to writhe through the rest of that orgasm with Michael still feasting on my flesh.

"Stop!" I cried.

He didn't. I lost track of Rudy. Lost track of time. There was nothing but Michael's mouth and my cunt and another pulsing, insane orgasm.

Finally, when I was a quivering, gooey mess, he relented. "Sweet and wet," he murmured, rising to his knees.

I watched, helpless, as he tugged my hips closer to that tree trunk he had for a cock. Shifters don't carry diseases that humans—like witches—can catch, so I didn't have to worry about STDs, and thanks to genetics and magic, witches don't get pregnant unless we consciously try to do so. So there was nothing for me to worry about other than the fact that he might rip me apart with that huge thing. He placed himself at my opening, then used brute strength to grab my hips and pull me onto him inch by glorious, fucking inch.

I was full long before he was done. Or so I thought. I gasped, and he smiled, slowly removing me from his cock. Glancing down, I saw him there, only about halfway in. There was more?! I watched him emerge, coated with my juices. It felt incredible. Then he pushed back again, further.

"Wait, wait," I begged, trying to get away. Or was I?

"C'mon, sweetheart," he crooned, clutching my ass. My thighs were draped over his forearms. "Take it. Take every last inch of me."

Goddess, he was stretching me apart! He touched every bit of me inside, the sheer width of him making him scrape against that oh-so-sensitive spot just inside my opening. It drove me crazy. I flailed in his grip, but he had a good hold on my legs and hips. Helpless, I dug my fingers into his thighs. Once more he pulled nearly out, then back again. Always slowly, always making sure that I felt every damn bit. It was torture. It was heaven.

It was in! I glanced down to see his nest of black hair meshing with my own. I looked up to see a look of unadulterated pleasure on his handsome face. "All the way in. Under your skin."

A part of me suspected he meant something else by that, but the rest of me couldn't have cared less. I rocked my hips, whimpering as my inner walls struggled to strangle him.

"Oh, yeah!" I twisted my head to see Rudy propped up against one side of the headboard, cock in hand, enjoying the show.

I would have reached to him, I'm sure, invited him closer so I could play with his cock, but Michael's abrupt tug and shove shocked all thoughts from my mind.

My eyes locked with his, and I gaped. His irises had expanded to nearly take over the whites of his eyes, the pupils had lengthened to slits, and his smile revealed elongated canines, both upper and lower. A faint memory tugged at my brain of my sister crowing about fucking her shifter and making him lose it. It meant he was way into it. I knew how she felt. Looking into those eyes, a savage joy slammed my heart against my ribs and punched my diaphragm.

Using his arms and his grip on my hips, Michael shoved strangled mewls of pleasure out of me by setting a rhythm and banging away. I clawed the bedsheet, the position giving me no leverage to push back. I was entirely at his mercy and loving it! The backs of my thighs caught his belly, and my calves braced his shoulders. I came, squeezing my thighs together. He transferred both of my ankles to one shoulder, allowing me to squeeze him tighter. He shoved into my pulsing cunt, an agonized snarl on his face. He roared and slammed my hips one last time, ramming home as he came.

He used my legs to support him while he gathered himself. Warmth suffused my body, not only from the orgasm, but from knowing that I'd wrung a pretty powerful one out of him. Shooting me a grin, his features fully human again, he kissed the insides of my ankles and released my legs to pull free. He eased back to the foot of the bed, content, it seemed, to lean against the footboard and breathe.

I was content to lie there and bask, spread-eagled and shameless, on the rumpled sheet. But my basking was short-lived. Rudy appeared over my head, braced on arms to either side of my shoulders, grinning down at me. Once he had my attention, he crawled down over my body, treating me to a view of his cock as he bent to swipe his tongue through my pussy. No doubt that he tasted the combined juices of me and Michael. I groaned.

"Yum," he murmured as he continued crawling. Once he was between my legs, he pivoted and very carefully, very slowly, lowered himself atop my sweaty body. "Remember me?"

I laughed, weakly, lifting my arms to circle his neck. "How could I forget?"

He lapped sweat from the base of my throat. "Mmm, good."

A little maneuvering, and I felt the head of his cock at my entrance. As I was already stretched and soaked, he slid in easily. He wasn't as thick, but I was sensitized, and I still felt every bit of him. I groaned, free to rock my hips in this position. I hissed when I felt him knock my womb. He really *was* longer than Michael.

He froze, eyes on my face. "Okay?"

I wiggled. Rocked a bit. Decided I liked it. "Yeah."

The relief on his face made me think his length had been a problem on previous occasions. "That's my girl." He pulled back and shoved in.

Goddess! To fuck one man right after another has fucked you. To know that the first was watching and enjoying the sight. To wonder what looked better to Michael—my limbs wrapped tightly around Rudy, or Rudy's slim, muscled ass as it pumped at me. The thought drove me crazy. I peeked at Michael over Rudy's shoulder, and he did indeed seem to enjoy what he saw. Even though his eyes were back to human, he looked every inch the sated cat, even licking his lips as he watched.

"Oh, Rudy!" I screamed when he changed his angle a bit and hit me just *there*. I bunched my hand in his hair. "Ah! Goddess!" I braced my ankles in the small of his back, and my entire body clenched. He froze, breathing hard into my neck as I jerked my hips, fucking him through my orgasm.

"That was fucking hot!" he muttered in my ear when I fell back. "Do it again."

"I can't."

"Oh, yeah, baby, you can."

Actually, he was right. But he had to barrel into me, pounding the entrance of my womb before my body again took over.

"No more," I begged, shaking after that one.

"One more." He bit my earlobe. "For me." He bit my neck, and another orgasm came out of nowhere. He'd found an erogenous zone I hadn't even known I had. I came with a scream, and he let it bring on his own this time, clutching me as his seed washed inside me.

The two of us lay in a sweaty mess.

After a few moments of simply breathing, Michael got up and sauntered away. Soon, I heard water running.

From his sprawl across my body, Rudy pushed up. He grinned at me, his shaggy hair wet with sweat and tangled from my death grip. "Shower time."

I whimpered. "I can't move." I was pretty darn serious! I didn't think my legs worked at all.

He chuckled. "Want me to carry you?"

"Oh, sure. *This* time you ask."

He laughed and moved off the bed. He tugged my leg to bring me closer, then bent to pick me up.

The bathroom was wonderful. All green and ivory tile and sparkling appliances to match the ivory. The huge shower took up one entire end of the room and could easily fit three people, with nozzles on two opposite walls, both detachable. A low, tiled bench ran the length of the third wall underneath a large, frosted window. The glass door was clear, providing an excellent view of Michael as he rinsed suds from his hair underneath one of the nozzles.

Rudy opened the door, then eased my feet to the floor. Michael was there to steady me, all wet and warm and...oh, *my*, the Goddess made him well! Water dripped heavily through the mat of black hair on his chest, swirling around a nipple that just begged to be sucked. I wanted to comply, but when Rudy let go, my wobbly legs would barely hold me.

Laughing softly, Michael caught me up against his chest. I wrapped my arms around his waist, pressing my cheek to his chest. Water from the nozzle behind him trickled over his shoulder and over my front, the warmth seeping a dreamy lassitude through my skin.

"Did we break you?" I heard his voice more through his chest than through the air.

"Probably." I sighed. "But I don't mind."

More water struck my back. A quick glance showed me that Rudy was behind me with a detachable showerhead, wetting me down.

"Then you don't mind being with both of us at once?" Michael asked.

I laughed. "Are you nuts?"

He chuckled, slipping his hands through my hair as warm water spilled through it.

"How do you feel?"

"Ridden hard. Just, please, don't put me away wet."

They both chuckled. "We won't," Rudy assured me.

The water behind me stopped, and a moment later Rudy's hands touched me, covered in soap. He had wonderfully strong fingers that massaged my skin.

"I actually meant your magic," Michael rumbled, pulling my hair out of Rudy's way.

"Oh. That." Reluctantly, I took a metaphysical inventory. "Something's blocking me. No, that's not right. It's like it's right *there,* but I can't reach the extra inch to take it. Does that make sense?"

"Yes."

Michael adjusted to allow Rudy to slide his soapy hands between us. He cupped my breasts, pinching the nipples lightly as he pulled me against him. That easily, they transferred me from one embrace to the other. It was Michael's turn to soap his hands, after which he knelt to soap my legs. Rudy reached up to the nozzle that had pounded Michael's back and twisted it so it produced a fine mist.

I raised my hand up to cup the back of Rudy's head, sliding my fingers over slick, wet hair. "What about you?" I muttered. "Shouldn't we wash you?"

"It's more fun to wash you," he murmured, licking the spot on my throat that had made me come before.

I shuddered, feeling the strange echoes of that orgasm.

Michael soaped my legs, then directed Rudy to rinse them. He soaped up again. His hands went to my pussy this time.

"I don't think I can take it again," I moaned as he ran slippery fingers through my swollen folds.

"Once more," he murmured, finding my clit and swirling it softly. "Then we'll take a nap."

Something about his intensity struck a nerve. I dragged open my eyes and looked down at him. "What are you doing to me?"

He raised his gaze, some gloating look on his face. A thrill of fear ran through me, not enough to push aside the wonderful, warm lethargy, but enough to clear my thoughts a bit. What was I doing?

But I was *way* too beat to fight. I could only watch as he stood. He pulled me away from Rudy, turned, and lifted me against the shower tiles. I hissed at the coolness of the sandstone at my back, but it took mere seconds for it to warm to my body heat.

Besides, I had a tremendous source of heat pressing against my front. "Wrap your legs around my waist."

"I can't."

Kissing me softly, he braced me with his body, then took hold of my ass in such a way that it was unnatural for me *not* to wrap my legs around him. "Just hold on, sweetheart," he murmured.

It was Rudy who reached beneath me as Michael lifted my body. Rudy positioned Michael at my entrance as Michael and I engaged in a soul-gaze.

"What are you doing to me?" I asked again.

I shuddered as he lowered me onto that thick cock of his, but I refused to close my eyes. He didn't answer until I was fully seated, bursting with his sex. "Taking possession."

"What?"

But that was all he'd say, and he made sure I couldn't speak any more, by lifting and lowering me onto his cock. I'd never done this before. Of the few lovers I'd had, none had come close to strong enough to take me against the wall. But Michael did it easily, no strain whatsoever showing, only pleasure.

I whimpered, my abused channel afire with raw sensation. I don't even think I came, but then, I don't think the orgasm really stopped. I was a confusion of pleasure as he used me as his tool. At the very last, before he set loose inside me, he smashed his lips on mine, gaining entrance with his tongue by brute force. Not that I fought him. On the contrary, my body seemed to be following his mind better than mine. It opened, accommodated, *squeezed* just when he needed it to wring a quiet, straining orgasm from him.

He held me for a moment, his forehead braced against the shower wall behind me. I buried my face in his neck, too wrung out to make sense of anything. Truthfully, at the moment, I didn't care. I'd never been fucked so well or so *thoroughly* as I'd been tonight, and I was determined to enjoy it!

Sounds of Rudy switching off the water and opening the shower door. Cool air wafted through the hazy steam, a welcome relief.

Michael took a breath and eased back, sliding his arms around me as my back left the shower wall. He lifted me a bit to ease his cock out of me. Twin little moans escaped us. Supporting my lifeless body, he exited the shower. I felt like a rag doll as he handed me off to the towel in Rudy's arms.

"Can you stand?" Rudy asked.

"Only barely," I admitted.

They both held me up and dried me off. Michael gently rubbed my hair with a towel as I propped myself against Rudy's chest. Then Rudy picked me up and carried me back out into the bedroom.

I never knew when my head hit the pillows, asleep before it happened.

Chapter Seven

Cocooned in warmth, I did *not* want to get up. I tried to convince my bladder that it wasn't full and didn't want me to move, but it wasn't listening. I ignored it as long as I could, but finally decided that it was not a good idea to wet the bed.

I shifted my arm underneath me so I could push up. A steely, hairy arm around my waist tightened, preventing escape.

I tapped it. "Gotta pee," I whispered.

Michael grunted and released me. I pushed up, then crawled over Rudy, who lay on his belly. He'd made a nice, solid body pillow, and Michael had made a heavy comforter. I never missed the lack of sheets and comforter, with such lovely bedclothes. The two of them generated a lot of heat, and I sorely missed it when I left the bed. The carpet was soft beneath my feet as I made for the bathroom. The bedroom itself was nearly pitch dark, but the frosted window in the bathroom caught the moonlight and cast a pretty bluish haze through the door.

Half asleep, I concluded my business and re-emerged into the bedroom. Rudy was there, handing me my cell phone, which was ringing. Yawning, he passed it to me and went into the bathroom.

The phone stopped ringing. I looked at the lit display. First, I was stunned to see that it was ten o'clock. We'd only been asleep for about two hours. I would have sworn it was almost morning. Second, I was pissed to see who had just called me.

Instant rage kept me immobile, until the phone started ringing again a minute later.

"You bastard!"

Instantly, Michael was up and halfway out of bed.

"Why didn't you answer your phone?" Roland demanded. "This is the fourth time I've called you."

"Fuck you! What did you do to my magic?"

Rudy scrambled out of the bathroom just as Michael turned on the light. Michael waved him to silence, and they both concentrated silently on me and my side of the conversation. Me? I started pacing.

"I told you not to cross me, Meg."

"You fucking asshole! I'm going to wring your neck."

"Such language. I take it that's why you tried to leash those shifters?" he sneered. "And, by the way, that was incredibly stupid. You could have gotten hurt!"

I stopped at the footboard of the bed. "What?!"

"Did they hurt you when they snapped the leashes?"

"Oh, that is fucking rich! You're pissed at me because I had the gall to protect myself from you? And then whatever *you* did to me messed up my spell to hold them?"

"Meg, you're lucky they simply gave up and went away. While I'm pleased to find out that you attracted two shifters, in order to hold one of them, you must…"

"Don't you *dare* lecture me!"

"Someone needs to teach you how to use your magic."

"And it's sure as the Goddess *not* going to be you, you jerk!"

He sighed. "Meg, you should just give in. You know you can't win."

"I know no such thing!"

"And together we can be a force to be reckoned with. With your power and my guidance…"

"I'll give you something to reckon, you pig. My foot up your ass!"

"Do not use such language, my love."

"Do *not* call me that!" I cried, stabbing my finger in mid-air despite the fact that he couldn't see it. "What did you do with my magic?"

"Are you all right?"

"Oh, I'm fucking dandy! Except that I don't have my *magic!* What did you do?"

Michael crawled down the bed to kneel close to me. Rudy crossed the room to sit on the side of the bed.

"You see, if you had studied as you should, you would know the spell I used."

"Oh, you are such an unmitigated ass!"

"Nonetheless, I have your magic safe with me. Accept my invitation and come to me tomorrow night, and I'd be happy to give it back."

"I'll tell you what I'll give you, you son of a bitch!"

"Join me, Meg. Make this a Samhain that we'll never forget. A time of new beginnings. A time when you and I join together to form a coven like no other."

"What planet are you living on? I've already told you, being your plaything doesn't excite me."

"It did."

"Actually, no, it didn't. You intrigued me for awhile, until you showed me what a shit you are."

Michael's big hand closed over mine, cutting off Roland before he could respond. Shocked, I stared at the phone and my hand, still held completely within his. "Oh, that's going to piss him off."

"Good."

I looked up into Michael's calm face. "Why'd you do that?"

"First, to piss him off." We shared an evil grin. "Second, to tell you not to let him know you've still got us leashed. He'll think you're helpless if he thinks we're no longer in the picture."

"I'm not…!"

"*And—*" The phone started to ring. "—I know the spell he used, and I believe I know how to break it. You'll need to meet with him somewhere in person. Try to make it neutral ground, someplace where there will be other people around, but not too many."

"What…?"

He released my hand. "Answer the phone."

"Bossy cat." Scowling, I flipped open the phone. "What?"

"Meg, I've been very patient with you. Do not upset me further." Oh, yeah, Roland was mad. But, true to form, he held his cool. An ice man, that one. "Let's keep in mind that your magic is literally in my hands."

I stared at Michael, trying to work out what was happening. His cool gaze gave me nothing. "If you've got my magic, what do you need me for?"

Michael shook his head.

"I have your magic, Meg," Roland explained, as though tutoring a child. "I need you to access it."

"Poor you."

I could almost see him gritting his teeth. I had that effect on him. "Meg, can you not understand how powerful the two of us together can be?"

"I don't want to be anything with you, Roland. I'm not that mad to control other people."

He grumbled, but remained relatively pleasant. "Come to me, Meg. Join with me. Let me show you what we can be together."

Trust me, Michael mouthed. How could I deny what I knew to be a very talented set of lips?

"When and where?"

"Pardon?" Good, I'd caught him off guard.

"As you put it, you've got my magic in your hands. If I want it back, I need to see you, right?" Before me, Michael nodded. "But I won't meet you alone, and it won't be at your house."

"You don't trust me."

"You think?"

"Then I'll allow you the choice. Where do you want to meet?"

"The plaza Halloween party. The courtyard right between my shop and Reilly's."

"The music store?"

"Yes."

He chuckled, the self-absorbed shit! "Very well. When?"

"When?"

Michael held up ten fingers as Roland answered in the affirmative.

"Ten o'clock."

"What of my party?"

"Do you want to do this or not?"

He sighed. "I don't know why I placate you."

I bit my lip on a number of choice words that burbled into my mouth.

"Very well, my dear. I'll see you then."

I closed the phone and stood there, looking deep into Michael's impossibly green eyes. "How do you know the spell?"

"I've studied."

I grimaced. "So? You're not a witch."

He smiled. "I've been leashed before."

I blinked. "Really?"

He nodded, sitting back on his heels. With that one action, he reminded me suddenly that we were all three very naked. Michael sat there, all calm and brawny and...yum. Rudy perched on the edge of the bed, watching us, all slim and cute and...well, yum.

I tried not to let it distract me. "Who? How'd you get free?"

Michael turned toward Rudy, who met his gaze curiously. Smiling, Michael reached out to slide his hands into the hair around Rudy's right ear and used it to pull the younger man toward him. Rudy went willingly, crawling further onto the bed to meet Michael's brief kiss, then settle happily with his head on Michael's shoulder. Both men looked at me. My heart stopped.

"It doesn't matter," Michael assured me, lifting his free hand to beckon me forward.

If I reached out, I could let him take my hand and pull me to them. I wanted to. But I bit my lip, struggling to remember what we were talking about. "This other witch taught you spells?"

He smiled, dark teasing in his eyes. "Yes. Not all witches are as clueless as you are."

I set my hands on my hips and glared at him. I don't think the fact that I was naked helped me look imposing.

Rudy laughed, skimming his hand along the trail of hair that led down Michael's chest to the cock that was waking up.

I narrowed my eyes at them, determined to have this conversation despite their attempt at distraction. "What's your plan to break Roland's spell?"

"Come here."

"I don't think I should."

"You don't trust me?"

"Should I?"

"You did earlier."

"Yeah, well…" Oh, brilliant comeback, Meg!

He tipped Rudy's face up with two fingers and gazed into his eyes. "Rudy trusts me."

"Rudy knows you better."

"Mmmm." He lovingly searched Rudy's face. "Yes, Rudy knows me well."

A huge grin lit Rudy's face.

Michael kissed him softly, his tongue darting out to sample Rudy's lips. My head spun at the sight. I had *never* imagined that seeing two men kiss would be so beautiful. Pulling back from Rudy's mouth, Michael put his hand on the back of Rudy's neck and pressed. Rudy's head bent and lowered down, down, down… My throat went dry as I watched, fascinated. Before he got there, Rudy's hand circled Michael's cock, aiming it for his open mouth. His lips closed around the head and slid down the shaft, and I watched him swallow it. I barely heard the little squeak that scratched the back of my throat as my own mouth fell partially open in jealousy.

"Do you want us, Meg?"

I tore my gaze from Rudy's mouth, raising it to Michael's face. He watched me carefully.

"I don't see how this is part of the plan to get my magic back."

"It is." He hissed, clutching Rudy's neck for a moment. Rudy grinned around his mouthful, but didn't stop.

"H-how?" I asked.

"If your link with us is strong enough, we could help you with the counterspell."

"Run that by me again?"

"Gladly." He grabbed Rudy's hair and looked like he was slowing the younger man down. "We're leashed. It can be a two-way bond if both sides are willing to open themselves to the other." His eyes were intent on my face, despite the fact that

Rudy's tongue was laving the head of his cock. "If Rudy and I are willing, you can tap us for the necessary power for a small spell. It should be plenty to supply what you need to counteract what Roland Parks has done to you."

"You can act as a conduit?"

"Yes."

"I've never heard of shifters acting as conduits before, only other witches."

He pulled Rudy up by the hair. "And we've already established that you know *so* much about magic."

Distracted by the glistening wet lips and lust-filled eyes on Rudy's face, it took me a moment to respond. "Bite me, cat."

He grinned, showing teeth that he'd allowed to go pointy. "Come here."

"I'm serious, though; it doesn't work. That part I do know. My mother and sisters have leashed shifters, and they've never been able to use them like that."

"I neglected to mention that it only works if you've leashed two shifters. One's not enough."

"And you know this how?"

"As I said, I was leashed before."

"Along with another shifter?"

He nodded.

I looked at Rudy, who, now that Michael had released his hair, was busy nibbling at Michael's shoulder. Michael answered my look. "No. It wasn't Rudy."

"Who *are* you?"

He chuckled. "Let's talk over dinner sometime." He licked his lips. "Meantime, the link works better the more intimate we are. So come *here.*"

"We've been intimate."

His grin was positively feral. "*More* intimate."

"How can we get more intimate?"

He crawled forward, and against my better judgment, I stayed where I was. In a very feline gesture, he butted his head against my chest first, rolling his head and sliding it up until he could nuzzle my neck. Silky, soft tendrils of his hair tickled my breasts and shoulders. He wrapped his arm around my waist and drew me to his chest as he straightened. With me securely pressed against him, he reached back to take Rudy's arm. The wolf came easily, allowing Michael to lead him off the bed and draw him to stand behind me. The two of them pressed me between them, as they had when we'd slept.

But we weren't asleep now. We were all very much awake.

"For this to work, the three of us need to be linked," Michael murmured into my left temple. Behind me, Rudy bent to nuzzle the right side of my neck. "You need to know what it's like to feel both of us inside you."

I stiffened. "Metaphysically?"

"Physically and metaphysically."

I shoved at his chest, but his grip on Rudy's shoulders trapped me between them. "Exactly what are you saying?"

He kissed my brow. "We fuck you at the same time."

"B-both of you?!"

Rudy's hand slid down my back and, very deliberately, into the crack of my ass. I jumped when he fingered that hidden opening.

I pushed harder at Michael's chest. "No way."

"Shhh," Michael soothed. "We won't if you don't agree."

That only marginally made me feel better. "Someone taught this to you? For the spell?"

"No. Some of it is theory."

"Theory? You want to fuck my ass on theory?"

"It can be amazing, Meg," Rudy cooed.

"Are you nuts? You're both huge."

"And we've fucked each other."

Michael had to have known the picture those words would put in my head. I'm sure it's why he said them. But that didn't stop the images from forming. Rudy on all fours, with Michael behind him. Or Rudy draped over Michael's back, doing him. I closed my eyes, hot lust expanding in my breast.

Rudy's fingers slid forward between my legs, sinking into my wet pussy. Goddess, they'd made me wet again. He pumped those fingers inside me, then pulled back to smear the wetness to my ass.

Michael cupped my face in his hands and turned me in to a tender kiss. Rudy continued to wet me with my own juices; then he slowly sank a long finger into me. I flinched.

"Relax," Rudy whispered, ghosting his lips over my shoulder and neck as he pulled out, then pushed his finger in again. "Resisting is what makes it hurt."

I disagreed. The fact that that particular hole was more of an exit than an entrance was what made it hurt. The fact that his fingers scraped enough, what the hell would his cock do?

I managed to tolerate the finger and even felt a dark frisson of pleasure when he pulled out. But when he started to press two fingers inside, I weirded out and pulled away from Michael.

"I can't do this," I gasped, wiggling to dislodge Rudy's fingers.

They exchanged a glance, but said nothing immediately. Then Michael nodded, and Rudy backed off.

"I'm sorry, I…"

Michael put the fingers of one hand to my lips to quiet me. He brought me onto the bed into a heated embrace that melted some of my tension. He broke free to gently push me onto my back. "Do you want to see?"

My eyes went wide, and I swore Rudy did a little happy dance from where he watched us. "Uh…"

"Say yes, Meg," Rudy begged.

I had to smile. He was too excited. "Um, ok."

Eagerly, Rudy pounced on one of the drawers in the bookcase beside the side of the bed. Michael moved back away from me, smiling, and accepted the small bottle of what I assumed to be lube from Rudy.

"Exhibitionist," Michael muttered, popping the top.

Rudy knelt before him, caressing Michael's hips and thighs, sliding one hand down to cradle his balls. "Hey, it was *your* suggestion."

Michael held up the bottle between them. "Give or take?"

Rudy paused, shot me a glance. He grinned, gave Michael a thorough kiss. "Take."

It became immediately apparent what that meant to them. Michael poured clear fluid into his hand as Rudy turned to face away from him. I fidgeted as I watched them, unsure what to do. The thought of this really turned me on; the fact of what I was about to see turned on some switch in my hips that didn't allow them to stay still. I grabbed a pillow and hugged it as Michael smeared his hand down Rudy's ass. Rudy squirmed and made happy sounds—overdoing it, I think, for my benefit. He reached out to draw my foot to his mouth and sucked on my toes while Michael poured more lube on him.

"Stop that," I admonished.

He grinned up at me. "Stop being so serious," he said. "Sex is supposed to be...ugnh, fun."

His eyes fell closed, and I looked back to see Michael's glistening fingers very clearly as they sank into Rudy. Two fingers at once, and Rudy obviously loved it. Michael pumped them in and out, then with a little more lube, added another.

Lips at my toes shocked me back into breathing. I looked down at Rudy, who was watching my face. "It feels good. I swear."

Michael reared up on his knees, poured a bit more lube on his palm, capped the bottle, and tossed it to me. I caught it on reflex, my eyes on his hands as he smeared the wetness over his cock. He placed his cock at Rudy's opening, then slowly pressed in.

Goddess! I remember how that monster cock felt inside me; I couldn't imagine what it felt like in Rudy's ass. But a glance at Rudy's face convinced me he loved it. He'd brushed back his hair, and I saw his face for the first time without his bangs as an obstruction. The pleasure on his face was unmistakable as he bit his lip to muffle a groan. I looked at Michael, and he, too, wore a look of utmost pleasure.

Was I really watching this? Were two beautiful men fucking each other before me? I could hardly believe it, could hardly *stand* it, as I watched Michael pull back and push *all* the way back in. His fingers dug into the meat of Rudy's ass, but I'm pretty sure it was Rudy who was pushing back and setting the rhythm. In and out. In and out. Michael's cock slid in and out, just as it had when he'd fucked me, except he was fucking Rudy, who'd also fucked me. The whole thing made some kind of cosmic circle that made a hell of a lot of sense.

Rudy clutched at the bed with one hand. I looked and found his other hand on his cock, fondling it as Michael drove into him. It was too much. I reached down and fondled my clit, slipping my fingers through my wet folds as I watched them heave against each other.

With a strangled grunt, Rudy came, spilling onto the sheet. Michael stiffened behind him, his handsome face drawn into a scowl of pleasure. I slowed my personal ministrations, watching them come down. Michael pulled out, and I watched his cock emerge, wet with copious amounts of lube and his own come. I bit my lip.

I cried out when Rudy pounced on me. I'd thought he was down for the count. I was wrong. He pushed my legs apart, caught my hand, and sucked greedily on my wet fingers. He grinned up at me. "It's *so* good, Meg."

I opened my mouth to reply, but only managed a groan as he dropped his head to suck in the clit that he'd exposed.

Michael left the bed while I melted underneath Rudy, who used his agile tongue to spread me open. He dug two fingers deep inside me, curling them to catch *that* spot. I shuddered, my hips arching off the bed at the sensation. He thrashed my clit with his tongue and managed to push one of his wet fingers into my ass before I realized what he was doing. He pushed it. Pulled it. It felt weird. It felt good. When he sucked my clit like that, just about *anything* felt good!

I came with a stuttering scream and an arch of my back that took my hips at least a foot off the bed. Rudy ate at me through it, moving with me and pushing back at my humping hips. He only relented a little when my butt touched the bed again. He played his tongue over my lips, my opening. I rocked and was surprised to find that he still had his finger buried in my ass.

Scratch that—he had *two* fingers buried in my ass. I squirmed. It burned, and I couldn't decide if it was a good burn. But his tongue was convincing me that anything he did was fabulous. He started in on my clit again and pushed his thumb into my pussy. He gently pumped both thumb and fingers into me as he brought me to climax again.

Michael was returning from the bathroom when I came back to earth this time. He had apparently cleaned himself off and now had a cloth that he used to wipe the lube from Rudy's ass. As I watched, he tossed the cloth aside, then climbed over Rudy until he was straddling Rudy's head and, therefore, my hips. He touched his nose to mine, forehead to mine.

"Feel it, Meg. I know you can. You're too powerful, too instinctive, not to. That other witch I was with couldn't do this, but you can." His words shocked me, even more because Rudy continued to distract me with fingers, thumb, tongue, and lips. "It's the perfect time of year. Samhain. Magic is rife in the air. You haven't been blocked from all your power, or else the leashes would be completely gone."

As he called my scattered attention to them, the leashes shimmered to view. I didn't know if only I could see them, or if he'd somehow made them visible. But when he raised his head,

I saw the faint yellow-white glow around his neck. I glanced down and saw the darker orange-ish one around the base of his cock and the yellow-white band around Rudy's neck.

"They're stronger each time we fuck you," he said. "Deeper. Connecting us. Let's complete the connection between all three of us."

I shuddered as Rudy pushed me over the top again. This one was a long, hazy spiral that wound my senses and flushed them down the drain into a maelstrom.

"Let us, Meg." His lips hovered over mine, breathing in my gasps.

"Oh, yes," I moaned, the thought too much to deny any longer.

Rudy slowly drew away from my pussy. Michael sank onto my body, his hips replacing Rudy's head. Deftly, he rolled, taking me with him until I ended up on top.

"Reach down and put my cock inside you, Meg," he murmured.

Eagerly, I complied. I couldn't resist pumping that thick organ once with my hand, just to make him moan, before I placed him and used my body weight to sheathe him deep inside. Even wet as I was, it took some maneuvering. And he'd had that whole thing inside Rudy! The memory of the sight boiled my blood, and my body seized in a massive shudder. More! I slammed down on him, grinding my groin to his. His sharp intake of breath sliced pure joy through my chest.

Then Rudy was there. I felt his hands on my butt, his fingers sliding through the crack, which my position straddling Michael already widened.

"Relax," Rudy soothed when my motion faltered. "Fuck him, Meg. Goddess, you're beautiful."

I whimpered, both at the compliment and at the fact that Michael took a nipple between thumb and forefinger and pinched it.

Wet fingers probed my ass. Just as Michael had done to him, Rudy prepared me, slathering tons of lubrication in my hole. I sank down on Michael's chest, moaning softly. Michael murmured soothing nothings in my ear and rolled his hips a bit, fucking me from underneath.

Rudy was ready. His fingers were gone, and I felt something larger and blunter nudge against my nether hole. I froze completely. Rudy leaned forward to press his chest to my back, easing his cock lengthwise between my ass cheeks. "I'll go slow," he murmured, kissing the back of my shoulder. "It'll hurt at first, but if you can get past it, I promise you'll like it."

"You better be right."

He chuckled. His cockhead teased against my anus. I comforted myself by rolling my hips against Michael, abrading my pussy with the thickness of him.

"Push out at me," Rudy said as he started to press in. "Relax and push out. It'll make it easier. Relax."

He kept saying that! Just because of that, I knew it was going to hurt like hell. But I was committed now. And truthfully, a part of me *really* wanted this. I did push back against him, grinding Michael at the same time.

"Shit!" I hissed. "That hurts."

"You're tight," Rudy groaned. His fingers dug into my sides.

I dropped my head and braced my arms to either side of Michael's neck. Michael fondled my breasts while Rudy pressed steadily forward.

"Wait!"

Rudy stopped pushing and started pulling. Oh, my! Now *that* felt kind of good. Especially since Michael decided to push a bit. Rudy was almost out before he started to push again, slowly. Michael ever so slowly edged out of my pussy, making way.

"Oh, fuck, Mike, I can feel you!" Rudy groaned, forehead pressed to the back of my shoulder.

He could?! The thought made me shudder more, even as I tried not to concentrate on the burn of Rudy's cock forging into my ass.

"Meg, Goddess, Meg," Rudy muttered, his lips fluttering over my back and shoulders. "You're so hot. So tight."

He pulled, and Michael pushed, and I fucking couldn't stand it. I squealed, squirming as best I could as pleasure, wet and dark and overwhelming, washed over me.

They kept up the slow pace, their hands keeping me as still as possible as they stretched me beyond anything I'd thought was possible. I cried out.

"More," I finally demanded, my fingers now clawing at Michael's shoulders. "Faster."

"You sure?" Rudy asked.

"Yes, damn it. Yes!"

The rhythm picked up, and I thought about dying. Dying right there would be good because I didn't think it could get much better.

"Feel it, Meg," Michael grunted. "Feel us."

"I can't... I can't do anything but."

"More, Meg. The leashes."

What was he talking about? How could I possibly...?

When I thought of the leashes, they flared back to life in my metaphysical sight. But more than that, they expanded, winding. The faded yellow-white around Michael's throat met the same from Rudy's and extended to somewhere around where my heart raced within my chest. Metaphysical sight has little to do with eyes, so I also saw the spells around their cocks—the cocks pistoning deep inside me—wind together, reach and latch around something in my belly. My womb. The connections snapped into place, and I stiffened, ramrod straight, as the most incredible surge of blinding pleasure roared through me. I don't know what my body did, but I'm pretty sure I was moving. Because they were moving. The spells were moving. Everything was pumping into me; everything was filling me; everything was pushing me to the breaking point, where I let out a scream. Pleasure and power burst from my shuddering skin and shoved into them, fucking them like they were fucking me. Both of my lovers roared, claws bursting out, fangs and eyes going bestial. For one agonizing, endless moment, we were one straining being struggling to mesh three parts into one.

Chapter Eight

I woke when the warm male back I was snuggling against tried to escape. I grumbled as he tried to slide out from under me.

Rudy chuckled, patting my hand. "Awake?"

"No." I nuzzled his shoulder and bit the muscle.

He shuddered. "Hungry?"

I blinked. Thought about it. "Actually, yeah."

"Good? I was getting up to make breakfast."

Sighing, I released him. "Fine. If it's for a good cause."

He rolled over quickly to face me and brushed a warm kiss on my lips. "There are new toothbrushes and stuff in the bathroom. Help yourself if you don't want to dig out your own."

As I watched his shapely little rear end lift from the bed, I realized that it must be morning because I could see clearly. I wiggled my behind, but the male body that had kept my back warm all night was gone.

Well, damn.

I snuggled down into the pillows, enjoying the smell of hot, musky sex I'd had with two amazingly gorgeous men. I giggled, breathing deep. I'd passed out completely after that last explosive orgasm, but as I was relatively clean—if really sore—I smiled warmly to realize that one or both of my lovers had tended to me.

Lovers. Plural. Amazing. In less than a day, I'd not only acquired two gorgeous shifters who seemed bound and determined to protect me, but I'd also acquired two amazing lovers who seemed determined to find my sexual limits. Part of me almost wanted to thank Roland for pushing me into casting the spell to attract them.

Unfortunately, Roland was a sobering thought. Experimentally, I tried a simple spell. Watching my fingers, I tried to get a flame to balance on the tips. It was a spell I'd done thousands of times, the first I'd ever mastered. It was also amazingly simple.

Nothing.

So how the heck had I connected the three of us last night? *That* I recalled with blinding clarity. I'm pretty sure I could even do it again, although outside of orgasm, I wasn't sure what good it would do.

Not that the orgasm wasn't a great reason.

I got up from the bed and went to use the bathroom. My body ached inside and out in a way I'd never dreamed possible. Especially my ass. How had they managed to talk me into *that?*

After cleaning up, I crossed the hall to the guest bedroom I hadn't used, to get fresh clothing.

They were both in the kitchen when I arrived, talking softly as Rudy stood over a sizzling frying pan. Michael stood up against the counter beside him, holding a mug to his lips. His other arm was crossed over his chest as support. Both of them were dressed in jeans and nothing else.

Rudy glanced over his shoulder, tossing his head to clear sunny brown hair from his eyes. "You're not a vegetarian, are you?" he asked, not quite hiding his horror at the thought.

"Nope."

"Thank the Goddess," he murmured, carrying the pan toward me and dumping a load of thick, crackling bacon onto a platter sitting on the counter. It looked like that was the third or fourth panful of bacon he'd prepared, because the stack was pretty high. Another plate, full of fluffy scrambled eggs, sat beside the bacon.

I hiked myself up onto a barstool that stood on the opposite side of the long, freestanding counter from them. I winced a little at the tenderness of my posterior.

"Sore?" Michael asked.

Why did that knowing smirk make my heart race? Bastard. "Gee, you think?"

Rudy grinned as he returned the sizzling pan to the stove. "You get used to it."

I snorted and noticed that I didn't say that we wouldn't do it again. Good Goddess, if I wouldn't admit it to them, I could admit it to myself. Having them both inside my body was *definitely* an experience that I'd repeat, sore body or not.

Rudy crouched before the oven to remove a cookie sheet full of rolls. Michael picked up a mug and gestured it toward me. I nodded eagerly, and he poured me a cup of steaming black coffee.

"Are those homemade?" I asked.

"Yep," Rudy replied, standing.

Michael met my eyes over the rim of his coffee cup. "Don't look at me. He's the domestic one."

I chuckled, grabbing a piece of bacon. "Why does that not surprise me?"

Rudy dumped the rolls onto another plate with a practiced flourish, then set the pan on the stove and went to the refrigerator. "Somebody has to feed him. You should have seen what he was like before he met me."

"At least I ate. You were half starved," Michael drawled, setting the coffee down before me.

"True," Rudy admitted as he worked, "I didn't even know how to cook then. But I think I've done rather well." He stopped just to Michael's side, bumping hip to hip. "Right?"

Michael smiled and reached out to loosely circle Rudy's trim waist with his arm. "You do very well."

I watched the exchange with amazement. I'd never had any gay friends in long-term relationships, and I'd certainly never seen morning-after prattle between two men. It was enthralling. Rudy pressed his hip to Michael's, his hand resting lightly on Michael's belly. The smile they shared told of countless hours just being together.

"How long have you been together?"

"A little over a year," Rudy told me proudly, breaking the near-embrace to retrieve plates.

I frowned up at him. "How old are you?"

He grinned. "Twenty, four months ago."

I arched a brow at Michael, who had turned away to pile food on a plate. I smiled. "How old are you, Michael?"

"Old enough."

Rudy laughed, filling his own plate. "Thirty-two."

"How sweet. A May-December romance."

Michael glared. "Hardly."

"Yeah, it's June-December," Rudy joked, earning him a smack on the head.

Michael pointed a fork at me for emphasis. "And, just for the record, *he* chased me."

Rudy nodded emphatically. "Chased him for two years, in fact."

"Jail bait," Michael grumbled.

I laughed. "Was this when you were leashed before?"

Like a douse of cold water on a fire, there went the levity. Both of their grins faded abruptly, and neither would meet my gaze. "I'm sorry, guys. I didn't mean to bring up a sore subject."

Rudy glanced to Michael for guidance.

Michael forked eggs into his mouth, chewed, then sighed. "No. You've a right to know." The look on his face was thoughtful, shadowed with pain. "Just...not yet. Let's get you through tonight and get your magic back. Then we'll talk."

Fair enough, I decided. Besides, I really wanted the light banter back.

Rudy came to the rescue. "Hey! Do we get to wear costumes?!"

Shortly after breakfast, I called Gwen, who had called my cell a number of times the previous night, both before and after Roland's call.

"Where *are* you? I called your house when I couldn't get you on your cell. I would have called the police, but..."

But she knew it was a bad idea to involve mundanes in magical affairs. They tended to get hurt or used as tools.

"I'm sorry. There was an...incident at the house. Michael and Rudy brought me to their place."

"Are you ok?"

"Yeah, I'm ok. Mostly."

"What does *that* mean?!"

I filled her in on Brent's visit, complete with losing my magic and Rudy and Michael coming to my rescue.

"Oh, my God, Meg—" Gwen was raised Catholic and introduced into the world of magic only in the last two years. The Goddess was a new concept for her still. "That's horrible! What are you going to do?"

I glanced down the hall from my seat at the kitchen counter. I was alone for the moment. Michael was in his office, and Rudy had taken the car keys and gone out hunting costumes for him and Michael, despite my assurances that they didn't need them.

"Michael thinks he knows a way to counter Roland's spell."

"Who *is* this guy, Meg? Do shifters normally know anything about magic?"

"Not as much as this one seems to."

"Do you think he's dangerous? Should I come and get you? Do you want me to call someone?"

"I *know* he's dangerous, but I don't think he is to me. I'm fine. Besides, the leash is still in place."

"Huh? I thought you said you lost your magic."

"I did. But the leashes are still in place. They're weak, though."

"Weak? And he didn't break it?"

"Nope."

"After his reaction yesterday, I would have thought he'd jump at the chance."

"Me, too."

Pause. "Meg?"

"Yeah?"

"What were you doing all last night in a house with two gorgeous men?"

I had to smile. She expected me to be coy. Fuck that. "Having amazing sex with the two of them."

She laughed. "Yeah, right." When I said nothing, she gasped, laughter gone. "Get out!"

My grin hurt my face, it was so big. "I shit you not."

"You bitch! Oh, you *must* tell me all!"

Michael stepped into the hall, catching my attention. How could he not? With only jeans on, he was a delectable distraction. I could see the amusement in his expression. Shit! I guess cats have pretty good hearing. He gestured for me to join him, then turned back to the office.

"I've gotta go."

"More sex?"

"Maybe."

"You bitch!"

"No, I think Michael wants to start in on this counterspell." I told her briefly that we'd be at the shop tonight and that I'd call later with the details.

"What's going to happen, Meg?"

"I don't know yet."

"You take care of yourself, and *call* me if you need me."

"I will. Thanks."

I hung up, put my cell in my pocket, then went to join Michael.

His office was one of those Spartan deals with very little furniture. The only comfortable place to sit other than the plush black carpet was behind the massive, high-tech desk. The desk itself was one of those strange things that was more a series of shelves attached to chrome pipes. I counted at least three desktop computers and a laptop situated on, in, and below the desk, and there were two LCD monitors facing the chair. A widescreen television sat in an entertainment unit within a recess on the opposite wall, both it and the accompanying hi-fi equipment dangling loose cords and cables like entrails. Obviously, he hadn't gotten around to finishing the setup.

Michael was seated cross-legged on the floor before the desk, a thick purple floor pillow underneath him. Another pillow sat before him. I took the seat when indicated.

I sighed. "This is where we learn words and meditate, right?"

He laughed softly at my grimace. "I take it this is not your favorite part of your craft?"

"I told you, it's not my craft. It's just something I do. I have to."

"Why do you have to?"

"Because, unlike other people, the magic will just happen if I don't learn some control. Other people have to *make* it happen. I have to make it *not* happen."

"Interesting." He watched as I adjusted my legs. "I've only known a few instinctives, and none very well."

I shrugged. Settled my hands on my knees. Blew out a breath. "Okay, chief, whatcha got?"

We spent the next few hours discussing the aspects of the spell Roland had set on me and what I could do to counter it. Michael was surprisingly knowledgeable, and what he didn't know, he had very good theories about. His whole idea of the counterspell was a theory, but though I did my best to poke holes in it, it was a good theory.

I didn't get bored, which shocked me. Unlike those who had tried to teach me magic in the past, he didn't try to instruct. We *discussed* the magic. He asked me plenty of questions. I was surprised to find that I knew a lot of the answers. It was like he was just presenting facts and theories to me and leaving the actual magic part to me. I'd never had anyone do that with me. It was kind of fun!

I'd come up with a workable theory of a spell by the time Rudy returned. Michael and I got up to stretch our legs.

I was shocked when I looked at the clock. "It's five o'clock! We've been sitting here for five hours!"

"Mmm." He slid his hand over my back, using it to propel me into his chest. "And I've been wanting to do this for five hours."

He placed his lips on mine, a soft meeting of skin to skin, with a warm, wet tongue to moisten the way. I parted readily to allow him to explore my mouth, loving the taste of him. Dark and spicy.

"Hey! What'd I miss?"

Michael lifted his head with a smile that matched mine. Together we faced the door to see Rudy leaning in the doorway, one hand braced on either side of the opening.

Michael held out a hand to him. "Nothing. You're just in time."

"Excellent!" He sauntered toward us, sliding his denim jacket down his arms and tossing it onto the very uncomfortable-looking leather couch. The move looked practiced, far too smooth for it not to be a show for our benefit. Not that I didn't enjoy it, as the move did make the muscles of his chest and arms move nicely under his sleeveless T-shirt.

I reached out to trace the design tattooed around his biceps as he curled his arm around me from behind. "Nice."

"Thank you," he nuzzled my neck. Michael curled a hand in his hair, gently kissing the top of his head.

Michael's hands slid to my waist, where his fingers could trace my bare belly beneath the hem of my T-shirt and above the waistband of my jeans. "Now, we do something about strengthening the link between us. Rudy?"

"Hmmm?"

I shivered as he nibbled that spot on my neck he'd found that drove me crazy.

"It's our job to keep ourselves open to Meg. She needs to feel us, physically and mentally."

"Not a problem," Rudy assured him, shoving a hand under my arm to take possession of my breast.

Michael sank to his knees, loosening my jeans. I leaned into Rudy, mapping his chest by pressing my back against it.

"Meg, relax," Michael prompted, sliding my jeans down. "You concentrate on the magic." He swiped his tongue over my navel. "Let us take care of your body."

When put that way, how could a girl refuse?

I sighed, closing my eyes and sinking against Rudy. I wasn't wearing much, so it didn't take long for them to get me naked. Michael teased the curls between my legs with his lips and breath, never quite touching anything good. Rudy supported me, one strong arm around my middle while the other hand played with my nipple. I let this go on until the teasing made me squirm.

"Michael," I warned, putting my hand to the back of his head to try and make him do something more serious.

He chuckled, sliding his hands up my thighs and hips as he stood. "Time to move to the bedroom." He lifted me easily from Rudy's embrace.

"Good," Rudy said, following. "Because this furniture you've got in here just isn't comfortable."

"It's *my* room."

"So you chose uncomfortable furniture to keep me out?"

"Ah! Deductive reasoning from the puppy. I'm impressed."

I buried my face in Michael's neck, laughing softly at their banter.

Michael took me to the bedroom and laid me out on the rumpled sheet, stretching his heavy body atop mine. My perked nipples scraped through his chest hair as he rubbed against me. When I tried to put my arms around him, he took hold of my wrists and pressed them against the bed. "Relax," he reminded me, lapping at the pulse at my neck. "Concentrate."

"How can I concentrate when you do that?"

"Do I have to tie you down?"

I was surprised by the thrill the thought gave me. I was further surprised when Michael raised his head. He met my gaze, amused, his long hair falling in a silky curtain to either side of his face. "Rudy, did you feel that?"

"Yeah! That was awesome." The bed beside us shook. Michael tossed his head to clear the hair from one side, revealing Rudy naked and stretched out beside us. "She wants to be tied down!"

I closed my eyes and groaned.

Michael pushed back, straddling my hips. His hands went to the waist of his jeans, slowly unbuttoning them. "Not this time," he said, eyes trained on my lips. "But soon, I promise."

I licked my lips when his cock emerged, angry red, with thick, ropey veins to decorate the shaft. "Promises, promises," I rasped, clutching the hands that I kept obediently above my head.

Michael climbed off to dispose of his jeans. Rudy inched forward, pressing his front against my side. He turned my head with the tips of his fingers and angled his lips above mine. He barely touched me, teasing me by nipping at my lips. I sighed, shutting my eyes. I could feel him more than physically. The leash around his neck and cock was still invisibly linked to my heart and womb. I turned my attention to that, and my awareness of him surged softly, sluggishly. I wondered what it would be like with my full powers.

The bed sagged again, and I turned my attention. How cool! I could feel Michael coming, sense him through the leash as much as I felt his body heat. We'd discussed that a long time today, what it was that I sensed—him, or the magic? What made it tangible? He'd told me that, even weakened, he felt this leash much more clearly than he'd felt his previous one. We theorized that it was a lot of my attraction to them and that the magic flowed along that strong pull.

He pulled my thigh toward him, spreading my legs. I lay completely limp as he tasted the inside of my leg, trailing up to my sex. He lay between my legs, scooping his hands beneath my ass, cupping it like a large slice of melon he was about to devour. I would have giggled at the mental image, but his light kisses around my pussy distracted me. Rudy smothered my smile by taking further possession of my mouth. Michael's thumbs spread my swollen folds. His tongue followed. The arch of my back and the groan were involuntary.

They both drank at me, mouth and pussy, neither in any kind of hurry. I subsided into languid bliss, letting them pleasure my body as I explored my link to them. Our connection pulsed with my heartbeat and, I think, in time with theirs, as well. I pulled them both to me as hard as I could, frustrated when that wasn't really enough.

"Relax, Meg," Michael purred into my cunt. "It's working. Just relax."

Rudy backed off enough to whisper against my lips. "It feels amazing, Meg. Like you're inside of me."

Warmth suffused me at their words, and they sighed in tandem. My excitement grew, and they responded to my growing urgency. Rudy spaced kisses down my throat, over my chest, until he could cup a breast in his hand, guiding it to his mouth. I *had* to move. I pumped my hips at Michael's mouth and dropped my hand on Rudy's hair, holding him there. They suckled me into a warm, rolling orgasm. Groaning, I sank into it and consciously pushed it toward them. They both gasped, twitching with me.

"Mike?" Rudy asked, voice strangled.

Michael pushed up. "Let's fuck."

I laughed and let them rearrange me. Michael knelt and hauled me up into his lap, straddling him. He kissed my lips when they arrived before his, and I licked my own taste from his lips and tongue.

"Ride me, sweetheart."

With his help, I lifted up and fit that monster cock at my entrance. I pushed down. "You feel so good."

"You, too," he muttered, holding me close.

We stayed still a moment, our bodies locked and the leash pulsing softly. We didn't move until Rudy was at my back, with wet fingers probing at my ass. I took a deep breath and turned inward, fanning the flame of our desire, dribbling it to them through the leash.

"Rudy," Michael groaned.

"Yeah, yeah. I'm there."

Both of their voices were strained. I felt Rudy behind me, positioning, then pushing.

My back bent, and I clutched Michael's head to my neck. At Michael's murmured behest, I relaxed and opened, and it just got better. Rudy panted, pushing further. His hands at my waist clutched, bit. I hissed, knowing he cut me with claws he couldn't sheathe.

"Sorry," he groaned, and his voice was octaves deeper than it should be.

I pulled Michael's hair, turning his face up where I could see it. Yes. His eyes had gone pure cat, as had his teeth. Even his lips and mouth had changed, the sides of his mouth dropping to cover the lower, like a cat's mouth.

The sight thrilled me, pulsing my connection with them, and two animal groans rumbled around me. Rudy pressed in, seated within me as far as he could go. He nipped the back of my shoulder lightly, and I felt his fangs.

"Shit, Meg," he growled.

"Take us, Meg," Michael rumbled.

And I could. I clutched Michael for support and rocked my hips, fucking them both as they fought to stay still. I knew that they were treading a fine line, barely maintaining control. I felt how close they were to slipping their human bodies. They held me, supported me, but it was time for me to take over. I swiveled, hardly aware of my physical body as I sank into our metaphysical link. Fur that wasn't tangible rubbed my skin as I lifted and sank. Smells of earth and animal and musk coated my skin. Their connection to my heart pulled, hauling Michael's chest against my breasts and Rudy's against my back. Their connection to my womb contracted, and each cock sank further into my body. I writhed between them, so close. So close! Just one thing more…

"Bite me," I demanded.

Neither could voice his confusion, but I felt it. I mashed Michael's face to one shoulder and reached behind me to pull Rudy's to the other. "Blood, damn it. Blood and sex. Bite me, now!"

Instinct? Command? Who knows what got them to do it, to overcome that hesitation and fear of hurting me. It didn't matter. Together they bit, sharp canines breaking skin. I howled in pain, but the orgasm struck me before it was done. I pounded them, pulling them, the leashed connection yanking orgasms from each of them.

How we stayed upright, I don't know. I sank in their embrace, whimpering. I *hurt!* During, I'd hardly been aware of the double penetration. As the sensation dribbled away, I felt every inch of each cock. Not to mention the bite wounds in both shoulders.

Rudy pulled away, awkwardly, and fell back on the bed. Trembling, Michael lowered me beside him, then stretched out at my side for a few moments. He tried to get up, but I stopped him. "Stay."

"You're bleeding."

"Not much. Stay."

He sank back. Rudy rolled over, and both of them pressed against either of my sides. Rudy laid his hand on my belly. Michael laid his over it. They let their fingers entwine.

I didn't think it was possible to be any closer to another person, let alone two.

Chapter Nine

"Isn't this a bit excessive?"

Rudy grinned, but didn't take his eyes off the street. He slumped in the driver's seat, both hands in the pockets of his denim jacket. Even though his mop of hair fell in his face, I had little doubt that those piercing blue eyes didn't miss anything outside the car as they settled from window to window to rearview mirror. Outside, people in costume made their way to the pedestrian mall and the giant, cheesy-looking spider that had been mounted over the main entrance.

"We're protecting you. That's what we're supposed to do."

I stared at the street, too, conscious of the traffic passing us by as we were parked underneath a tree. "I told Roland ten o'clock. Do you really think he'll be scouting around before that?"

"I would."

"Why?"

He shrugged one shoulder. "I put myself in the guy's shoes. If I really wanted a girl that bad, and I didn't care what her feelings were about it, I'd come early, scope out the place, and take her early if I could."

I blinked at him across the darkened car. He swiveled his head to meet my gaze, some of his soft hair falling to the side to reveal those sparkling blue eyes. His ever-present grin was there, but I was starting to get the feeling that there was a lot more to Rudy than met the eye.

"You would?"

"Yeah. *If* I was an obsessive, egotistical jerk." He flashed teeth. "Which I'm not."

I laughed. Despite the tension, despite the fact that we waited here for a sign from Michael that he hadn't found anything suspicious and dangerous to me, despite the fact that I might very well become Roland's plaything in another hour or so, Rudy made me laugh. What a precious man!

I sighed, toying with one of the jagged edges of my skirt. "I should probably just let him keep my magic. It's never done me any good anyway."

Rudy backhanded my arm lightly. "Hey!"

I smiled. "Okay. One or two good things have come from it. But it's the only reason Roland wants me. It's not like he'd want me without the magic."

"Why wouldn't he?"

I snorted. "Please. I'm not the type of girl guys pant over."

He reached over to cup my chin in his fingers, turning my head toward him. He'd leaned in and was mere inches from touching my nose with his. "Then they're stupid and blind. I happen to think you're gorgeous."

"That's the leash talking."

He trailed a knuckle down the line of my neck to softly graze my collarbone. "The leash wouldn't make me like you. Or want to wrap yards and yards of your soft hair around my hands and use it to hold you down while I taste every curve you've got."

My heart raced as I stared into his eyes and heard his words. Where had that husky quality come from? Where he dredged up all that sincerity?

"You're a beautiful woman, Meg, and both Michael and I look forward to getting to know you real good after we get this Roland character out of the way."

I stared at him, clenching my hands into fists to avoid grabbing him. "Why didn't you break the leash?"

"Don't want to."

"Why?"

He considered me seriously. "Michael and I love each other; I know that. But it gets to be too much sometimes. We *need* someone else. For balance." He brushed my cheek with the back of his hand. "I think that's why we were both attracted to you. You're the third. You're the balance." He traced my lower lip with his thumb. "Damn, I wish Michael hadn't told me I couldn't kiss you."

I drew in a stuttering breath. We'd made the connection that last time we'd had sex. Even though my magic was weak, I felt the leash humming. I had to concentrate and *hold* it tight. Michael was concerned that if we got distracted by fooling around, I'd lose the connection to both of them.

Rudy glanced down the street, then sank back into the driver's seat. "You're being paged."

Near the entrance, Gwen stood beside a potted tree at the end of the pedestrian mall. Actually, she stood *on* the pot so that we could see her above the milling, costumed crowd. Michael had said he'd send her out if the coast was clear.

"This is it," I sighed, reaching for the door handle.

"Let's make this fast, huh? I want to get you and Michael back home."

Yes, he made me smile over my nerves.

I walked toward Gwen, easily avoiding anyone in the sparse crowd. The main party had started about an hour ago, so the people around me were the latecomers. I felt Rudy's attention on my back like a warm, safe cloak. Somewhere, unseen, I knew Michael watched me as well.

"There you are," Gwen crowed, spying me.

I waved my broom at her. She hopped down, adjusted her Little Bo Peep skirts, and we started down the walk to the shop. Between her crook and my broom, we managed not to be jostled too much by the crowd. Still, I kept a wary eye out, and bless her heart, I think Gwen did, too.

"Did you see Roland today?"

"Nope. And he's lucky. I would have clobbered him." She shook her shepherd's crook.

I laughed. At all of five-foot, Gwen was hardly menacing. Well, at least until she opened her mouth. *Then* she was a force to be reckoned with.

"Where's Michael?"

"Don't know. He came in, told me what to do—" She arched a brow at me, silently telling me that she'd borne that outrage for me. "—then left." She laughed. "I must say, though, I approve of his costume."

"I'll bet!"

"And I *will* hold you to that promise to tell all, you slut!"

Friends. Gotta love 'em.

We got to the shop ok, but I didn't go inside. I followed Michael's instructions and stayed in the little courtyard between our shop and the music store. A few sturdy iron table-and-chair sets were strewn around a funky modern art sculpture that looked more like a kid's toy than anything artistic. Surprisingly, there was no one in the courtyard. Plenty of people passed by the opening, but no one came in to join me. Then again, I could hear the band playing at the open air amphitheater down the way, and that seemed to be where most of the crowd was headed.

I sat in one of the iron chairs. Then stood, too antsy to be still. I considered going into the shop to get a cup of coffee to keep me busy for a few minutes, but a voice stopped me.

"Meg."

Chapter Ten

I turned. Roland stood at the edge of the courtyard, flanked by Brent and one of the men he'd had with him yesterday. A Roman senator's toga draped Roland's slim build, part of the white-and-violet tail draped over his bare shoulder. He even had a golden leaf crown on his curly brown hair. The men flanking him were dressed as Roman centurions.

"I approve of your outfit," he said, looking me up and down with a possessiveness that I didn't appreciate.

"Shouldn't you have dressed as the Marquis de Sade?"

"Very funny." He held out his hand. "Shall we go?"

"Go?"

"Yes. To my house. To a *real* Samhain celebration, not this—" He glanced disdainfully over his shoulder. "—farce."

"I don't think I want to go to a party at your place, Roland."

He stared down his long, straight nose at me. "I don't think you have a choice."

I held out my hand. "Hey, Roland, why don't you just give me the little ball with my magic and go away. No harm, no foul." Hey, it was worth a try, right?

He laughed, but there was no humor in it. "Oh, Meg, you are droll."

"That's me. Drolly Meg." I wiggled my fingers. "Hand it over."

"Did you think I brought it with me?"

My blood ran cold. Actually, I had. Michael had. The whole plan hinged on that.

Roland's smile grew. "What did you think, Meg? That I'd give you back your magic, you'd recover and be able to escape me?" He stepped toward me as I stood frozen in shock. "I am not stupid, my dear."

Apparently not. He took my hand and started to draw me away. I wanted to scream. I wanted to call for Michael. But I didn't. He didn't know. This could still work, couldn't it? I had to get to the ball before I could start anything in motion.

Gwen raced out of the shop, stepping in front of Brent, who led the way. She held her crook across her body, almost as though she knew how to use it as a weapon. "You're not taking her anywhere."

"Go find your sheep, Bo Peep," Roland advised, holding fast to my wrist.

"Let her go."

"Don't make me hurt you, little girl."

"Fuck you."

Roland sneered. He raised his hand and flicked his fingers, as though batting a moth from his face. Gwen stumbled out of her solid stance, not catching herself until she thudded against the wall of our shop.

"Hey!"

Roland rounded on me, squeezing to hurt my wrist. "Do *not* toy with me, Meg. Not tonight. I won't tolerate it. I've been patient until now."

My blood ran cold. I knew he was an icy bastard, but this behavior was new. Economy of motion and emotion—that was Roland. Tonight, for him, he was being passionate.

"It's ok, Gwen," I said lamely, not taking my eyes from Roland's steely blue gaze. "Roland's just taking me to a party at his place."

He nodded, straightened, and turned.

Gwen pushed from the wall toward us, but halted when Roland held up his hand, palm out toward her.

"Don't think to call any authorities," Roland advised her. "Go back inside. Meg will call you tomorrow."

Gwen didn't take her eyes off me. I tried to convey my thoughts with my eyes. *Tell Michael and Rudy where he's taking me.* She knew where Roland lived, even if she'd never been there.

She ground her teeth. "Meg?"

"Just going to a party, Gwen. I'll see you later, and we'll talk about those guys you met."

Roland lost patience and hauled me away, toward the parking lot.

I sat in the back of the limo, trying not to shake. Roland went on and on about how wonderful this was, how fitting our life together should start on Samhain, witches' new year. It was, indeed, a powerful time and one I did *not* relish spending with him.

He tried to put his arm around me, but I squirmed away. When he pushed the issue, I went so far as to sit on the floor of the limo. Brent, seated across from us, had to move his legs aside. His thick features very carefully did not smile, but I think I saw the glint of amusement when I glared up at him.

Roland was not amused. "Meg, you're being childish."

I put my thumb in my mouth.

I heard the growl, but totally didn't expect the fingers that bit sharply into my shoulder to turn me around, nor the resounding slap across my face. I stared up at him in horror.

"You *will* learn to obey me. Do you understand me, Meg?"

"I understand that you'd better not do that again."

His eyes narrowed to angry slits, making his lean face resemble nothing so much as a spitting cobra. How come when Michael slitted his eyes at me, it melted my insides, but when Roland did it, they rolled in nausea?

"Or what, Meg? Don't you understand? You're mine now. I've been very nice about it until now. And I can continue to be nice." He slapped me again. "But *don't push me.*"

My mother. My oldest sister. One of my aunts. These are the only people who have ever gotten away with slapping me. I'd sought and achieved revenge on the few others who'd tried. I sat quietly in the limo, glaring daggers at Roland until he slapped me again. Then I glared daggers at my hands, determined that with or without my absent shifters, I *would* make Roland pay.

Chapter Eleven

Roland's house was as ostentatious as he. One of those gorgeous showplace homes that look really nice but that no one can actually live in. We parked, and he hauled me inside. We went straight through the marble entry, the black-and-chrome living room, and the sparse, art deco formal dining room, and exited through the sliding doors to the landscaped backyard.

There, a small group of people were gathered. Roland, his two centurions, and one more bodyguard were the men present. The five women were clustered about a bonfire on a paved patio area above the pool. They were all dressed in skimpy outfits that made my witch's costume look like a nun's habit. All talk ceased when Roland pulled me outside, but I don't think he noticed. The women stared at us, and it was only then that I noticed that they were penned on the patio by a spell. I could see it wavering at the edges of the pavement like heat waves off pavement.

Pig!

These were the poor members of his coven. I didn't even want to use the word to describe what he'd done. A coven was supposed to be a good thing. A gathering of witches who had reached an accord. A group of like-minded people who agreed to use their powers together, usually for the protection of the group. But that's not what this was. Roland had *forced* this accord. None of the women in that circle showed their magic, so they were either very powerful, or not at all powerful. I was betting on the latter. He'd overwhelmed them, taken them hostage, and forced them into a so-called accord. Oh, he might have done it with seduction, might have convinced them to join, but the end result was the same.

I mentally clutched my leashes. I was actually kind of surprised that Roland didn't see them, but they were weak to the magical sight. They were a thing more felt than seen by any but me, and I wasn't sure Roland could feel anything. I took heart from the echo of furry bodies and warm strength. I couldn't tell if they were close or not. I tried to monitor the feel of it. Did that sense of presence mean that they were close? Or was that my hopeful imagination?

Roland drew me toward a courtyard of pounded earth beside the patio. A circled pentagram was burned into the ground. Ornate stands held lit torches at each of the five points. Even without my magic, I could feel the power of it, and it stank of Roland. This was his main focus.

Which made it dangerous. "Oh, hell no!" I fought to free my wrist from his grip, digging in my heels.

Roland held on. "Meg, the time is now. I am finished toying with you."

"No! I'm not going in there."

"No? That's the only way to get your magic back."

He snapped his fingers, and Brent brought him a bag. Roland pulled that small ball out of it. I grabbed for the ball, but

Roland wrapped his long fingers around it. I snarled at the fingers and couldn't believe it when that fist came at my face. He caught me solid on the jaw, throwing me sideways. I stumbled and fell.

Right into the circle of power.

Roland stepped in with me before I could scramble out. He spoke a word, and the circle flared to life, enclosing us.

Still smarting, I pushed to sit. "You fucking bastard."

"You will learn not to use such language."

"What are you? My father?"

"From this moment forward, I am your *everything*."

"Oh, man. You're not full of yourself or anything."

He hit me again, and this time I tasted blood. My lip poured blood over the teeth that had cut it. He was *so* going to pay for that!

He stalked to the center of the circle and spent a moment to loosen his toga. It fell in a white-and-violet puddle at his feet, revealing his naked body to the torchlight and moonlight. He was actually quite a good-looking man, if you liked tall and slim. He kept himself in good shape, even though it looked like he'd never get any muscle mass. His slimness was entirely different from Rudy's. Rudy was sleek, but he had curves and definition and decided bulk to his muscles. If it were possible, I'd swear that Roland had had his muscles painted on or sculpted, rather than doing anything physical to acquire them.

Looked like hitting me excited him. Either that, or the power surrounding us. Because his cock was at three-quarter mast.

He snapped his fingers. "Come here."

I wanted to fight, but even I know when to be quiet sometimes. He still held my magic in that ball, and that was what I had to get back. I got to my feet and walked to him, glaring. I almost expected to get hit again, but I guess he figured he had the upper hand.

He held the ball in his fist between us, fingers facing up. "Take my hand."

I took a breath and brought my spell to mind. Would it work through a circle of power? Those circles were designed to keep magic in or out. What did my hold on the leashes count as?

Well, I wasn't going anywhere. Might as well do what I could. I put my hand on Roland's.

His grin of triumph was sickening, even if it was cool and understated. He reached out to grip my shoulder with his free hand, then opened his mouth to start his incantation.

I stared at our hands. Once he'd begun, I started muttering my own incantation. Contrary to myth, the words aren't really important. Not if they don't mean anything to the spell-caster. The words are to help the focus, to help guide the magic. You can do magic without the words, but it was harder and tended to get away. The only visual I can give is a water hose. Use a hose and you can direct where the water goes. Without the hose, you pretty much just get everything wet.

So I clutched the feel of the leashes linked to my heart and womb, and I used the words that helped me to define the theories Michael and I had discussed earlier in the day. My words were lost in Roland's exuberant voice, my actions unclear to him as he crowed to the moon. My words were empty at first. The circle wasn't mine, so the magic was sluggish at best, but I pushed it, clutching the hand and the ball inside my hand, reaching out, desperately searching the furred presence that would help me do this.

Was that a cough I heard? Or was that one of those short, feline barks that big cats make? I'm pretty sure that was definitely a bark. Whatever, I felt the fur, felt the muscle, and dug my metaphorical fingers into it until I touched two warm, familiar souls.

Weak, weird magic burbled within me, and I channeled it down my arm. I clutched at Roland's hand and the ball inside it. His chant reached inside me, sought to settle a spell like the leash on my soul. I fought it back, wrapping myself in my dual layers of bestial protection. My chant gained volume as I siphoned their connection to me, taking all they offered until that weak warmth touched the ball in Roland's clutches.

A feline scream pierced the night, followed by human, feminine shrieks.

Roland's chant faltered, his concentration broken despite his exuberance. I knew what was out there, so I didn't stop chanting, didn't take my eyes from our hands as that strange magic I took from Rudy and Michael touched the ball. Like to like kissed through the veil of Roland's spell. Real light flooded our hands. It does that when two strong spells collide.

Roland snarled, pulling his hand to try and free it, but I held fast. He gripped my shoulder, and though he unknowingly found Rudy's bite mark and it hurt, I held fast. My magic flooded back into me, sinking into my being and overflowing into the animals that shored me up.

Out of the corner of my eye, outside the haze of the circle of power, I saw a black jaguar, then a wolf flash by. But I couldn't concentrate on them. Didn't really know if they were real, or a reflection of my inner sight. I wasn't done with my spell, and it took all my concentration.

Roland fought me. Not physically, but he tried to counter my chant. He was good. He was also more educated than I. But I had brute strength on my side.

I lifted my gaze to his. I let all my hatred show. How *dare* he hit me! How *dare* he try to pen me. Me and other women. Other witches. How *dare* he!

I dug my fingernails into the meat of his thumb, drawing blood. He stood toe to toe with me, speaking, but I couldn't make out his chant. Couldn't afford to try. I gathered magic, gathered myself, gathered the brute force of my will, and abruptly slammed it at him, right between the eyes.

He choked, eyes rolling up into his head. He fell to his knees. I held on to his hand, channeling the force of my rage into him. I didn't even chant now. Didn't need it. I was spilling power all over the circle, but it didn't matter. He thought he'd drain *me?* Yeah, well, fuck him. I'd drain him.

His lips moved, but I cut off his words by slapping him with my free hand. He was stunned in the magical sense as well as in the physical. In my unreasoning rage, I reversed my attack and pulled. I'd show him what it was like to be without magic!

I pulled and pulled. I wasn't sure what. I'd never done anything like this before. I had a vague thought that this probably wasn't a good thing. It seemed that I had some of his thoughts now. A memory? Was that a spell?

In shock, I stopped. The world halted. I stared down at Roland's slack face. His circle of power resonated around me. No. *My* circle of power.

I dropped his hand. Both he and the innocuous little ball—empty of anything now—fell to the ground.

I dropped the circle.

Immediately, I was surrounded by two furry bodies. A wolf, tall enough to reach my waist, pressed against the front of my legs. A jaguar slid against the back of my legs, just brushing my ass. Anxious, I reached down to dig my fingers into real fur. I dropped to my knees, uncaring who else was present, and buried my face in the ruff at Rudy's neck.

And wept.

Chapter Twelve

I'm hazy on the details that happened right after that.

We left Roland's house without further confrontation. I didn't know at the time if anyone offered resistance. All I knew was furred warmth, then naked-man warmth. It was Rudy who picked me up and carried me away. I know that because I remembered his sweet summer scent.

I curled into his arms and shook. Shuddered. It was like the chills, except that I was far from hot. But neither was I cold. I was full to bursting with raw power that I had no idea how to control.

A flash of a woman whom I'd never met. But I knew her. Rather, Roland had known her. Sweet Goddess, did I have his memories?

A car door opened, and Rudy and I sank into the darkness. His hand cradled the back of my head, pressing my face into his neck as he murmured to me. I absorbed his heat, pressing gladly into his naked chest as another car door opened. A minute later, the car moved.

I whimpered.

"Meg, sweets, do you hear me? Mike, she won't stop shaking."

"Power shock," I heard Michael say. "She lost it and sucked up his power."

"Shit! Can they *do* that?"

"Obviously."

"Is that why he dropped like a stone?"

"Yeah."

I groaned. My teeth chattered.

"Mike! What do I do?"

"Meg, do you hear me?"

I groaned. Couldn't form words. Words didn't mean anything. I understood them, but only in passing. My mind was a cacophony of color and sound that made very little sense. What if I just released it? Would I explode?

"Meg!"

No. Can't release it. Gotta pull it in. But that was like trying to gather feathers in the wind. No, feathers in a tornado when you're standing in the eye of the storm.

"Fuck her."

"What?"

"Fuck her. Now. She needs the connection. Needs the release."

"You've got to be kidding!"

"Do I look like I'm kidding?"

I whimpered, cuddling into Rudy's chest. Oh, yes! That was a better thought. Better than exploding. Fuck me silly, wolfman, so I don't have to try and control a storm.

I tried to help him as he arranged me to straddle his lap, but I couldn't seem to turn on the part of my brain that worked my limbs. I barely knew they were my limbs.

Silky hair twined in my hand as I fucked the screaming girl from behind, my cock raw from taking her before she was ready.

My cock! Oh, no! Nonononononono! I did *not* want Roland's memories.

Lips pressed at my temple. Warm, male lips begging me to come back. Rudy. Fingers probed between my legs, and I hissed at the shot of red lightning that cracked the storm inside me.

"Goddess, she's wet!"

"Power will do that," Michael said.

Oh, yes! There it was. The head of Rudy's cock at my entrance. Seizing control through the storm, I managed to dig my fingers into his shoulders and drop heavily forward, impaling myself in one hard glide. Did he gasp? Or did I? Long and hard, Rudy rammed into the mouth of my womb. Pain. Pleasure. Easier to focus.

Beneath me, Rudy cried out, but I had to trust that he was all right, that he was strong enough to take this, because I *had* to ride him. My hips took on a life of their own, rolling into him, grinding against him, the frantic, mindless fucking of animals driven by a need more than a want. I know I bruised something inside me, but failed to care. Fucking him held the storm at bay, hovering over and around me, but not battering at me. The pleasure-pain kept my concentration. I had use of my body again, and it was far preferable to the resounding storm of power. This was me. This was Rudy. This was *my* experience. I pulled up and slammed down and drew blood from his shoulders with my nails. I came, howling, only realizing as I came down that Rudy's own howl echoed mine.

I slumped against the back of the front passenger seat, opening my eyes finally. I saw Rudy through a haze, my inner sight picking up magical residue in the air. Through it, I saw very clearly the wolf superimposed on the sweaty, panting man slumped in the backseat.

The car stopped with a hitch, shoving Rudy forward against me, then dumping us both back on the seat. I hadn't righted myself before the back door opened and Michael's huge, hairy arms gathered me up.

Oh, the smell of him! The feel. He was all feline strength and grace as he carried me inside. I circled his neck with my arms and squirmed until I could wrap my legs around his waist. His cock nestled against my dripping, swollen folds, and I tilted my hips to slide against him lengthwise through my sex.

He growled, a sound entirely alien to a human throat. The hands that grasped my ass were tipped with claws. Tilting my head back, I saw his cat shaped eyes briefly before he dropped me. I bounced on the mattress that I only dimly realized was his and Rudy's. Before I could move, he flipped me onto my belly with my knees tucked beneath me. He draped over my back like a heavy blanket.

"Let it go, Meg," he growled in my ear, his chin bumping in my shoulder, digging into the wound he'd made the previous night. Clawed hands snatched at my thighs, parting them so he could push inside me.

I screamed.

"Let it go, Meg. Fill me up. Give me what you can't handle."

I didn't know what he meant. What a ridiculous thing to say when *he* was the one filling me with that thick, hard cock. He was abrading my already bruised pussy, and it was wonderful, even as I was sure I was going to die from it.

He bit my shoulder, jaguar teeth piercing skin. "Damn it, Meg, pay attention," he slurred around his teeth and, I'm sure, my blood.

Blood.

Blood of a woman who wouldn't do my bidding. A weak witch. Her life's essence pouring into a chalice for me to drink.

I screamed, incoherent with fear. Too much! With Roland's memory surged the power, power that hadn't left me, had only abated for brief moments after my orgasm with Rudy. I scrambled at the mattress, witlessly trying to escape, but Michael surrounded me, pinned me down. I couldn't get away. I couldn't escape.

He battered at me. Bit me. "Damn it, give it to me."

I let go and vaguely aimed the storm at him. He froze, his entire muscular body seizing. For one, bright, too-clear moment, we were one. Michael, me, and Rudy, who I couldn't see but I knew was near. The storm spread out between us, thinned, and it was like I was in a plane that suddenly broke above the clouds. I could see the power for what it was. See that it was too much for me. But it wasn't too much for *us*. Using practices I'd known since learning to work my magic, I tucked the power away, filled every nook and cranny of each of us that could take it. Stored it up and thinned it out into manageable pieces. That which wasn't essential, I let dissipate into the mattress, the walls, the floor, the nightstand, those things that belonged to Michael and Rudy and were, by extension, a part of them.

I breathed in the fitted sheet bunched underneath me, drenched with sweat. My sweat. Sweat dripping off Michael, who still wholly encased me underneath his body. We didn't move. We just breathed. I could hear Rudy panting somewhere off to my left.

Michael moved first, stretching his jaws to remove his teeth from my shoulder. "Is it done?" he asked, voice gravelly.

"Yes."

"Good. Now I'm going to fuck you."

He shoved forward, pushing a gasp from me. He was still inside me. Still hard. Harder, maybe, now that the desperation was over. I clutched the mattress and moaned.

"Feel good?"

"Yeah."

"Need me to stop?"

"You do and I'll kill you."

Laughing darkly, he eased up off my back, bracing himself on both brawny arms to either side of my shoulders. He slammed into me. No smooth, slow teasing this time. This was a ravenous taking, a beast laying his claim. He braced me with hands on my waist and took me.

Chapter Thirteen

We slept. I woke happily nestled in the curve of Michael's body. My cheek was on Rudy's chest, my chest and belly mashed against his side. Rudy's hand was, I think, caressing Michael somewhere, because the arm beneath my head kept moving. Michael's arm was draped over me, his hand settled just below Rudy's nipple. It was hot as hell, and I was a tad uncomfortable, but I kept my mouth shut because I was loving the closeness.

"Is Roland dead?" I asked finally.

Michael tensed, then relaxed. "Probably. If not, he's very likely a vegetable. I think you destroyed his brain."

"I've got his memories. Some of them, at least."

Rudy clutched my hand where his and mine lay on his belly.

"It's ok. I think. I haven't had one flash before me since you fucked me silly."

We all laughed.

"What happened?"

Michael rolled off me. "I'm not entirely sure. When the circle fell, Brent and the women in the circle passed out. We'd already taken care of one of the other shifters." He sat on the edge of the bed, facing away. "I didn't pay much attention, I'm afraid. I ran to you."

Tears blurring my sight, I reached a hand toward him. He gripped my fingers, but wouldn't come closer when I tugged.

"Thank you."

He smiled, a bit sadly, and kissed my fingers before rising from the bed and padding toward the bathroom.

Beside me, Rudy twisted, forcing me to back up a bit. We ended up on our sides, facing each other. He cupped my chin in his hands, thumbing away some of my tears. The comforting smile on his face was priceless. "You're safe. We've got you."

I had to smile. "Thank you."

"You're welcome." He kissed the tears on my cheeks. The gentleness only made me cry harder.

He gathered me in his arms and held me close as I cried. I wasn't unhappy. The tears were more of a release, the ability to let go after a horrifying event.

He pushed me to my back and lay on top of me. His lips found mine, kissing me through the soft crying. It was enough to stop the tears. Soon, I was kissing him back, twining my body into his.

He entered me slowly, settling inside me as though it were the most natural place for him to be. And it was.

He was slow and languid, in no hurry to rush our pleasure in each other. After the hurried fucking from before, this was like a homecoming.

The bed moved, and we both peeked over Rudy's shoulder. Michael positioned himself behind Rudy between my spread legs. He held a tube in his hands. Lightly, he patted Rudy's back. "Gather your legs up."

I couldn't miss the eager look on Rudy's face. Without leaving my body, he bent his knees until my thighs were draped across his, my hips secure in the bend of his body.

I watched Michael pour clear liquid into his palm. "Meg. Do you mind?"

Rudy nipped at my jaw. I stared at Michael, spellbound. Was he intending what I thought he was intending?

He lowered his wet hand, out of my sight. But when Rudy tensed and sighed happily, I could certainly guess what he was doing.

Michael's eyes met mine. "Do you mind?"

"No."

Rudy licked my neck, and I think he got a little harder inside me. Michael's gaze dropped to watch whatever he was doing with his hands. Rudy rocked into me. Michael poured more lube into his palm, closed the tube, and tossed it aside. Even though I couldn't see his hand once he dropped it, the movement of his upper arm told me he was pumping his cock.

He edged forward, and I'm pretty sure I knew the exact moment he penetrated Rudy, because Rudy tensed, then groaned, then just seemed to melt on top of me. His chest pinned my breasts between us, and his forearms cushioned the back of my shoulders. His hair brushed like fragrant feathers against the side of my face as he buried his nose in the pillow beneath my head.

Michael adjusted and continued to push, his eyes on what was happening between them. But I was part of it. Rudy's arms slid up under me, clutching me. His mouth suckled my ear, nipping it. I heard his breathless groan as Michael slid endlessly forward. I watched Michael until he stopped. Remembering what it looked like to see Michael buried inside Rudy made me wiggle. Which made Rudy squirm. Which made Michael groan. Michael caught my eye, grinned, then slowly pulled out.

Rudy hissed, his fingers clutching my shoulders.

Michael took it slow a few times. He settled his hands on Rudy's back. "You ok?"

"Oh, yeah," Rudy moaned.

"Harder?"

"Please."

He did, and this time I echoed Rudy's hiss. The strength of that shove pushed Rudy into me. About that time, I realized that, in this position, Michael could fuck us both.

He did. Just a bit faster and harder at first, until Rudy was trembling and mewling. I echoed Rudy, shoving forward with my hips to take as much of Rudy as I could. Caught between us, Rudy cried out, clutching the mattress beneath me. Michael took our cues and picked up the pace. The bed shook with the force of what he did to us, and we both loved it.

I came. That triggered Rudy's shattering release. Michael wasn't far behind.

We fell in a tumble of sweaty bodies. I was too tired and too sore to move and relished the feeling.

Michael broke me out of my bliss by crawling up beside me and leaning over me.

"Put the leashes back."

I blinked at him. "Huh?"

"The leashes. They're gone. Put them back."

I struggled to clear my sight. Realized what I was doing and switched to inner sight. Indeed, the glowing pulses around their necks were absent, and the tugs on my heart and womb were gone. I must have lost them in one of the many magical explosions of the night.

I met his gaze. Licked my lips. "Are you sure?"

He did me the honor of not making light. "Yes."

"It's all over. You don't have to."

"I want to."

He glanced at Rudy, who nodded emphatically.

"Why?"

Michael wanted to dodge the question. I could see that. His big shoulders, sweaty from our exertions, tensed. He took a deep breath, glanced at Rudy again, then said, "Because we need you. And you need us. The leash makes it complete."

Troubled, I looked from one to the other. "The leashes are a sign of ownership. I don't want to own you."

Michael snorted. "And I don't want you to. I'll fight you every step of the way." His face grew strangely tender, a softening I'd yet to see on those harsh features. "But I do wish to be joined with you. We've already found something special. I don't want to lose that. Or lose you."

I glanced at Rudy. Who nodded with a grin.

My heart surged and my soul sang. I brought up the leashing spell, and settling it on their bodies, their souls, was the easiest spell I'd ever cast.

Jet Mykles

As far back as junior high, Jet used to write sex stories for friends involving their favorite pop icons of the time. To this day, she hasn't stopped writing sex, although her knowledge on the subject has vastly improved.

An ardent fan of fantasy and science fiction sagas, Jet prefers to live in a world of imagination where dragons are real, elves are commonplace, vampires are just people with special diets and lycanthropes live next door. In her own mind, she's the spunky heroine who gets the best of everyone and always attracts the lean, muscular lads. She aids this fantasy with visuals created through her other obsession: 3D graphic art.

Only recently, through the wonders of the digital age, has Jet, a self-proclaimed hermit, been able to really share this work with others. It was through a series of images posted to the erotic art website Renderotica and encouragement from the fabulous Angela Knight that she finished and submitted a story to Loose Id.

In real life, Jet lives in southern California with her boyfriend of nine years, his daughter and father and nine cats. She has a bachelor's degree in acting, but her loathing of auditions has kept her out of the limelight. So she turned to computers and currently works in product management for a software company, because even in real life, she can't help but want to create something out of nothing.

Visit Jet on the Web at www.computerotika.com.

WOLFE'S GATE

Raine Weaver

Dedication

Dedicated to THE HOOD.

Chapter One

Scarlett pounded frantically at the door, desperately pleading for asylum. Her hands were quickly becoming numb, her voice gone hoarse from screaming. And despite the fog of fear that clouded all rational thought, she dimly wondered how she'd managed to stumble into the middle of a B-grade horror film.

It wasn't the rain that scared her. Even though she'd become thoroughly soaked when she hadn't been able to raise the hood on her treasured little red Miata. Even if the rain had come down in such a torrential downpour the car had slid off the road. Even if her new three-hundred dollar heels were oozing with mud. Even though she was shivering and lost, and her heart had threatened to burst during her mad dash down the road. She was a big girl. She could handle it.

But the *storm*. The special effects had done her in. Lightning that seared every layer of sky, and thunder that sounded like the earth cracking open. These things had always frightened her, even as a child. That had never changed. But now she couldn't run off and cringe in her closet, praying for it to go away.

Now she was lost in the dark, at the mercy of the worst storm she'd ever experienced. And seeking sanctuary at the house of a total stranger.

"Hey!" she screamed as the sky exploded around her. "I know you're in there. I can see your shadow. I see candlelight!" She let loose with another volley of blows against the door. "Open up, for the love of—"

The door slid quietly open.

Scarlett blinked the rain out of her eyes and took a step back. Silhouetted in the orange-gold light that permeated the room behind her, a slim, striking woman, her complexion as pale as her ash-blonde hair, stared coolly out at her. "I'm sorry. You have the wrong house."

"No, wait!" Scarlett threw her forearm against the solid, wet oak. "Don't close the door. You don't understand. I need—"

"I said I'm sorry. But *believe* me." The woman pushed harder, her vivid green eyes cold and unsympathetic. "You have the wrong house."

Fear clashed with fury for a brief moment. Diplomacy would've been the sensible thing to try. But she'd left her common sense about half a mile down the road, when the wind had torn her cell phone out of her hands and she'd begun her sprint for the house, silhouetted by fleeting moonlight and half-hidden in shadow.

Scarlett clamped her fingers around the edge of the door, determined it would not close. "Okay, now look. I know I'm a total stranger. I probably wouldn't let you in either. And at any other time I can be as well-bred as the next person. But this isn't that time. And if you think I'm going to let you leave me out in this storm, you are one crazy bitch."

Frowning, the woman swatted at her clinging fingers as they pushed and pulled for possession. "Let go! I'm trying not to hurt you—"

"Then open the goddamn door, lady!!"

The woman disappeared from view, as if she'd suddenly been yanked away, and the door swung open again. Wide open. And this time the amber light was nearly obliterated by a massive dark form that made her loosen her death grip and cautiously retreat.

He moved forward, as if unaware of the driving rain, with black, wavy hair that blew fiercely in the breeze, and the most chilling ice-blue eyes she'd ever seen on a human being. "What do you want?"

Somehow, somewhere, she'd taken a step back in time. With his cold, angry gaze, the billowing white shirt open nearly to the waist, the broad chest shadowed with a thatch of dark hair, this man did not belong here. He might have commanded a pirate ship, or been a rakish, rebellious highwayman, or lord of the manor on the moors of old England—yes. But in twenty-first century *Ohio?!* "I... I..."

"You have interrupted my evening. Been rude to my guest. Disrupted our small Halloween celebration. And now you stand there gawking." His voice was rough-edged and whiskey-hoarse, his thick brows furrowed beneath a pronounced widow's peak. He took another step toward her. "So, I ask you once again, young lady. What is it that you want?"

Him. The answer sprang immediately to mind, nearly tumbling off her tongue. She wanted *him.* Tall, handsome and commanding, the man was totally hot. He had the swarthy skin of a gypsy beneath a perfectly-trimmed doorknocker beard. That whispering voice of his was deadly seductive, as if he could kiss or kill with equal force, and do both very well.

She'd completely forgotten it was Halloween, and now, staring at this captivating stranger, she nearly forgot she was standing in the middle of a deluge. But only for a moment. Only until the sky lit up in satanic fury above her again, making her flinch. "I... I..."

"Speak!"

Scarlett placed her hands on her hips, his anger making her indignant, despite her pathetic appearance. "Oh, well gee, I am *so* sorry I interrupted your little Halloween soiree! Well, trick or fucking treat!" With a hand sore from hammering his door, she pushed back the dripping red hair that insisted on veiling her eyes. "Look, I don't mean to disturb your special evening with your lady friend—but in case you hadn't noticed, there's a nasty storm going on out here. See? Rain and everything." She spread her arms wide, then quickly crossed them over her breasts. Her silk blouse was soaked, transparent. She hadn't bothered with a bra. And he was obviously well aware of that. His eyes focused there, seemingly fascinated, diamond-blue and intensified by the lightning reflected in his eyes. "Your sorry-ass roads are flooding, this place is the sole sign of life I've seen in the past ten miles—and look!" She gestured wildly, trying to point a shaky arm. "See that dark little speck down the way there? That's my car, stuck in a ditch, so mired in mud the freaking wheels won't even spin."

He continued to watch her, standing firm as the rain thrashed them both. Scarlett wiped water from her eyes, flinching as white-hot heat split the night. "Look. It's dark. I'm lost. And I'm all alone. Please."

She struggled with the word, furious when her voice trembled with tears. "*Please.* Just let me wait out the storm."

And still he stood silent and immovable, even as the earth around them shuddered, angry and deafening.

"Very well." He stood reluctantly aside at last, scowling. "Enter."

Despite his invitation, he maintained his post in the doorway, so that her chest had to brush against his in passing. Scarlett walked forward with as much dignity as she could muster, ignoring the tingling of her nipples that flared with the brief moment of contact.

She was mistaken. What she'd assumed to be a candle or two turned out to be dozens of them. Arcs of dancing flames flickered along the walls, up the stairway, in a small circle in the middle of the room. Fluttering behind the fine iron filigree of a spiral staircase, they turned the cathedral-ceilinged room into a huge magic lantern.

Candles far warmer and more welcoming than the five sets of eyes locked upon her right now.

She'd also been unable to tell how massive the place was from outside. Nothing short of a small mansion, it was decorated in an elegant color scheme of ivory white and pale gold, with lush, cranberry drapes and immense oriental rugs that even her unpracticed eye could tell were both antique and expensive.

Her rescuer seemed to study her, gently swishing a generous dose of brandy in the large snifter he held in his hand. Six-foot-five, she guessed. Tanned, sexy, and solid as a brick wall. Aware that she was making a puddle in the middle of a very expensive Turkish rug, Scarlett hugged herself, trying to somehow contain the water that slid in huge, trailing drops down her body. She felt even more lost now, and very small.

"I'm sorry I said... I mean, I'm sorry to barge in on you this way. I'm not usually so excitable, I promise. I don't normally even use swear words, only when I'm...well, when I'm scared. Or in trouble. It was just—just the storm..." She squinted at her surroundings, inhaling the strange smell of the candles. It was a strange, subtle scent, like nothing she'd experienced before. Exotic and elusive—and, somehow, seductive.

Her audience silently watched her squirm. "Hello," she ventured, trying to break the spell of silence.

"I am Grayson Wolfe." The large man spoke at last, his voice barely more than a throaty whisper. "And despite the circumstances, you are welcome to Wolfe's Gate. My home." He drew a half-circle in the air before him with the glass. "Allow me to introduce you to my friends. You've met Disa."

Scarlett turned toward the woman who had denied her entrance, and barely received a nod. She was slim and willowy, with fine, white-gold hair that fell straight in a blunt cut to her shoulders. Her lips were pink and pouty, appealing to men, probably; but her eyes were jeweled and hard, and her nails seemed talon-sharp and bloodless. There was arrogance and mistrust and envy in her eyes as she glared back at Scarlett. Good. This was a good thing. They instinctively disliked each other, and both acknowledged it. Scarlett gave her a covert wink and quickly turned her attention to the next.

"Alana."

A trim, tiny creature, the girl's skin was as tan-dark as Scarlett's, her hip-length hair thick and shiny black. She smiled and spoke so softly that Scarlett couldn't hear her over the thunder, but she returned the smile anyway, happy to receive even a small welcome.

"William. Will, we call him."

Will raised a glass of white wine to her. About five-foot-six, square-jawed and bandy-legged. His brown hair was flat-topped, his dark eyes unreadable as Alana snuggled against him, obviously claiming possession.

"And this is Jacob."

Jacob flashed a full-blown smile, his eyes blatantly taking in the curves of her figure—even though his arm was draped around Disa's shoulders, his hand moving easily inside her sweater against her breast. The four of them were seated on a champagne-colored French provincial sofa, and there was an undercurrent of something far more than friendship between them. For a moment, she considered taking her chances back out in the rain.

Jacob laughed at her obvious discomfort. "Welcome to Wolfe's Gate, Ms....?"

It was a stunning room, full of beautiful, strange people. In her disheveled state, she was distinctly out of place. "I'm sorry," she murmured, attempting a grin. "Seem to have left my manners in the storm. Scarlett. Scarlett Grier. My friends call me Red."

"Do they, now?" Grayson Wolfe blinked at the mop of wet hair weighing heavily on her shoulders and sipped his drink. "And where might you have been going in such a storm, lass?"

His accent was all-American, but his language, everything about his demeanor, cried old European wealth. "My grandmother lives here. In the area. Somewhere. I think." Gawd, did she sound as idiotic as she thought? "I haven't been here since I was a child, so I'm a little fuzzy on the details. But if you have a phone I could use, I think I remember the number. I could call her, and—"

"Is she expecting you?"

"Well, no, but—"

"Then there's no sense in dragging an old woman out into the storm, or worrying her, now is there?" The master of the house nodded, his mouth forming a long, severe line. "You can spend the night here. This storm will not end soon."

There was something about that strong, dangerous voice that discouraged argument. There was also something about the way he tasted the brandy on his lips that made her want to melt into her sopping-wet panties. "I wouldn't dream of imposing."

"You have no choice, Red." His smile was more like a grimace as he spoke her name. "The reason you've seen no lights for the past ten miles is because it's all my property. Every inch of it. Now, I'll be happy to see you safely on come morning, but there's little to be done about the flooded roads tonight. There are several vacant rooms in the house. You'll be comfortable enough."

A queasy uncertainty crawled through the pit of her stomach. She didn't frighten easily, but this man was just too much...*man*. "Isn't anyone leaving tonight? Anybody with a four-wheel drive?" She cast a pleading eye upon his guests. "Anyone going home? Toward a town? Anywhere?"

"There are guest cottages on the property. My friends are staying in them." Grayson placed his brandy on top of a marble-mantled, empty fireplace and turned to lightly touch her forearm, sending a spark through her that put the lightning to shame. "And unless you plan to pay for that very expensive rug you're ruining, I'd best show you the way. Shall we adjourn to your bedroom?"

Chapter Two

He'd left her alone for a moment. She was glad of it. It gave her a little time to take in her surroundings and attempt to still her raging heart.

The bedroom was large and quaintly decorated, situated on the third floor of the house that seemed to expand with her awareness. Dusty-rose and white, it boasted its own bathroom, a free-standing floor length mirror, and pale oak furniture that held fragile china ornaments, lending a feminine touch. And even in the dim light of the two candles he'd left on the mother-of-pearl dresser top, every object in this room was also obviously very, very expensive.

Now that the roar of the storm had died down to a whisper, she couldn't resist the urge to explore. Scarlett wandered over to the window. It was oddly made, triangular in shape, and pulled open to showcase the courtyard in the rear. Ringed by a tall wooden fence, it was all velvety grass, azaleas, and large, imposing oaks. In the spring it was probably bursting with blooms. Even on this chilled, misty fall night there was a stark beauty to the old trees, standing sentinel in the perfect landscape.

"I hope the room is comfortable?"

She whirled at the sound of his voice. Not a sound, not even a stirring of the air in the room had betrayed his entrance. The man was some kind of demon. "It's fine. Lovely. Really. Still, I'm sorry to interrupt your...celebration."

He cocked his head to one side, hands behind his back, his expression unreadable. "Celebration?"

Geez, the last thing she wanted to do was offend her host. She'd have a fit if he tossed her back out into the rain. She'd just assumed it was a party, with the abundance of wine, the multitude of candles...that Jacob person copping a feel right in front of her... "I mean—"

"You mean the *ceremony.*"

His hoarse voice spoke the word with a kind of reverence that sent a chill through her. She glanced down at her shoes, encapsulated in mud rapidly hardening to the consistency of cement. It'd be tricky, but if she had to run for her life they'd have to do. "Ceremony?"

Wolfe nodded slowly, taking a few tentative steps toward her. "*The* ceremony." His tone was solemn, his eyes glowing in the near-darkness as they blatantly skimmed her body. "We had the ritual meal. The wine. The candles, the storm. All we needed was the sacrifice." He stood over her, all powerful, intense masculinity, and she swallowed hard. "And there you were, knocking obligingly on the door."

That was her cue. She should definitely be on the run by now. Instead, she stared into eyes that had changed from ice to smoky-blue, and found she could not move. "Um...er, don't you need a virgin for that sort of thing?" Her voice was shaking, and she couldn't tell whether it was from fear or excitement. "Because if you do, I'm afraid you'll be disappointed."

He was staring at her mouth, watching her speak, his irises growing darker as she nervously licked her lips. "I somehow doubt I would be." He smiled, a wide, sinful smile that softened the hard angles of his face. "You've watched too damn many old movies, lady. A little storm, an old house, and you're ready to run. The power is out from the storm, Ms. Grier. Thus the abundance of candles. Rest assured, we're a simple group of people. There's nothing sinister here."

She released the breath she'd been holding, hating her warped imagination. The storm had destroyed her nerves. "Still, I'm sorry to intrude on you and your guests this way."

"Not a problem. My guests have retired to their cottages, so there's just us in the house. Make yourself at home."

"*Us?*" She shivered.

"I brought you something to wear to bed. You'll be wanting a hot shower and a good night's sleep."

Scarlett watched, fascinated, as he placed a satiny white gown on the bed. He was still damp from the storm himself, and his shirt gaped open, revealing the lush trail of black hair that narrowed at his waist, like a marker pointing the way to treasure. With shallow, measured breathing, she moved closer, holding the gown up for inspection. "Very pretty." Hiding her embarrassment behind lowered lashes, she bit her lip. "And do you make a habit of keeping women's nightgowns handy, Mr. Wolfe?"

"Gray. Call me Gray." He grinned again, and her heart shifted back into high gear. He was capable of an easy manner that was nearly as hard to resist as his gruffness. "People visit here often. And women have a tendency to leave things behind."

She didn't believe him for a minute. This man would have women. *Lots* of women. They'd be pounding at his door in the middle of the night...

"I would fetch your luggage for you, but—"

"Oh, there isn't any." She silently cursed herself as soon as the words were spoken. Damn, he knew she was a loose thread, and that nobody knew she was here. If the bastard killed her as she slept, she'd have nobody to blame but herself. Nervously fingering the satin, she noted the spaghetti-nothing straps and how short it was. About one size too small. It would be tight, but dry. "It's beautiful. And like everything else here, very expensive. A set?"

He slipped his huge hands into his pockets, and she shivered again, sure those baggy trousers held a wealth of jewels. "Excuse me?"

"Was it a set? A matching set, with panties? It's so short, I figured..."

"Yes. There are panties."

Her tired eyes scanned the bed, took in the floor around them. "Did you forget the bottoms?"

"No." There was no smile, no humor, no trace of discomfort in his tone. His eyes glittered like pale sapphires against his ruddy complexion. "No. I didn't forget them."

Her breath faded to nothing behind her parted lips.

He knew.

He knew she wanted him. And he obviously wanted her just as much. A flush of embarrassed desire spread from her breasts to her neck and face. Now it wasn't a question of how they felt—but how they intended to proceed. Had he selected this particular gown with care? Would he take active advantage of the absence of the panties? Or did he intend to lie in his bed alone, thinking about it, wanting it, dreaming about it?

And how was *she* supposed to sleep, thinking about him thinking about *her?!*

His subtle brazenness made her uncharacteristically shy. "So what happens now?"

"Now?" Gray slid his hands from his pockets, jingling a large set of keys. "Now I lock you in this room. You get a restful night's sleep, and I will send you safely on your way in the morning. Goodnight."

"What?! Oh, no, no, wait!" She nearly made a grab for him as he opened the door. "What d'ya mean, 'lock me in'? You can't do that!"

"Of course I can. My house, my room, my keys. My rules." He spread his arms wide, and all she could see was that hard wall of well-hewn muscle flexing within the loose confines of his shirt. "You have a bed. Something clean and dry to wear. There's a small bathroom for your comfort. You'll do well enough. Despite your shy, introverted demeanor, I must also consider the safety of my guests. And you're not likely to go a-wanderin' bare-bottomed through the house and over the countryside." His eyes darkened to royal blue as they slid over the gown she clutched in her hands. "And as long as I hold the key, you can be sure no one else will have access to your room."

Damn him. He was going to leave her waiting, wondering whether he intended to take advantage of his "house rules."

She could be bold, invite him to stay. Jump his bones here and now, wrap her legs around his waist and hump until he humped back. That predatory look in his eye was not her imagination. And he was still here, lingering, even after he'd made his announcement, key in hand, poised at the door.

As if he didn't want to leave. As if he *expected* her to invite him to stay.

She'd be damned if she'd give him the satisfaction. He might be lord and master of these people, but his rules didn't govern her. She'd get him to make the first move. Or let him lie in bed, thinking about her here, in this shortie-nothing of a gown, warm and butt-bare.

Let that bulge in his pants keep him awake, as it would her. "I will not be held prisoner in this room, Mr. Wolfe. If I have to pick the lock, or break the door, or shimmy out of the window, I—"

"I'd suggest you behave yourself, Ms. Grier, or I'm liable to take you over my knee and give you a sound spanking." He nodded at the garment draped over her arm. "Something I might enjoy with that particular nightgown."

She felt a warm flush on her buttocks as he spoke, vividly imagining the scene. And enjoying it far too much.

He could read her mind. She was sure of it as he approached and lifted her chin, holding her eyes. "And I suggest you stay away from open windows, Red. You'll catch your death."

He wheeled and left the room as quietly as he'd entered, with only the sound of the key turning in the door as a goodbye.

A shudder, frighteningly similar to a small orgasm, rippled through her body. Damn, she *liked* this man. She'd met men with attitude before—but *this* one actually seemed to have the goods to back it up.

Turning to face the large mirror, she stared at her reflection. She looked awful. Her hair was limp, her face still pale and tired from her ordeal in the storm, and the clothes she wore could probably not be saved.

But if she could tempt Grayson Wolfe looking this ragged, she could steal his soul on a better day. And tomorrow would be a better day. Carefully carrying the delicate nightie into the bathroom, she turned the water on as hot as she could stand it, humming happily to herself.

If she had her way, Wolfe's Gate would be the gateway to *many* things.

* * *

Gray prowled the perimeter of the great room. He couldn't seem to feel the buffed wood of the floor against his bare feet, or hear the thunder that shook the house with sound.

With every third or fourth circle, he would pause in front of the small bar, grab a bottle—*any* bottle—by its neck and take a hard swig before continuing his march.

Twice he'd stopped before the staircase. Once, he'd even climbed to the second floor before regaining his senses and retreating. He could hear the shower running, smell the delicate rose scent of the bathroom soap. If he focused hard enough, he was sure he could see right through the walls. That magnificently wild mane of auburn hair. The tawny skin. Five notable freckles, two on her nose. The large breasts the rain had so kindly revealed to him. And the long, long legs. Dear God, the legs that were made for stroking, for locking around him as he slid inside her, home at last. He closed his eyes, his mouth going dry as he imagined her standing beneath steaming water that ran between her breasts, pooled in her navel, streamed teasingly between her thighs. Sparkling drops in the dark red hair of her pubis, yielding to the creamy lather of the soap…

Gray vigorously shook his head, trotted over to the bar, and chose a single bottle of Kentucky whiskey. Returning to the stairs, he sat, turned the bottle upside down, and swallowed until he nearly choked. He had to stop this. The girl had come seeking sanctuary, and the more he dwelled on the temptations of her body, the more danger she was in.

"Grayson?"

She was biracial, and had managed to combine the best of both worlds into one healthy, luscious morsel. He could suck on that full bottom lip forever, twine his fingers through that thick mass of hair, dig fingers deep into that wicked-round bottom, suck, tongue, and taste those tits until…

"Gray? Are you all right?"

He pulled his lips back over his teeth. Because he was frustrated. Because his friend had caught him at a weak moment. Because the full moon was just rising over the hills surrounding Wolfe's Gate. "I would be. If I took just a few steps, climbed a few stairs." Grunting, he glared at the figure in the doorway. "Thought all of you had retired for the evening."

Will loped into the room, a half-smile upon his face. "The guest cottages are woefully low on liquor. Your visitors drink too much." Sizing up the selection at the bar, he picked one bottle and cradled it under his arm. "And how is the lovely Scarlett Grier?"

Gray turned the bottle up again, then savagely wiped his mouth. "Too damn lovely for her own good. I should've left her out in the storm."

"She's half-black, I think. The elders wouldn't approve. 'Maintain the purity of the race,' and all that shit."

"Then they wouldn't approve of me either, being half-human as I am."

"That's different. You're a born Alpha."

Will picked up a bottle of Gray's favorite twenty-year old single malt Scotch, considered the risk, and carefully put it back. "Why not take the girl if you want her? It wouldn't be unpleasant for her. Even I sense the attraction she feels for you."

"No. I always swore I wouldn't. You know that. My own mother—"

"Was a human, taken by your father. I know." Deciding to go for quantity rather than quality, Will grabbed five bottles at random and turned toward the door. "But you said she eventually adjusted. They were even happy in their time."

"She shouldn't have to 'adjust.'" Gray put his bottle down on the step. He was hornier than he thought. He'd just snapped at his closest friend in the world. "I don't want an uninitiated woman. Too much trouble, too dangerous for her. The jealousies, rivalries, risk of discovery...no. There are plenty of our own females to choose from. What I need," he murmured, rising and stretching, "is a good night's sleep. I'm off. Enjoy your evening, Will."

"She seems like a pretty strong woman to me, Gray. But it's your choice, of course." Will shrugged, hesitated in the throes of a thought, then grinned. "You must, at least, find the irony of it amusing."

"Irony?"

"That little Red, who couldn't get her ride's hood up on the way to Grandma's house, should stray from the forest path and stumble upon the big, bad Gray Wolfe?"

Gray barked a sharp laugh, heading slowly up the staircase. "Well, our very existence proves that God has a sense of humor, doesn't it?"

His sharp ears heard the lock click into place as Will left, detecting the heart of the storm now centered 13.72 miles away from the house. The rain had softened into a whispering mist, and the thunder played in the background like the rolling wheels of some great military machine.

He paused on the second floor, mere yards away from the door of his own bedroom. The shower was not running in the room directly above his. She'd finished, used one of his towels to daub drops of moisture from her body, then slipped that short bit of satin fluff over her head, allowing it to drape over the stiffened peaks of her nipples. And by now she was in bed, locks of burnished brass spread across his pillow, round, taut buttocks exposed...

Gray shook himself like a dog waking from sleep and entered his room. The massive old bed would give him little comfort tonight. Carelessly tossing his clothes to the floor, he kicked them aside and stood before the only square window in the house, drinking in the night.

She was the most tempting piece of ass he'd encountered in over five hundred years. No use even pretending he'd sleep. Forcing her bedroom key so deep into his fist that he drew blood, he watched the watercolor-moonlight paint the landscape around him, and fought the urge to howl, the instinct that seemed keener tonight than it ever had in his long, well-regulated life.

Chapter Three

Red turned over on her side once again, sighed, and finally gave up. It was ridiculous to keep trying. There was no way in hell she was going to sleep this night.

Rising, she tiptoed quietly across the room and tried the door once again. Still locked. The bastard had actually imprisoned her and failed to take advantage of it! Wasn't there an unspoken, barbarian law somewhere that insisted a captive woman should be ravished at least once during her brief stay?

Huffing angrily over to the window, Red pulled it open and pressed her forehead to the screen, inhaling deeply. The room was comfortable enough, but her body felt heated, tightly wound.

There was a freshness to the air, now drained of the nervous energy of lightning. All was silent and moist, the fine rain beading on the browning leaves and lush grass beneath a full, ghostly moon.

Halloween, she mused. She couldn't imagine a child coming to this property, even for candy. It was built almost like a fortress, with high walls and fences surrounding the main compound of the house, and the guest cottages planted at the four corners of the rear.

The guest cottages...

Red leaned closer to the screen, trying to peer through the mist and rising fog.

The guest cottages whose doors hung wide open to the night...

Something moved across her field of vision, something pale and lithe, drifting weightlessly across the lawn. A fairy without wings. The creature was dancing, its arms raised toward the moon as it pirouetted twice, attempted a graceful curtsey—then fell flat on its fanny with a shrill, drunken laugh.

Pressing her nose against the metal mesh, Red blinked several times to be sure. No, she was not mistaken. The fairy was none other than the ice-bitch, Disa.

And there was something else, something crawling out of the nearby bushes, something feral, slinking toward her on all fours. And still she laughed, offering the bottle in an unsteady salute as the beast crept forward, slowly making its way to her long, extended legs.

Slapping the bottle away, the hulking creature ignored her giggling protests, easily pushing her legs apart and forcing her onto her back. And in the soft, wet grass, it burrowed between her thighs with its body and made a hard, sharp lunge with its hips.

Red's mouth opened in a silent gasp, her hands flattening against the screen. Dear God, what was it? As far as she knew, no predators that large existed in Ohio. Was the woman being attacked?

On the verge of screaming to attract Gray's attention—
anyone's attention—the cry died quickly in her throat as Disa's
pale, spidery legs lifted and locked behind the creature's
humped back, her greedy cries audibly urging him on.

It was a man. She could see him now, hips gyrating upon
hers. Probably Jacob. Her fingers were twined in his hair, too
long to be that of Will with the blunt cut. Red retreated,
stepping to the side of the window, suddenly worried about
being seen. The white gown would shine in this darkness. And
her rapid, excited breathing would be easy to spot beneath the
bodice.

Ridiculous. They would be—should be—too caught up in
what they were doing. She stood boldly before the window,
pressing her heated forehead against the damp wire. Amazed
and guiltily delighted at the undoing of the prim, prissy Disa.
Red gleefully watched as Jacob did her, and did her well.

His arms were behind her back, barely cushioning his
blows, his hands locked around her shoulders. He seemed
oblivious to Disa's vocals, every athletic stroke eliciting a moan,
a high-pitched cry, his name.

Red felt the room warming as she watched the slender
bodies move like mating minks, leaving a wide trail across the
wet grass as he slammed forward again and again, driving her
clinging body helplessly across the lawn.

Her own nipples straining against the tight bodice of the
gown in response, Red tore her eyes away from the couple. The
strange people, the spooky setting—it was a fantasy within a
dream. The gnarled limbs of the old trees twisted and curled
above them, forming a surreal canopy over the entire yard.
Leaves, heavy with water, hung limp from the branches, shining
with the light from the cottages. And above it all the full moon,

spectral and pale behind the veil of mist, melting into shimmering slivers that glanced off everything below.

There was another noise, a *woman's* noise, beneath Disa's shrill raving. Earthy and gruff, the sound drifted up to her window from the largest oak in the garden. Red squinted, could hardly see the source.

But she could see enough.

Will. She recognized the bandy legs, the short, sturdy figure. And Alana, pinned against the great oak, her arms back and wrapped around the trunk in the posture of a sacrifice. Supported by Will's hands grasping her buttocks, her legs were folded around him, her head swinging senselessly from side to side. Unlike Jacob, Will was going for quality, not quantity. With every stroke of his hips, he ground hard against the small woman, who gave a guttural groan with each movement.

It was bewitching, watching the four of them. Something like a memory buzzed in her brain, of hunters and the hunted, of harvest festivals, of celebrating life among the ashes of the dead. With shallow breath, her hands crept to her nipples and squeezed the sensation there from painful ache to wanting.

Will was pounding harder into the woman. She reached for him, and Red could see the bloody gouges of her nails striping his shoulders, was certain she could feel the rough bark against her own back. His legs were stiff, his buttocks dimpled with strain as he thrust harder, almost violently. Alana's body was helplessly tossed, her long hair veiling their faces.

Barely aware of what she was doing, Scarlett's hands slid beneath the skirt of her gown as the girl cried out in a gut-wrenching yelp and went limp in Will's arms.

Allowing her to slide senselessly to the earth, he turned, his expression wild, and charged the other couple. Grabbing Jacob by his hair, he tossed him aside as if he weighed nothing. In the next instant he had dragged Disa to her knees and was kissing her hungrily. Laughing hysterically, she ran her long talons sinuously down his torso.

Disa's eyes sparked green-gold as she reached for Will, still hard after his marathon session with Alana. Perching on her haunches, she tasted the tip of his gleaming, wet hardness with long, languorous licks. Hungrily taking all of him into her mouth, her eyelids fluttered shut in ecstasy.

Raising herself to all fours, Disa seemed to swallow him whole. She didn't miss a beat, barely seemed to notice when Jacob approached from behind. He pulled her hips upward, mounting her, pumping away at the same furious pace he'd used before.

The image was hypnotic. She couldn't look away. Jacob rode her hard from the rear, pausing only occasionally to give both pale cheeks a sharp swat before plunging forward again. He almost seemed to derive no pleasure from the act, but held her hips in a vise-like grip, his rutting noises slicing through the soft rain.

Will rolled easily in and out of her mouth, unhurried, unworried. This was a man who savored sensation, a man after Red's own heart. His fingers slid through her hair, stroked her face each time her lips slipped over him, her cheeks hollowed, body vibrating with Jacob's violent thrusts.

Red's fingers skirted the damp hair beneath her gown, teasingly touching her feverish flesh as her clit began to tingle. If she listened hard enough, she thought she could hear the woman purr. Disa was in heaven. Every pistoning push of Jacob's hips made her body lurch forward, her mouth sink onto

Will as his face, turned toward the moon, shone like that of some dark angel.

She felt her own body turn hot, moist at the thought of being taken by the two men, both so different, both so hungry for her. To let go beneath that full witch's moon, to be unable to tell where the pleasure from one began and the other ended. And if one of those men was Grayson Wolfe...dear God!

Alana. Where was she? Red's finger probed deeper between her folds, her eyes scanning the yard. She wasn't with the others, and there was only one other person missing from the ménage.

Gray. An astonishing feeling of envy possessed her as she searched the shadows. The girl must be with Gray. Her curiosity was almost as great as her jealousy. To see him in action, find out what he was capable of...

"*There.*"

The soft voice was just below her window. Red stood on tiptoe to glance down. Alana was crouched there, still naked, her arm around the neck of an enormous dog. Its hair was coarse and straight, silver-gray and stippled with pearl-white drops of rain. Its vivid blue eyes stared up at Red as the girl pointed and spoke again. "There. At the window."

Scarlett ducked and, dropping to her knees, crawled back into the bed. Yanking the covers up, she shivered beneath the sheets, suddenly cold. For what seemed hours, she lay still. Listening. The voices were still there, their moans little more than low howls, still laughing and grunting long after the moon rose to pour across her bed. She drifted into an uneasy sleep, exhausted, and dreamed of gypsy orgies around roaring campfires, and demonic dogs that guarded the gates that led to the abodes of the damned.

Chapter Four

"Good morning."

Red squirmed beneath the embroidered sheet, still half-asleep and dreaming of the night. Dark bodies writhing to an inaudible beat, the woods coming alive, gathering beneath her window, waiting...worshipping...

But the deep, masculine voice and the smell of strong, hot coffee was enough to lure her to waking. Reluctantly prying her eyes open, she pushed away from the thick down pillow. "Morning already?" she murmured drowsily. "Feels like I just—"

"Just went to bed?"

Red was awake immediately, grabbing the sheet and pulling it upward. She was still furious with Gray. But she'd fully expected him to awaken her this morning, hopefully with something more than a cheery word.

She had not counted on this. "Jacob. What are you doing here?"

With a big, satisfied grin, he shoved a mug of steaming coffee at her. "Hell, I thought you looked good caked in mud. You're a damn fine looking woman in the morning, Red."

She accepted the cup, still holding the sheet tight. He wore khakis and silk, and a bit too much aftershave. And he looked thoroughly rested, as if he'd slept all night. "You've got awfully big eyes, bud, for somebody who wasn't invited in."

"All the better to see you with." He laughed, a low, growling sound. "And I like the way that gown doesn't fit you."

She supposed he was trying to be charming, but the situation was beginning to make her uncomfortable. "Gray said he was the only one with a key."

"So he is. I scaled the outside wall."

"Impossible. It's a sheer drop. And you were carrying *coffee.*"

"I think you already have some idea how athletic I can be."

He was a liar, but attractive enough. She'd seen what he could do last night, secretly admired the way he handled himself. But there was something creepy, covert, about him that she just didn't like.

And he wasn't Grayson Wolfe, the man she *really* wanted in her bedroom. "I appreciate the coffee. *Gray's* coffee," she added carefully. "But I think you should leave. Consider waiting for an invitation next time."

"You watched us last night. I felt your eyes on my back."

The mug froze on Red's lips as he playfully tugged on the sheet. "I said you'll have to excuse me. I need to get dressed."

He began to pull the sheet down by fistfuls at her feet, still smiling. "You should've joined us. Always room for one more."

Alarmed now, she kicked at him, wriggling to the other side of the bed. "Look, I don't want to cause a scene, but if you don't get out of here—"

Sweeping the bedcover impatiently aside, he grabbed her free arm as the coffee spilled, tossing her on her back and falling on top of her. "I can do even better than last night. Let me show you."

"N-n-no!" She twisted her head to avoid his kiss. Summoning all the strength she could manage, she shoved the heel of her free hand forcefully against his nose. It should have worked, should have slowed him down enough for her to squirm free and make a run for it. Blood poured from his nostrils as he hovered over her, staining the gown, her shoulder, the sheet.

Jacob smiled, a smug, deadly sort of smile, and pressed her deeper into the mattress with his body. "Nice defensive move. Stimulating foreplay. Now it's my turn." He effortlessly snapped the thin strap of the gown, baring her left breast. "Tit for tat."

He was so heavy upon her she could barely breathe, let alone scream. He was pinning her wrists, nudging her legs apart with his knee. If only she could manage a kick in the groin, an elbow to the eye, she could...

Before she could complete the thought, he was gone. Just *gone,* vanished into thin air. She was free. Pushing up to her knees, heart bobbing in her throat, she scrambled toward the end of the bed, staring dumbfounded at the scene before her.

Grayson Wolfe had silently entered the room, and was glaring at the body of his friend, tossed like a doll against the wall with such force he'd broken through both plaster and drywall, laying bare the studs.

Red gaped as Jacob slowly began to move, peeling himself away from the mold he'd made. Jerking one limb free at a time, he finally fell to the floor and blinked up at his friend. He seemed remarkably unharmed, but dazed. "I... I didn't know." He faltered. "You can't fault me if I didn't know the bitch was yours."

Slowly shifting her eyes to Gray's face, Red felt a bit of that fear. It was dark with fury, his teeth clamped in a silent growl, his eyes narrow and savage. What in the name of God was going on here? Had he really managed to fling the man halfway across the room? He wasn't even breathing hard!

Jacob raised himself to all fours, eyes shifting between Gray's mud-stained boots and the escape route through the door behind him. "You know I would never presume, never think of stepping outside my...my..." He paused as if waiting for an answer. Cowed. Not once did his gaze rise to meet Gray's.

He stood slowly, carefully, and with shoulders slumped and eyes focused on the floor, made his way to the exit. "My sincere apologies, Ms. Grier." The words were mumbled, barely coherent. He behaved like a dog that had just been disciplined, although Gray had yet to speak. "Please forgive my intrusion."

For long moments after he'd gone, Red knelt on the mattress, staring at the smashed wall, the white dust on the floor, the blood on the sheet. Left-over adrenaline from her near-escape still flooded her veins, and she turned on Gray with a vengeance.

"*You.* This is all *your* fault." With as much dignity as she could muster, she scooted across the bed to stand and face him, pointing an accusatory finger. "Simple group of people, my ass! You and your gang of hyper-sexed houseguests! You're busy locking *me* in a room while that—that animal of a friend of yours roams free. He should be caged and tested for rabies!"

He didn't seem to be paying attention. He was staring at her, but his eyes weren't focused on her mouth. With a start, she remembered that her gown was ripped, her bare breast obviously holding his interest. It only made her more furious. "Hey! The tit is not talking to you! *I* am. My mouth is actually moving, and with a three-digit I.Q., I'd appreciate a little—"

With an effortless sweep of his arm, he gathered her to him, crushing her mouth beneath his with such force it bent her backward over his arm. Her eyes flared wide as her outraged protest was smothered by the passion of his kiss, dying quickly into a low, astonished moan.

Arms flailing helplessly in the air and completely off balance, Red grasped his shoulders. But there was no danger of falling. He held her firmly, a mass of muscle, completely in control.

His tongue slid into her mouth just as his large hand found and gave a possessive squeeze to her exposed breast, and the drawn-out moan that had been simmering in her throat became a whimper of surrender.

He seemed to sense the moment, and swung her through the air in an arc. Red was barely aware that her feet had left the floor. She only knew the immense power of his arms, the feeling of his tongue and lips moving slower, erasing all doubts with easy confidence, the urgent, guttural sound that vibrated in his throat as she met and dueled with his tongue. He drank deep, long draughts of her, intoxicating her in the process. Every nerve-ending in her body sang as he strummed her body with the skill of a master.

And then she was on top of the mother-of-pearl dresser top, his body wedged determinedly between her legs, her fingers tangled in his hair as he ripped what was left of the gown from her bosom, his lips hungrily fastening on a stiff, sensitive nipple.

Red arched into him, audibly purring as he greedily suckled one nipple while deftly squeezing the other between thumb and forefinger. He was like a drowning man, intense and single-minded, drawing as much desire from her as he evoked in himself. He nipped, suckled, mercilessly tweaked her nipples until she writhed, forgetting to breathe.

He'd seduced her with one fiery, overwhelming kiss, and without speaking a single word.

Forcing her back with the weight of his body, he tore his mouth from her breast and eased the gown up with a smooth motion of his hand. He nuzzled her navel and inhaled deeply before the slightly abrasive feeling of his beard edging lower betrayed his intentions. "Jesus." She shivered in anticipation. "Wait…"

With the gentlest of touches, he spread her wider, running his huge hands with surprising smoothness along the inside of her thighs, nibbling teasingly at the soft skin. She felt herself yielding, her desire to maintain control lost in the touch of his lips. "Wolfe…wait." She was nearly panting, barely able to manage words. "We barely know—"

His tongue slipped into the moist folds of her flesh, talented, teasing. Red's back arched at the shock of familiarity, her hands gripping the edges of the dresser.

Huge hands grasped her buttocks possessively, pulling her toward him as his tongue mastered her, as if he knew every super-sensitive spot, as if he'd been there a thousand times before.

Within seconds, she was mewing. Within moments, she was quivering, her hips moving helplessly beneath him. "God!" she gasped in disbelief, her eyes screwing shut.

She felt him smile against the hot, swollen lips of her sex. His tongue flattened, curled, lapped up every drop of her increasing wetness with an appreciative growl. He was enjoying it as much as she was.

Red was teetering on the edge, muscles tightening, searching for his hardness to hold onto. Without a word, without warning, he slipped two large fingers deep inside her, nestling there for a moment before establishing a rhythm in and out of her that her hips matched immediately. Her body slid along the satiny surface of the mother-of-pearl with every push of his hand, pumping back for more every time he withdrew.

As if he'd been waiting for just the right moment, he pulled her hard against him, found her clit, and sucked.

Red bucked beneath him, helpless in the throes of the most intense sensation she'd every known. With an eagerness that stunned her, she gave into it, into him, contracting around his fingers as a thin, high-pitched scream sounded in her ears. Her body burst into one taut, trembling mass of energy until, spent, she went limp beneath him.

Some moments passed before she was able to open her eyes, even more before she could focus. Her inner muscles were still contracting, hungry for more. And Gray was...

Grayson Wolfe was standing beside her, silently watching the expression on her face. With the air of a connoisseur, he passed his finger, still wet with her juices, beneath his nose, as if inhaling the scent of a fine wine on its cork. His mouth melted into a wolfish smile that matched the gleam in his eyes. Leaning forward, he whispered to her.

"Good morning."

Turning, he left the room without another word.

Red sat straight up, waiting for the blood that had flooded her groin to creep back to her brain. Damn. Her sex was still pulsing, her entire body vibrating. This wasn't just about the sex. This was about a man who knew exactly what buttons to push to get her going. And damn, he was good at it.

"Scarlett?" A soft female voice sang with a tap on the door. "It's Alana. I have clothes for you, and a little breakfast."

She leaped from the dresser, eager to get going. She'd already had all the breakfast she wanted.

But maybe, with a little female persuasion, she could make a reservation to sample the main course.

Chapter Five

"My God. You're a magician!"

Gray resisted the urge to smile as she approached. Leaning against the rounded trunk of the little car, he kept his arms firmly crossed before him. In a few minutes she'd be gone. He simply had to keep his hands to himself until then. "Not at all. Just the lowly lord of the manor."

"You got it out of the mud." Her lips parted in wonder as she ran her hand over the hood. "And it's clean. How did you manage that?"

She had a glorious smile, open and full of honest delight. There was no deception in that smile. Pity he wouldn't be able to see more of it. "Jacob helped me push it out of the ditch early this morning. Before he decided to make his unauthorized 'rounds.' And before he wisely left the compound a few minutes ago," he added dryly. "Will cleaned it up, but the seats are still wet. He covered them with plastic for you. Even your little ride's hood is working properly now, Red." He couldn't suppress a slight twitch of his lips. "You're looking well-rested."

"Yeah, well—the late-night show is great, and they serve one helluva breakfast in this joint."

He studied her as she inspected the car. The pants fit well enough, but the ribbed tank top was a little small for her. It stretched teasingly across her breasts, revealing hard, pebbled nipples, and baring her midriff whenever she moved. Gray made tight fists of his hands, trying to stem the hardening of his cock.

"You're looking less Heathcliff-ish yourself today," she countered. "But you'd probably look good in anything. And better without."

Her eyes briefly skimmed his body, finally coming to rest on his crotch. There was admiration in her gaze and invitation in her smile. Damn, he liked everything about this woman. Mind, body, and spirit.

And he had to get her away from here as soon as possible.

Tossing her the keys he'd found still dangling from the ignition, he took a last, lingering look at her midriff as she effortlessly caught them with one quick hand. "My apologies, Ms. Grier, for your unpleasant evening. I wish you well, and hope you find your grandmother in the best of health."

She stood by the driver's door, fingering the keys with an uncertain expression. "That's it? You're just going to send me on my way—and that's it?" A shy grin with a trace of devilment lit up her face. "You could always invite me back for lunch sometime."

Tucking his hands in his pockets, he sauntered away from the road, clearing the path for her to leave. "I'm afraid you have to go. I still have guests, and there's work to do."

Still she lingered, as if she didn't believe him. Another minute, and he was likely to toss her over his shoulder and drag her into the bushes. He tried one last tactic. "Disa will be lonely now that Jacob's gone. I must see to her...comfort."

It worked. That red hair betrayed not only a lively spirit, but a fiery temper. "Thanks for the warning. Wouldn't want to waste my time with somebody who pumps anti-freeze into the ice princess." Slipping into the toy automobile, she slammed the door.

He couldn't resist a laugh. She was so completely different than any woman he'd ever known, all willfulness and fire and passion. Magnificent. With a wave and a toothy smile, he called back to her as he headed for the house. "I enjoyed having you for Halloween, Scarlett Grier."

The red roadster peeled out of the driveway, engine racing—but not before he saw the anger vanish from her face, saw her grin. Then saw her laugh as she glanced back and gave him the finger before turning her attention to the road ahead.

Gray laughed again, licking his lips. The taste of her was still there. Scintillating. Seductive. Now *that,* he thought with regret, was a woman worth throwing away all the rules for. If only...

* * *

"Walker? You're looking for Elise Walker? Oh, I'm sorry. Mrs. Walker passed away some three months ago."

Red's shoulders sagged in defeat. The stars were stacked against her on this trip. "Guess she won't be coming to the door then, huh?"

The man laughed, slapping the molding with the flat of his hand. "Well, she'd be kinda messy-looking if she did, wouldn't she?" He extended the same hand with a big smile that displayed a slight gap between his front teeth. "How do. Lucas Sterling. Can I offer you a cup of coffee, little lady?"

He was medium height and weight, with a dense scrub of light-brown brush on his face. Lucas Sterling said he was the second cousin once removed of her grandmother's second husband's sister-in-law. Or was it the third?

Everything about Lucas was easygoing. He wore plaid shirts and oversized jeans with holes in the knees. He did odd jobs around the area for folks because he couldn't stand being chained to a nine-to-five. He was as open and friendly as Grayson was gruff, and invited her to stay in the small house before she'd even decided how to ask the favor.

"Of course you'll stay here." He smiled as he showed her around the house. "Belongs to you more rightly than it does to me. I just happened to attend the old lady's funeral—heart attack, y'know, died peacefully in her sleep—and started fixing things up after the rest of the bereaved left. Guess I haven't had sense enough to stop. I'm surprised you didn't hear about Mrs. Elise, though. Didn't your mother—"

"I haven't spoken to my mother in ages." Red surveyed the interior with barely polite interest. Gone were her grandmother's dozens of doilies, knickknacks, everything that made the place country-quaint. It was all tools and woodcrafting machines, all about Lucas. But it didn't matter. She didn't plan to spend much time there anyway. "Mom's busy. We don't spend much quality time together. Are there two bathrooms?"

And the best thing about Lucas Sterling was that he seemed more interested in bragging about his power tools and plans to renovate the property than whether she was female or not.

"You're traveling all alone? With no directions, no luggage? And you spent the night at Wolfe's Gate?" He shook his head, impressed. "I don't think anybody in these parts has been allowed to even walk in the door. Wolfe's a very rich, very private person. But I'm glad to hear he is, a least, a gentleman."

"And is that 'gentleman' married? Gay?"

"Not from what I hear." His mouth twisted. "Not from the parade of women I hear comes and goes through that house. Lots of strange goings-on, people say. But not to worry, cuz. You can bunk here, upstairs, and I'll take the couch. I want you to treat this place like it's your very own."

Perfect. A safe haven and base of operations.

Leaving Lucas with a big thank-you hug, Red set out in search of the nearest strip mall. The sun was beginning to burn off the morning fog, and she relished the feeling of the wind on her face.

She had one charge card. It would do. She just needed one or two suggestive dresses. She'd noticed Wolfe watching her legs. He liked them. A few sexy underthings. A quick shampoo and cut, and a repair job on the manicure the albino heifer had ruined in their tug-of-war for the door.

Remembering the feeling of Wolfe's mouth on her sex, she whooped, hitting the gas pedal with a purpose. The little red car devoured the road, as if glad to be back in business. She would return there by evening, ready to sample whatever he might have to offer for dinner.

This particular big, bad Wolfe didn't stand a chance.

Chapter Six

It had given her immense pleasure to park before the great house, knock politely on the door, and have it opened by Disa. The Norwegian beauty seemed distinctly unhappy at the sight of a clean, stylish, well-mannered Scarlett.

Almost as much pleasure as coming upon Grayson Wolfe shoveling dirt from a wheelbarrow into one of several holes in the ground. Sweating, shirtless, and drop-your-drawers gorgeous.

She'd intended to appear aloof, arrogant, even mysterious. But the unabashed admiration in his eyes, the way he carelessly dropped the shovel and wiped his mouth as he watched her approach, made her smile and put a bounce in her step, despite the pinch of her new shoes.

She'd chosen well. The black dress bared her shoulders to the sun that burned bright and hot, emphasized her waistline, and flared into a full, flirty skirt. A plunging neckline made it obvious she hadn't worn a bra, and the black thong seemed to incite more movement in her hips when she walked. A sapphire-blue stare of raw male appreciation made the purchase more than worth the price. She'd worry about how to pay for it later.

Red stopped a few feet before him, deliberately looking him over, making sure he knew she was doing so. The minute strands of silver at his temples were deceptive. There was no gray on the chest, the hair so thick she wanted to pillow her head there. Biceps that bulged with every movement, shoulders so broad you could park a Buick on them, and abs you could play a game of jacks on. Her smile broadened as she parked her hand on her hip and tilted her head. "Disa told me I'd find you out here. And that I should be careful, and watch my step," she added cheerfully. "Referring to those holes, I assume."

"If you were trying to be careful, you wouldn't have shown up here looking like that." He bent slightly backward, stretching, and she carefully studied the movement of every muscle from the flat stomach to the flex of the shoulders and neck, ending at the quirk of a confident smile as he caught her. "What are you doing here, Scarlett?"

"I didn't get to thank you for coming to my rescue." She bent confidingly forward, allowing him to view an inch more cleavage. "I thought you might like to have me for lunch."

Grabbing his bottom lip between his teeth, he chewed, seeming to consider it. "You do enjoy being the bad girl, don't you?" Reaching for a kerchief in his back pocket, his eyes flared as the breeze toyed with the hem of her skirt. "You shouldn't have come back, Red. You don't know what you're playing with here."

The kerchief slid from his back pocket, and she imagined holding on to that taut, tight behind for dear life. No, she didn't know what she was playing with. But she wasn't going to leave until she did know, every slow, glorious inch of it. "I hear you're a wealthy man, Wolfe. Don't you have somebody to do this kind of work for you?"

"Yeah. But he's got the week off. I don't like having people around when I've got company." Retrieving the shovel, he jabbed it forcefully into the ground and wiped the perspiration from his brow. He had more hair on his arms than some men have on their heads. "Damn groundhogs. I've had to keep my alpacas in the western corral, afraid they'll stumble into one of these shitholes."

"You have alpacas? The little llama-looking creatures?"

"Why so surprised?"

She bit her own lip, choosing her words carefully. "You just don't strike me as the shepherd sort. More like a horseman, I think."

"I'm working on that too. Just being very selective. Horses have a tendency to be...well, a bit skittish around me. Meanwhile, the alpacas are a great investment. Their wool's worth a small fortune, you don't have to slaughter them to get your money back, and they're really very...well, sweet." He paused, flushing. "My favorite is a charming young fellow named Schmooze. I'd introduce you—but not with all these freaking holes in the ground! I hate the idea of killing the varmints, but—"

"I'm surprised they'd come around with the dogs loose."

"Dogs?"

"Yes. I saw one last night. Huge, majestic-looking beast, with eyes—"

"I'm taking a break." He interrupted her train of thought, then further confused her senses by moving closer, a sheen of sweat gleaming on his taut skin as he lowered his head, close enough to kiss her. Close enough to entice her to kiss him. "Care to see the property?"

She could barely breathe. Something about this man sizzled, sent off waves of heat that made her weak in the knees. "Yes. It looks very...impressive."

Turning his head slightly, he whispered in her ear, his beard making her cheek hot and flushed. "And you look good enough to eat." He nuzzled her neck, and she resisted the urge to sink her teeth into his shoulder. "Last chance," he whispered. "Run, little girl, run."

Red felt her eyes go wide in amazement. How incredibly intuitive of him. How'd he manage to guess that was her standard method of dealing with her problems? A wee voice, stifled by an overload of female hormones whispered to her. *He's right. He's giving you a chance. Take it, get the hell away from this strange place, this man that makes you want to melt and pour yourself all over him.*

"Let's start by exploring the inside," she murmured. "I mean of the house, of course."

"Of course." Brushing his hands across his jeans, he gallantly offered her his arm and a devastating smile. "As long as you're *willing* to stray off the woodland path, I'd be a fool to refuse, wouldn't I? But don't say you weren't warned..."

Chapter Seven

"Now this is interesting." Red took the two stairs down, blinking hard in disbelief. "I have a ten-year old VCR that eats tapes. You have a twenty-five-seat home movie theatre, complete with concessions."

"Is that what this is all about, Red?" His voice was quieter than usual, and she barely heard it as she gaped at her surroundings. Huge flat screen hanging against the wall, flanked by dramatic black velvet curtains that swished open as they entered. "Is it the money that interests you?"

"Don't be ridiculous." Stadium seating with cherry-red velour, complete with cup rests—except for the first two rows. Four full, beautifully upholstered royal blue seats, two in each row, more like thrones than chairs, lay temptingly before her. This, she was sure, was where he sat. And perhaps did other things. "I just ran away from a high-paying job because I couldn't stand it anymore. Your money doesn't interest me." Red peered around the room at the spotlights, the speakers hidden behind huge masks of Comedy and Tragedy, the adorable old popcorn machine behind a well-stocked bar. "But you do seem to have an abundance of it."

Gray shrugged, his eyes narrow as he watched her caress the chairs. "Live long enough, and you collect stuff. Antiques. Money. *Things.* What kind of work did you do?"

"I was a TV weatherperson."

He laughed. It was the first time she'd heard it, a sly, sexy, rumble that made her want to run a finger along his diaphragm, trace the source. "A weatherperson who's afraid of storms. Not good."

"It wasn't just that. I was out sick last week, at home channel-surfing. I moved from station to station at news time, and it suddenly struck me that every woman on every channel doing the weather reports was exactly the same. Well-dressed. Smiling. Plastic. Basically carbon-copies of each other. I didn't want to do that, didn't want to *be* that anymore. So, I did what I always do. I ran. Hopped in the car and took off for wherever the road might lead me. Just left it all behind. No problems, no worries."

His eyes sparkled periwinkle-blue. "And that's how you handle all your problems? Even man problems? Or are all of your men well-trained?"

"I like nice men, of course. Doesn't everybody? And I never have man problems. If it gets to be a problem, either he's gone or I am."

"Good thing you had your grandmother to run to. Did you find her well?"

"I found her dead, unfortunately. Heart attack as she slept. There's some relative living there now. But at least he doesn't have naked people frolicking in the yard. Can we watch a film?"

"But you've only seen half of the property."

Her mouth dropped. She'd counted fifteen rooms in the house already. Each of them exquisitely decorated, as if he wanted to anticipate the needs of his guests. This man knew how to live. "I'd rather we got to know each other. Let's relax. Take in a movie."

Gray rubbed the back of his neck, obviously uncomfortable. "I should finish my work. And you, Ms. Grier, really should leave."

"Not afraid of me, Wolfe, are you?" Swishing her hips in a tempting, exaggerated motion, she sashayed down to the second row and took a seat in one of the big chairs. "Oh, c'mon. I've never had a private showing before. It's just one movie. I promise I'll be good. Then I'll go away if you want me to."

She faced the screen, hands folded demurely in her lap. Dammit, was the man going to make her rape him? She wasn't mistaken about the mutual attraction. She could see it in his eyes, the way he watched every movement she made, the way they darkened every time she came near him. Even the way he was trying to get rid of her indicated a little caring beyond a quick kiss and a hump.

Why was he making this so difficult?

"All right then." He sighed. Assuming the chair beside her, he slouched into the seat, legs wide, and pushed two buttons on the chair's arm console. The theater immediately darkened, and the choppy sound of old, deteriorated reel tape crackled in the air. "Since you insist on doing this, we'll watch *my* favorite movie."

"And that would be...?" She waited through his silence, through the whining sound of melodramatic violins, until the film's title flashed on the screen.

"*The Wolfman?*" She gasped. She was hoping for something sexy.

Suggestive. Possibly pornographic. Obviously, she wasn't getting through to him. "You've got to be kidding me."

"Great movie. Fine acting. Circa 1941. A bright spot in a rather bleak year. The sinking of the Bismarck, bombing of Pearl Harbor—although DiMaggio's hitting that year was, as I recall—"

"'Recall'?"

"As in, recall the facts, Red. I'm a bit of a history buff."

Fascinating. Yeah, he was definitely trying to get her into bed. Uh-huh. "Tell me why this is your favorite movie."

"I relate to the tragic hero. Would you like a drink?"

"No." No, nothing to numb the senses. She wanted to feel every single sensation of sex with him. "I'm not big on horror films, but—is that him?"

"Yes. Larry Talbot. Can I get you *anything?* Cotton candy?"

She had a sudden, dizzying vision of licking whipped sugar from around his erection, letting the taste of him dissolve on her tongue and enjoying every puffed-pink moment of it. "No. He has such a sad face!"

"Lon Chaney, Jr. Master craftsman. Popcorn?"

"No."

"Taco?"

"Nope."

"Raisinets?"

"No, thank you. Fellatio?"

"Huh?"

"Do you enjoy being blown, Mr. Wolfe?"

She could feel his body heat rise next to her. Even in the darkened room, she could see the crotch of his jeans steeple as he shifted in the seat. "If you don't behave, I'm gonna have the usher put you out," he grumbled. "Watch the movie."

With a sinfully smug grin, Red stood before him, effectively blocking his view. Boldly reaching for his pants, she quickly popped the snap and slowly pulled the zipper down, one metal tooth at a time. "I predict a warm front coming up from the south," she murmured, watching a large muscle tighten in his neck. "Possibly complete with stiff winds and blunt-force conditions. I would recommend you seek shelter inside some warm, soft place, and—"

Gray grabbed her arm and pulled.

She tumbled sideways, awkwardly landing in a sitting position in his lap. "Do you know what you are, Ms. Grier?"

"Yes." She squirmed, the jaws of his zipper biting into her butt as he held her fast by her waist. "Horny."

"You, Scarlett, are a caution. A tease." On the verge of turning to protest, she felt his fingers at the crown of her own zipper. "And the sexiest, most mouthwatering woman I've had my paws on in ages." She felt cool air on her spine, and shivered. "Now, sit very still, and keep your eyes on the screen. I'm going to have to teach you a few things."

Red sat very still, very erect, as he peeled her dress open— all the way down to the line of her black thong. She could feel his hardness pressing against her behind, his breath hot upon her bare back. "Don't you want to know *why* I identify with the hero of this movie?"

His voice was a dangerous whisper near her ear, and she tried to laugh, to release some of the excitement that was already making the thong damp between her thighs. "Why?" She chuckled nervously. "Does he have a hard-on too?"

"No. But we do have something in common." He ran one light finger in a zigzag motion down her spine, and her hips wiggled despite her best intentions. "I'm a werewolf too."

Red blinked, blinked again, and tilted her head to one side as an old gypsy woman drove her cart onto the screen. "You are a...what? What the hell did you say?"

"A werewolf. Wolf-man. A man who can change into an animal." He slid the dress down her arms, baring her upper body. "And you have no idea how much you bring out the beast in me."

Scarlett sat frozen in place, thinking fast. Okay. She was in trouble here. Shit and dammit all to hell! Why did the sexiest man she'd ever met have to turn out to be deranged??!

"You don't believe me. I didn't expect you to. But I can prove it." With one hand he swept her hair away from the back of her neck and proceeded to plant sweet, soft kisses there. "I saw you in the window last night. I saw you touching yourself."

She reached for the top of the seat before her and held on tight. God, it was worse than she thought. He was not only demented, he was a peeper. A perv whose caress was like a drug, whose heat against her wet warmth made her want to try her first lap-dance.

The only question left to be answered was whether she'd make a run for it before she got laid, or after. A tough call, considering the apparent size of what she was sitting on. "You sicko. You were hiding in the bushes, weren't you? Watching me."

"No. I sat right up front and watched you, in plain sight." His huge hands slipped beneath the wide skirt of her dress and slowly slid smoothly up her feverish thighs. "I saw you do this. I saw your fingers find your sex, saw you struggle with the urge to join the others. I saw you touch yourself." His fingers barely brushed the crotch of her panties, and she nearly rocketed off his lap. "Remember the dog?"

She tried to turn, to call him a liar to his face...

That face that held those ice-blue eyes. The same eyes she'd seen staring at her from the face of that dog. "No, I still don't believe it. You're making this up."

"I tried to avoid this. God knows I did." His hip gyrated beneath her, against her, and her eyes slid closed as her head drifted back against him. With the deft touch of a practiced hand, his finger slid beneath the fabric of the thong, gathered it, and ripped it from her body in one forceful tug. "But as they say in the movie..."

His hands moved up her sides, soft as a whisper of air, drifting slowly to the front of her body and skimming the surface of her breasts even as she sighed.

>*"Even a man who is pure in heart,*
>
>*and says his prayers by night,*
>
>*May become a wolf when the wolfbane blooms,*
>
>*and the autumn moon is bright..."*

She was leaning against him in unknowing invitation, offering the side of her neck as he nibbled, bit with more force, kissed it sweetly away. And when the soothing hands suddenly became demanding, capturing her breasts from behind and pinching the nipples hard, she cried out, bowing back against him, giving him just the leverage required to yank the rest of the dress past her hips and toss it to the floor.

He inched away for only a moment. She felt his hardness come to life behind her, beneath her, as his chest heaved against her back. "Do you know what happens to bad girls who stray from the safe forest path?"

"God, Wolfe," she whispered, bringing one of his hands back to her breast. "If I have to endure a lecture, can I at least get a little bit during class?"

"That's it. That's exactly what happens." He was thick and hard, soft silk over steel against her bare ass. Adjusting her position in his lap, he raised her slightly until the round, hot head of him was poised at her entrance. Red held her breath, felt herself becoming wetter with each passing second, her lower lips swelling in anticipation. "Watch the movie. I'll continue with your 'lesson.'"

She was burning up, dying to feel him inside her. "But I want to see you, and—"

"You don't understand. I need to have you keep your eyes on the screen. Having you this way is dangerous enough, but if I see your face, your pleasure, I can't promise you…" She felt his forehead briefly fall upon her back. He felt feverish. "You have to listen carefully. This is important." He accentuateded his request by pushing forward ever so slightly, just enough to widen her, enough to prepare the way.

Red tried to relax. The prodding head felt *enormous*. Even if she had to listen to nonsense, she was going to enjoy this Halloween treat. She could always make her getaway later.

"It's nothing like the movies, y'know. It'll all make perfect sense to you, if you just open your mind." Gray eased the crest of his rod into her, just the head, and she gasped. God, he was huge and hot, his need pulsing, burning. Her interior muscles contracted and wept, greedily seeking more as she stared at the screen, seeing nothing.

"Is your mind opening a bit, Scarlett?"

God, yes. Wide open and receptive. She tried to move, to draw him in, but he held her still and motionless against him. "Yeah. Nothing like in the movies, you said. That's a good thing, Wolfe—because if your hair becomes anything like this guy's jacked-up fro when you change, I don't think I want to—"

"Unlike what the movie crappola you've been subjected to all your life tells you, being a werewolf is not a curse. I know. I was born with the *blessing*." He slid another throbbing inch inside, two inches, and she adjusted her hips, heart pounding. Wider. She had to widen her thighs to accommodate the massive size of the man. She wanted as much of the blessing as she could handle.

"My people are special. Gifted. Slightly different genetically. The senses are stronger, reactions faster. We're more sensitive to our surroundings than most people." He carefully slipped more of his thickness into her, feeding her a little at a time until she trembled, her nails digging into the fabric of his jeans. Still not home yet, and her muscles were stretched and straining, her heart pumping every bit of blood to her lower body. She was drenching the man in her juices, and he was still all caution and control. "I didn't just let you in because I pitied you for being out in the storm, Red. I could smell your sex, even in the rain and wind. And I responded like the animal that I am. I wanted to taste more."

This was unbearable. She was not a naturally passive woman. Grasping his hands, she placed them on her breasts. Tears sprang to her eyes when he pinched her nipples, and she closed her eyes to the sight of the screen werewolf being caught in a trap.

"The body manifests the thoughts and emotions of the mind," he whispered, squeezing harder. "We are all beasts, Scarlett, barely a tick of the evolutionary clock beyond living in caves. Your people hide behind manners and clothes, thoughts and reasoning. My people have learned to control the animal. But it lives in our nature, in our cellular structure. When not kept very tightly under control, we physically become what we feel. What we *are*." His big hands kneaded her breasts into sensitive, aching need. "Tell me you understand." His heart pounded forcefully against her back. "Tell me you remember what it is to feel like an animal."

He drove completely into her, deep, hard, before she could answer, before she could think. The force of it nearly pushed her off his lap, and might have been painful if she weren't so completely, utterly wet. Her sheath grasped and constricted, sending a short burst of rippling pleasure through her immediately. He'd sent her over the edge with a single thrust.

Her body locked on his, wanting more. To her dismay, he held her fast by her hips, unmoving. Only the frenzied beating of his heart against her back betrayed him. "Listen, Scarlett. I know what you want—what we both want—but you have to listen." He gasped the words rather than spoke as the screen werewolf strolled with his beloved through a fog-laced cemetery. "I swore I'd never do this, promised myself I'd never take a human female. But I had to have you, would've *killed* to have you. And now it's important for you to understand—"

"I don't care!" Her nerves were raw with need, softening around him in invitation. "I don't want to hear it, and I don't care. Can't we deal with your delusions later? I just want the sex, Wolfe. Why can't you just—"

His hand slipped between her thighs, a single teasing finger probing her folds as he sank deep inside her. Finding its prize, the finger feather-stroked her clit, and she moaned in frustrated ecstasy.

And with long, slow, measured thrusts, he began to move his hips in sync with that finger.

"I have to maintain some small control." He was murmuring nonsense into her ear, and it didn't matter now, nothing mattered now, as long as he continued. "If I let go completely, I might involuntarily change. I don't think I'd harm you, but I could become too rough, too careless, and I wouldn't want to risk..."

A harsh sound grated from his throat, and she felt him swell and harden within her. "But God in Heaven, you feel so good..."

His free hand pulled her legs wider to accommodate him as his other played her clit. Free to move at last, Red slid away, paused for a deep breath, then sat hard upon him, grinding, demanding. Feeling the pressure building in her groin, she increased her pace as he pumped faster in and out, still in control with short, hard thrusts, and that determined finger driving her mad.

In a rush of sensation, it washed over her. Her entire body shook from some fiery inner core and she convulsed around him, feeling nothing but his steel rooted inside of her.

He went still beneath her. Hot, throbbing, hard as stone, but still—except for that finger that still tormented her, that massaged with increasing pressure, began to increase in pressure, that wouldn't allow her to come back down to earth. "Wolfe?"

She could barely speak, barely breathe. Her hips still churned on top of him. Her body could not get enough. "Wolfe, wait. I need a minute here to—"

She heard a rasping snarl behind her ear, felt herself lifted, floating in space for only a moment. "Gray? Wha—"

She was suddenly tossed over the chair in front of them, arms folded into the seat, butt high in the air. Before she could react, he grunted and joined with her again in one piercing, violent push. Alternately pulling her against him and stabbing into her, the shadowy figure behind her put all of his force into his hard, piercing thrusts, pumping savagely away. Her sex heated, tightened, taking it all, craving more.

Red managed to grab the armrests, silently exulting in making him lose control, bowing her back to tempt him further. She screwed her eyes shut, the black and white film flickering beyond her lids, as his heavy sacs banged against her bottom. "Yesssss..." The hissing sound from her throat grew louder with her excitement, and her nails clawed at the chair as he expanded to impossible thickness, burning inside her.

He was coming, stiffening, the head of his cock red-hot as a low growl built in his chest. The first waves began, a slow pulse in her sex, quickly building to blue-white oblivion behind her eyes. Intense spasms of charged heat possessed her body as he drove deep, fingers tightening, and exploded inside of her. His primitive roar reverberated through the theater, his hot, creamy lust spurting inside her, filling her, overflowing, until her own climax wracked her mind and body.

With ragged breathing, bone-limp and exhausted, Red slowly came to her senses. He had fallen forward upon her, effectively pinning her beneath him, still joined with her. And, incredibly, still hard.

"Oh, my, Mr. Wolfe. What a big cock you have." She was sore and slightly dizzy, smiling at the grumbling sounds of the wolfman in the forgotten film. "I'd hate to see what you're like when you lose control!"

His hand landed on the top of the chair to her right, and she moved to touch it.

With a horrified gasp, her fingers froze in mid-air as her eyes flared wide in disbelief.

It was not a hand. It was an enormous furred paw, clinging to the chair with pale bronze claws.

As her heart stopped cold in her chest, she felt another fall to her left, effectively trapping her beneath him. No, not him. *It.* It was an animal of some sort, something that had possessed Gray. Something that *was* Gray. Her mouth fell silently open as she remained very, very still. Petrified. She could feel the breath of the beast on her back, but could not make her fear-frozen body recoil from the sensual sliding of its fur against her spine.

With a curt snarl that sounded surprisingly like anger, it pushed against the seat, propelling itself away from her. She heard the sound of the animal rushing away, saw a dark, muscular form on all fours just before the door of the theater slammed open and afternoon light punched through the darkness.

Closing her eyes, she slumped over the seat, wordlessly giving thanks to God that she was still alive.

And cursing herself as she realized she was far from ready to run. The danger, the strangeness of it was as powerful an aphrodisiac as Gray himself was. She was aroused and ready to go again.

Never had she felt more alive. Having the oh-so-controlled Grayson Wolfe and being frightened nearly to death had been the most exciting, erotic things that had ever happened to her in her life.

Chapter Eight

Gray stomped through the house, tossing doors open, overturning anything in his path and not sparing even a glance at Will and Alana as they huddled together in the Great Room, whispering solemnly.

His pace slowed as he made his way through the kitchen. He considered a quiet, gentle approach, thought better of it. Best to remain true to his nature. With a casual jerk of one hand, he ripped the kitchen door from its hinges and stepped out into the garden.

This night was gentle and cool, and after his bout of exercise he appreciated the caress of the breeze, the stark bright moon. Allowing his bare feet to sink deep into the dewy grass, he walked straight to the great oak tree.

"I knew I'd find you here."

Red sat quietly on one large, protruding root, her feet tucked beneath her. Watching him.

Gray hooked his thumbs into his pockets, at a loss for what to say. She wore the sundress, and the memory of what lay beneath stirred his blood to desire once again. "I should apologize for my...sudden exit. I'm sorry. Don't have any idea how long I've been gone. I lose all sense of time when I..." He fumbled for words, concentrating, focusing on the dry, whispering leaves overhead, the sharp edge of the denim against his hand, her hair dark fire in the moonlight—anything to keep himself from taking her in his arms again. "I was eight miles away, going at a full gallop, before I realized what I was doing."

Kneeling beside her, he reached over to lay a comforting hand on her shoulder, and to see if she would scurry away. There was no movement, no sound. No expression. He'd rather have her curse him than this strange, strained silence. "Red? Are you all right? Please tell me I didn't hurt you. I think I remember that much, but...tell me."

Scarlett rested her chin on her knee, peering up at him. "Doesn't your superior nature tell you these things?"

"No. The male of *every* species is at a loss when it comes to the female, I think. And I was so hungry, so impatient to have you, I forgot to tell you about the incantation for your own safety, and—"

"Incantation?"

"An old wives' tale that happens to be true, in this case. To bring the werewolf back to human form, you would repeat his Christian name three times. Nothing magical about it. It's just a matter of reminding the beast of his humanity, and—"

"Where did you go?"

She was, he thought, still in a slight case of shock. She wasn't asking about the most important thing: the change. He shifted uncomfortably, curling his toes into the damp grass. "I had to run. Had to burn off the energy, the exhilaration of the mating, and..." He tried to clear his throat, clogged with some emotion he couldn't identify. "And I had the urge to run out and get you something, bring it back as a present. Dead rabbit. Possum. Something like that."

"Please tell me you *didn't!*"

He barked a short laugh. "Not to worry. Came to my senses in time. And I figure you're more the venison or squirrel sort anyway."

"For future reference, I'm not into wild meat. I don't want to see the eyes of *anything* staring back at me, okay?"

His heart began to race. Was that hope he was feeling? She'd spoken of the future! "Understood." Her expression was little-girl guileless, and for a moment he thought he'd do anything in the world to keep her from being disappointed with him. "I feared you'd be gone. I thought you'd be afraid."

"Afraid?" She slowly stood, straightening her skirt. "I'm amazed. A little stunned. It's like finding out the Martians have been here all along, isn't it?"

"So why did you stay?"

Rising, Red swirled her fingertips through his chest hair, her lashes provocatively lowered. Gray firmly clenched his teeth as he remembered there was nothing beneath that trim little dress. "I had a dream last night. There was a woman. Here. Pinned against this tree, like an offering."

Gray's nostrils flared, taking in the scent of her. He was dying to have her again, his hardness painful in the confines of the jeans he'd retrieved. "Interesting dream."

She flicked his nipple and, again, he was fighting for control. "There was a man. He was having sex with her, pounding her senseless against this tree. The air was fresh, and their bodies were wet. It was pure, raw, uncompromising lust."

She shrugged. "I wondered what it might be like in the moonlight." She gave him a tentative peck on the lips. "Where somebody might see us." Another quick kiss. "Especially Disa."

He gathered her into his arms. "That fantasy just might work for both of us." Fingers trembling slightly, he reached behind her for the zipper again, cursing when it caught in the fabric. Without a moment's thought, he grabbed the neckline in both hands and pulled, ripping it apart, baring her body to him.

Her eyes widened and she laughed. "Effective, if a little cliché. You werewolves have a problem with women wearing clothes, hmmm?"

"You won't be needing them." His gaze was fastened on her nipples, puckering in the chill of the night air. "Spend the night with me." He gently traced the undersides of her firm breasts, his mouth going dry. "We can discuss our future later."

"Our 'future'? Hold up now, Wolfe—I'm not talking love and marriage here." Her fingertips began to drift toward his abdomen. "I just want another taste of the good stuff you've got stashed in here, and—"

"I swore I'd never consider a human female." He shook his head, marveling at the fever consuming his body. "But I think it would be at least several decades before I tired of you."

"Smooth talker, aren't you? Gives me the warm-fuzzies, just thinking about..." Red paused, blinking. "Several decades? Um...exactly how old are you, Grayson?"

At last, the questions were coming. But he couldn't wait long enough to answer all of them. He needed her *now*. "It doesn't matter. Why don't we—"

"*Ah, ah, ahhh.*" She held up a hand between them. "A girl's got a right to know these things. I'm not sure I want some grandpa's old grinder working on me, y'know?"

He barely touched the tips of her nipples, heard her inhale sharply. Anything, anything to get inside of her. "Relatively speaking, I'm rather young. Seven hundred and forty-five years old."

First the questions, now the disbelief. Her mouth ovaled. "My God. You're not kidding, are you? Oh, my God…"

"I'm the Alpha male of this particular pack. My descendants originally came from Germany, and—"

"And the others?" She wanted information faster than he could speak. "Disa, Will, Alana, Jacob? Centuries old?"

"Except for Disa—yes. She's all too human. Some women hang around the pack for the excitement. The sex. Or the appeal of being with powerful men. I thought you were like that, at first."

Her eyes held a challenge. "And now?"

"Now? Now I know better." He inched forward, palming her firm breasts, his mouth watering. Forcing her to back up as he approached, he continued until she was wedged between his body and the tree. "You're a strong, independent woman. Your natural inclination would be to resist a man who was too aggressive. Too demanding. A man who took what he wanted." His mouth sank slowly toward hers, fascinated as he watched the large brown eyes close in anticipation, the moist lips part slightly, inviting. Irresistible.

Gray tasted her, nibbling, teasing as he hurriedly unzipped his jeans and stepped out of them. He knew she needed to know more, knew there were a thousand things he wanted to tell her.

But not right now. Right now he needed to bury himself inside her more than he'd ever needed anything.

Prying her legs apart with his knee, he found her hot core with one finger and inserted it. She was already soaking wet.

He was damned.

Wickedly wiggling the tip of his finger, he smiled as her arms slipped around his neck, felt her trembling as he pushed deeper, whispering in her ear. "I suppose you've always had *nice* men, yes? The kind of man who would be gentle and sweet. The kind you could control." He sucked vigorously on her throat, tasting her, resisting the urge to draw blood. "He'd make polite conversation until you felt relaxed. Ask if you might consider having sex, take you to some expensive, romantic place to persuade you?"

With one quick motion, he grasped her hips, lifting her off the ground and roughly entering her with one hard, stabbing stroke.

Her gasp inflamed him. He had to pause, even as the blood of the beast roared in his ears, even as he thickened inside of her. He would not lose complete control this time, would not allow the change to scare her away. "And he'd never think of fucking you out in the open, in the moonlight. And he'd take it slow and easy, just as you thought you liked it. It would never occur to him to hump you so hard it would make you scream and ask for more."

Her legs wrapped around his waist, her walls tightening around him like deep, warm velvet.

Gray pushed with his legs, sinking deep, and deeper still. "Tell me you want it, Red. Tell me."

"Damn you, Wolfe." She practically hissed the words. "Shut up and give it to me."

He withdrew only enough to thrust deeper, and she laughed softly, tossing her head back. Quickly establishing a fast rhythm, he stroked mindlessly in and out of her heat. His fingers dug into her taut buttocks, pulling her violently against him as he pushed, unable to get enough. A soft whimper tore from her throat, became a moan that ended in sudden silence as her eyes clamped shut and her body shuddered against his.

"God, Wolfe," she groaned breathlessly. "That's it. More. Please. More…"

Her hunger pushed him right to the brink. He felt his nails harden, curve, the longest one piercing the skin of her right buttock. His teeth grew sharp against his bottom lip, and he clamped onto her neck, not drawing blood but needing the feeling of flesh between his fangs. She would have cuts and bruises afterward, and the skin on her lovely back would be scraped raw by the bark of the tree.

He couldn't care about that right now, couldn't think. He was so swollen with blood he hurt, unaware of anything but the need to go deeper, faster, to feel her grow tighter around him, to burst inside her.

She was chanting his name, whispering at first, then louder and louder as he increased to a frantic pace. A light went on in one of the cottages, but the lodger wisely stayed inside. A vortex of fallen leaves, gathered by a sudden breeze, swirled like a serenade around them. He saw them through a crimson fog, didn't care. The pressure in his cock had built to explosive force, ready now, peaking as he made one last, massive thrust and ground into her with a savage snarl as her sex rippled around him and her screams echoed in the night.

* * *

Red felt herself slowly drifting downward from the blazing white light that had seared her body into blankness. Lowered by a pair of gentle arms, she slowly opened her eyes to find herself in darkness.

She was on her side, the humped root that had served as a seat now cradling her head. Unable to focus immediately, she reached out for her last memory, for the man who had so easily rocked her entire world.

"Wolfe?"

He wasn't there. Her hand found the mossy base of the tree, the grass slick with dew. But there was no man by her side. "Wolfe?" she repeated, stunned by the hoarseness of her throat. Until she remembered she'd been screaming. Loudly. And the sensations that had accompanied those screams...

Forcing her aching body into a sitting position, she saw him, magnificently naked in the moonlight. He was a few yards away, pacing frantically in a large circle, muttering to himself.

"Gray? What are you doing?"

He ran his long fingers through his hair and swore, increasing his speed.

What was *this* about? Had she missed something along the way? "Boy, those decades slipped by fast! Tired of me already, Wolfe?"

He stopped, his form gleaming gold in the light. "I have to go. Have to run." He shook his hands as if shaking off water. There was something odd about them, something different she couldn't quite make out in the shadows. "I know you don't understand. No time to explain." He began jogging around the perimeter of the yard, his eyes never touching hers.

"I've got to burn off the rest of the animal energy, try to avoid the change. Away from you," he panted. "Not sure it's safe for me to be here with you."

Red blinked, bewildered. "Not safe? But what—"

"Stay there. Rest. I'll bring a blanket, wine… God!" The word seemed wrenched from his body, and he nearly doubled over. "Must go. Can't hold it…"

He took the nearby fence in one athletic leap and charged the nearest stand of woods at top speed.

"Wait!" She called after him moments after he'd disappeared, waving his jeans in the air. "Don't you want your *pants?!*"

The shutting off of the cottage light that had been burning was the only response. More darkness. Rolling the denim into a ball, she slipped it beneath her head and stretched like a satisfied cat, sore, satiated, sighing. "Cigarette, Ms. Grier? A little after-sex cuddling, hmmm?" She easily mimicked his voice with her newfound hoarseness. "Let's just bask in the afterglow here, why don't we? God, you're good, Red!" She giggled at her own cynicism, curling into a half-fetal position. "You are the hottest woman I've ever—"

She saw the shadow move from the corner of her eye and started, suddenly alert. Smaller than a man. Breathing hard. The bristling fur that formed a ruff around its neck gleamed silver in the moonlight, the ears pointed and perked as it approached.

"Oh, my God." Raising herself slightly she stared, wide-mouthed, marveling. "Gray? Is that you?"

The beast pranced toward her with gleaming teeth forming a canine smile. It warily slowed within inches of her, carefully sniffing the soles of her feet, its strong legs and huge paws firmly planted in the turf.

"Wow." It was unthinkable. Miraculous. He was gruff and powerfully built, and apparently every bit as suspicious as Grayson Wolfe the man. Idly wondering whether he'd allow her to touch him in this form, she cautiously eased an open palm toward him. "I'm really not into the foot-fetish thing, Wolfe," she laughed softly. "Why don't we try…"

Her words died away as the creature's eyes narrowed, its ears flattening. Baring ivory-white fangs, the tail stiffened slightly as a low growl issued from its throat.

"No, no, Gray, *sshhhh.*" Pulling her hand back, she spoke soothingly. "It's all right. It's only me. It's all right…"

The low growl became an angry snarling noise as the beast eased closer, saliva dripping from the tip of its tongue.

This was wrong, all wrong. In a fugue-like state of fear, Red suddenly realized what it was.

She was in trouble.

Even as her heart swelled into her throat, even as her limbs stiffened with fear as she thought of flight, she tried to assure herself that Gray would not harm her. He would come to his senses any moment, or she'd find it was some twisted joke, some terrible mistake. Afraid to rise and run, she began to inch away on her back, propelled by elbows and hips. Maybe it wasn't even *him.* But the animal shook his great silver head, even as she remembered something Gray had told her: "I'm the only silver wolf here…the only one…"

And other words. Something he'd told her about an old incantation, a method of bringing the man back, out of the beast. Trying to clear her throat of fear, she sat up to face him. "Grayson Wolfe," she whispered.

Nothing. Three times. He'd said three times. Dear God, if only he didn't kill her before she managed it.

"Grayson Wolfe." Her voice shook at the vicious expression on his face. Either it wasn't taking effect—or it wasn't Gray…

"Grayson Wolfe!!"

With an impatient snort and a bark-like warning, the wolf sprang.

Red screamed, scrambled to her knees, and nearly gained a footing. The surprisingly dense weight of the creature caught her back, knocking her to the ground, its claws ripping into her skin. Instinctively turning sideways, she lashed out with one heel and caught it squarely on the left eye socket.

A loud yelp. The teeth clamped onto her foot, sinking in. Her fingers clawed, uprooting grass, troweling into soft earth. Tasting blood, the beast latched onto her leg, fangs tearing it open and worrying the flesh as she screamed one last, helpless time.

The night became suddenly cold, and she shivered as her strength ran out of her, too weak to move. The moon seemed to darken as sleep overcame her. Maybe another storm coming, she thought vaguely. She was too tired even for fear. There was a voice, a shout beyond the hungry humming of the animal. A light flared, then another, and another as her knee slid in the thick, slippery pool of her own blood, and she gave herself to the merciful deadness of the dark.

Chapter Nine

Gray shuddered as he hovered over the still body. Wiping his forehead with his arm, he unconsciously smeared her blood over the satin-cold sheen of perspiration that clung to his skin.

His fault. God in Heaven, it was all his fault.

"Grayson."

There was a hand upon his shoulder. He turned, blinking, unseeing, in response.

"Gray, she has to go." Will's face came into focus, grim and drawn. "I know you're upset, but the girl needs a hospital."

Shaking him off, Gray moved to the other side of the bed. "Don't be an idiot. How do you suppose we'd explain a wolf attack inside my very civilized compound?"

She might have been asleep. Her face was peaceful, her breathing shallow. Only the mangled left leg and abundance of blood betrayed the truth. "Where are the damned women?"

"Alana is fetching bandages, antibiotics. Disa is packing. This is all a little too real for her." Gently lifting Red's limp wrist, Will checked her pulse. "I understand your duty to protect the pack, Gray. But the girl could die, and—"

Gray was on him immediately, his hand stretched tightly around the thick throat as his friend's eyes bulged in surprise. "Say that again, and I'll kill you. Understand?" His own blood was on fire, and only a supreme effort of will was preventing him from changing at this moment, from wreaking vengeance on everyone, friend and foe alike. "She lives. If I can do anything about it, the girl lives."

Will silently nodded, releasing her arm as Gray loosed his choke hold. "What can I do?"

"Get out." The sight of her blood had seriously shaken him. He didn't think he'd ever enjoy the taste of it again. "Check the area. Put your nose to the ground. I think I know who did this, and—"

"Jake." Will's voice was low and sure. "You think it was Jacob."

He barely nodded. "See what you can pick up. If you find him, get him away from here. *Far* away. For good. Because if I find him, I'll rip out his fucking throat."

Will shuffled his bare feet and zipped the trousers he'd never fastened in his haste. "I came running as soon as I realized something was wrong. It was a tough call, y'know? I mean, I knew the two of you were out there together, and she'd already been screaming anyway, and..." He slapped the back of his neck in frustration. "She was alone when I found her. I brought her inside, called out for you. I did my best."

"You probably saved her life. And when I can spare the energy to be more civilized, I'll be sorry for the way I'm speaking to you." Gray raised the injured leg slightly, watching the blood soak through the impromptu pressure bandage and into the sheet, thread by thread. "Now get out. And tell your woman I need her *now*."

* * *

Alana entered the bedroom, placing her small silver tray on the dresser. The Alpha's eyes were fixed on the broken figure on the bed. He didn't seem to notice her at all.

But she noticed him.

Still in the raw from his run, he was gloriously naked, a fine beast, whether in animal or human form. Turning away, she busied herself with the gauze and tape, taking advantage of the mirror to watch. She belonged to Will, of course—if not by decree, in her heart. Loved him deeply. But if she couldn't still enjoy the sight of a man like Gray, she'd have to be nearly as dead...

Nearly as dead as the woman in the bed.

"You know why you're here." His tone was clipped, urgent.

"Because I know the old ways." She nodded, using forceps to retrieve a wad of greenish gauze from a steaming crystal bowl.

"And because you know how to keep your mouth shut."

She turned to stare at him openly now, waving the bandage to cool it. "I didn't know you intended to—"

"As a child, I remember seeing my mother cry a great deal, Alana." He barely seemed aware that he spoke. "Whenever she thought of the family she'd been separated from. Whenever we were forced to move yet again because of suspicious people. Whenever my father disappeared without a word for days, whenever the moon was full..." He smoothed the wild red hair with the gentlest of touches. "Even then I remember thinking, 'how fragile these humans are!' Swore I would never harm one. Or have one."

Alana's lips parted in unspoken amazement. He was already smitten with the human. "This girl is not fragile. She'll survive. I've seen worse."

"You've brought the ceremonial knife? Sterilized it?"

She lowered her eyes, remembering her place, and spoke carefully. "You realize, Wolfe, that what you plan to do will bind you to this girl forever?"

"Quiet. Quiet now." Removing the bloodied wrap, he focused on Scarlett's legs, alternating between the whole, shapely one and the gaping wound in the other. "I need to concentrate. Concentrate on my *fury...*"

Alana waited patiently as the huge silver wolf loomed over the unconscious figure, taking in every scent. Slowly, with the care he might give in cleaning a cub, he ran his long tongue along the jagged edge first, then inside, mixing his healing saliva with her blood.

It was the first time Alana had seen him taste blood without the desire for it. She was sure it was the last time he'd taste it without desire for the girl.

Stretching the herb-soaked gauze out to its full length, she waited for him to finish, now understanding at least one reason for the tears of a human female.

Chapter Ten

Raining again.

Red frowned in her semi-sleep, listening carefully. Yes, there was the breathless, whispering sound of sheer sheets of water blown lightly across the roof. She waited apprehensively for the thunder that never came, then relaxed. Rain, but no storm. She was safe.

Only then did she attempt to pry her eyelids apart, slowly, carefully. The room was brighter than the gray skies that crowded the window. And a large, imposing figure sat silently beside her bed.

The overhead light burned her eyes. She closed them, attempting her first—or last—deep breath. The creature beside her was either Death incarnate, or Wolfe. Or maybe both. "So...am I going to be served with gravy, or without?"

Her eyes flickered wide enough to catch his response, a scowl that carved creases into his entire face. He did not seem amused. "Scarlett?" Gray slowly shook his head. "I thought you'd never wake up."

Beneath the cover of her lashes, her gaze cut quickly across the room, searching. They were alone. "That was the idea, wasn't it?"

Bending over her bed, he lightly palmed her forehead—testing for fever? "How do you feel?"

"Cold. Sleepy. Numb. Stupid."

"Scarlett—"

"Are you...are you going to kill me? Is that how this works?" She couldn't feel her left leg. She couldn't feel much of anything. His face wavered like water before her, and the corners of her eyes burned like acid. Making a determined push, she saw the movement of her leg wrinkle the sheet covering her body. Thank God, it was still there.

"No, of course not. No one will harm—"

"Then may I leave, please?" Her body was beginning to wake up, to feel the pain not known in sleep. Her leg, her back, her hand—everything seemed to be on fire. But more than anything else, she wanted to get away from him before the hot tears spilled over. "I won't tell anyone. I promise. What do I need to do? Do you people have some kind of vow, something to sign in blood? I will."

Gray sighed, then shook his head. "I think you've shed enough blood already, Red. I know you probably don't understand. You've been out of it for a day and a half, and—"

"What?" The dry, raspy word squeaked out of her throat. "A day and a half?! That's not possible. I have to go." She wrestled her shoulders from the bed, gasping as a wave of dizziness possessed her, almost grateful when he firmly pushed her back down. The cold eyes became fierce blue steel as he held her in place.

"Red, if you try to get out of this bed again, I'll screw you so hard you won't be *able* to walk for a week. Understand?"

Even now—dizzy, lame, dazed, and wounded, her body responded to the promise of his words. Pulling the sheet up, she lay silent. The sizzling sound of the rain was all that passed between them for several moments.

"Scarlett. You can't leave yet." He sat gingerly on the edge of the bed opposite her wounded leg. "I have to protect my people. Can't have too many questions asked about that injury. And you need a little more time to heal. Not as much time as you normally would, but time. Just rest for another day or so. Alana and I will take care of you."

"I don't get it. Don't understand any of it. What happened? Why would anybody want to attack me?" Memories, flashbacks to the attack clicked through her mind. "And what do you mean, 'I won't take as much time to heal'?"

"We suspect Jacob. He's been unhappy about his place in the pack for some time now. This may have been his form of revenge for my handling of the incident the other day. I'll deal with that problem. Don't worry." He struggled to maintain control, to keep the delicious image of him tearing Jacob apart from possessing him. "As for the other...you've been treated with certain herbs and medicinal remedies passed down through generations. We know these wounds, know how to treat them."

A sudden thought made her empty stomach turn over. "Oh, shit, Wolfe! I'm not going to become... I mean, I won't be like..."

"You've watched too damn many old movies." He nearly grinned. "I told you, this is about genetics, plain and simple. If I had six toes and bit you, you wouldn't grow an extra toe, now

would you? But you'll carry a *bit* of your adventure with you."
He leaned forward, whispering. "I licked your leg."

Scarlett went very still beside him. "Perv to the end, eh,
Wolfe?"

"My people have a natural ability to heal faster than average
humans. Possibly because there aren't many of us, relatively
speaking. We were a hunted people. We needed to evolve
defenses. Whatever injuries we suffer in our animal forms are
healed by the time we finish 'the change.' Our saliva has a
natural healing agent. It's helped your leg already. That—and
this."

He held her palm before her face, and she felt herself shrink
away from him. A pentagram. A large pentagram, carved into
her hand by some very sharp object. Neatly drawn and also well
on the way to healing, it was a bloody reminder of the position
she was in. Had she really flirted with the danger of all this,
really tried to accept it as some sort of rational possibility?

"Pentagram. Okay. Also a little cliché, but—"

He silently held up a single finger and, to her dismay, she
immediately went quiet. She'd never *obeyed* a man in her life.
But then, this was no ordinary man. "You need to learn stillness,
Scarlett. Acceptance. It isn't the circumstances of your life you
run away from. It's yourself. What you intuit, what you want.
What you don't want to know. Things like this."

Spreading his fingers wide, he revealed the same pentagram,
carved into his own palm. "It hasn't healed yet. This I did as a
man. My blood mingling with yours via this ancient symbol, to
strengthen and heal. It means you carry me with you wherever
you go now. So there can be no running away. It means I've
shared the most sacred part of myself with you. Now—will you

listen?" His voice became as soft as the rain. "Allow me to care for you."

The dual nature of his sentence made her tears escape at last. Forgetting the brand on her hand, she wiped her face with her palm, then sucked in air as the salty tears burned the wound. "I'll need to contact my cousin. In-law. Once removed, or whatever he is."

"I'll get Will to take care of it."

"And I'll actually be allowed to wear panties?"

His mouth twitched. "If you wish."

"Then I'll stay. For a while."

He lapsed into a broad smile. "You must be parched. I'll get you water, have Alana whip up a nice broth—"

"So you were wrong?" She tugged the sheet up to her chin. The recklessness and small trust they'd shared had not returned with consciousness. "I mean, it wasn't an out-and-out lie, just a mistake, right?"

"Mistake?"

"You told me you were the only silver wolf in the vicinity."

"Yes, I did."

"But the animal that attacked me was a silver wolf, Gray."

His body stiffened, and there was something of the look of a cornered animal in his expression. "I'll have that broth brought up for you." His voice was unnecessarily loud as he shouldered his way through the door. "Yes. A mistake. I made a mistake."

* * *

Will poured two fingers of the Macallans into each of the finely-etched Waterford snifters. Gray watched him sip, savor the taste as he swallowed all of his in one gulp.

"I don't believe it for a minute."

Gray shook his head slowly, twisting his lips into a humorless smile. "You sound like one of those pathetic humans who refuses to believe in the reality of werewolves. The ones who can't accept truth, even when it bites them in the ass."

Will shook his own head, resolute. "There's no way in hell you would've done anything to hurt that girl—even in your altered state."

"One silver." Gray helped himself to another drink, keeping the bottle beside him. "I'm the only silver in our pack, Will. Unchallenged, my territory covers nearly one hundred twenty square miles. I don't suppose some vagabond werewolf strayed that far out of the way." He grimaced, at last feeling the whiskey. "And we both know we can't always remember what we've done once we 'return.' It had to be me."

Pausing as Alana passed through the Great Room with another tray, they listened to the crackling of the season's first hearth fire compete with the peaceful patter of the rain. "If you did, by chance, injure the woman, you can't blame yourself. You know that."

"What I know is that I swore I would never..." Grabbing the whiskey, Gray pushed away from the sofa and planted himself before the stone fireplace, turning the bottle upside down in his mouth. "Never harm one of them. Never. Especially a woman. And certainly not *this* woman. But she had those lips, those taunting, tempting lips, and breasts you'd kill to touch, and...and..." He closed his eyes, his head falling loosely back.

"She has the spirit of the wolf, and the fragility of the woman. How the hell was I supposed to resist that?"

"Grayson, I've known you for six hundred years. I've seen you enraged, drunk, vicious, sexually obsessed. But I've never seen you like this." Tapping a forefinger on the side of his glass, Will cautiously cleared his throat. "There is another possibility, you know."

He wasn't in the mood for conversation. Or for making excuses for himself. "Is that right?"

"There's always the chance that one of us has become a true master of the metamorphosis. That he's not only able to change from man to wolf, with all the variations in-between, but able to assume the form of any other werewolf." He tasted the scotch. "Even *you*."

"You're talking about the old legends. The myths about Proteus, shapeshifters, or the werewolves who can go beyond the ordinary change." He shrugged. "Fairytales. Bullshit. Impossible."

"Like the legend of werewolves?"

Gray's voice echoed from the high vault of the ceiling. "Yeah. Like that."

Will tossed back his drink, squirming in his chair. "Gray? My own father had the ability."

"What? What's this you're telling me?"

"My father was one of those shapeshifters. He had complete, absolute control over his molecular form. The wolf, the man, anything in between—and anyone else he chose to replicate."

He nearly laughed. "You are *serious?*"

"I am. Is it so hard to believe? One step, one thought, one emotion beyond what you yourself are?"

Gray turned, considering. Considering Will's claim. Considering the consequences if true. He felt the hair at the nape of his neck bristling. Turning his cut-glass gaze on his friend, his voice took on a deadly edge. "And tell me, William. Did you inherit this peculiar ability of your father's?"

William slid the glass across the table, facing him without flinching. "I have no grand designs on leadership, Gray. I'm quite content with my role as a Beta. And we've been friends for a long time. You can't lash out at everybody. You'll need someone to trust."

"As I trusted Jacob?" He pushed his hair away from his face, cursing. He'd had too much to drink, and too little sleep in the long hours of tending the girl. This was not the time for a confrontation. "Apparently, what I need is someone else to blame, so I don't feel so guilty myself. Any sign of our old friend?"

"Hard to tell. The persistent rain's made tracking difficult. And there are multiple scents now. Others from the pack coming, seeking your approval of their unions."

"They refuse to let go of the old ways. I've told all of them repeatedly they're free to mate as they wish." Everyone except him, apparently.

"And what about the girl?"

The alcohol was beginning to numb his brain. Thank God. "Scarlett will have to leave."

"But you've just asked her to stay."

"Doesn't matter. She isn't safe with me. I don't have the control…" He paused, focusing on the large log being devoured by flame.

"You could explain, tell her you think you're responsible, ask her to understand…well, the nature of the beast."

"That's exactly what I can't do. She'll either run, or find it fascinating, irresistible. And I'll wager she'll find it challenging—that damn spirit of hers. I'll have to make her leave." The bottle shook in his hand. "We can't always have what we want, Will. You might ask Alana, who waits, patiently warming your bed, about that."

Will stiffened, shook his head, and headed for the door. "Then I'd best go. Maybe I can be useful there, at least."

Dammit, this was not what he wanted! This man was like a brother to him. "Will! I'm sorry. That was vicious and unnecessary."

"Yes. You've become as deadly with words as you are in battle." Swinging the door wide open, Will hesitated, his foot on the threshold. "Oh, and to answer your question, Gray? Yes. I will sleep happily with Alana tonight. And yes, I did inherit my father's ability. Will you rest easily knowing that?"

"No. But I don't want us to become enemies. I need you with me, Will. I count on it."

Will's shrugged slightly without turning to face him, his voice unusually tight. "Don't worry, Gray. You won't be able to take a step without me."

Chapter Eleven

Scarlett puckered up for the huge, soft lips, amused by the absence of teeth at the top. "Mmm-wah!" she exclaimed, laughing with delight. "That's the best kiss I've ever had."

Gray grabbed his heart, trying his best to look wounded. "You really know how to crap on a guy's ego, Red."

"Lack of ego will never be your problem, Wolfe." Lightly rubbing noses with her new love, she hummed contentedly. "Will it, Mr. Schmooze?"

The pure white alpaca hummed with her, offering his long neck for a good scratch. With huge, half-closed eyes, he allowed her to sink probing fingers into his fur. "I can't believe how thick and soft this is! And if he isn't the sweetest—"

"You're shivering."

"No, I'm not." Still, she pulled the oversized leather jacket he'd loaned her closer, lifting the collar against her neck. The wind was coming faster now than it had been when they left the house, but she hated the idea of going back. The sporadic sunlight, the fresh air, and being back on her feet were the highlights of the best two days of her life.

Two days of Grayson Wolfe. Two days of his non-stop care and attention. He'd fed her when she was still weak, when the rawness of the pentagram made holding things difficult. He'd read to her from his favorite books, an astonishing array of myths, heroic legends, and passionate poetry. He moved her bed so the waning moonlight swam across her sheets at night, and he was there as the sun rose to pull the sheers so she might awaken gently.

And last night, when a dream of the attack had awakened her with a scream, he'd joined her in bed, holding her so tightly that nothing could harm her, until she relaxed in his arms.

"Careful," she'd whispered against the warmth of his chest. "You don't want me getting used to this."

She'd thought he'd stiffened slightly, but he pulled her even closer. "Exactly what is this thing you have about running, Red?"

"Oh, abusive childhood. Teenage runaway. The usual dreary story." She'd nuzzled his neck, feeling surprisingly comfortable telling him her secrets. "My father liked to prove his manhood by beating the two women in his life. I left first. My mother didn't stay long afterward. When I finally came back home, she'd remarried. A nice guy. But she was so busy trying to please him twenty-four-seven, she couldn't waste time on being a mother.

"So, I ran again. Since then, I've become very good at it. That is how it's done, right? Run away *before* situations become unbearable, *before* somebody hurts you. Saves a lot of wear and tear on the heart."

"Just as I thought," he'd murmured as she drifted into smiling sleep. "A fragile little thing."

She could never have imagined the man who barked so harshly at her when she first appeared could have been so kind.

She would never have imagined herself falling in love in such a short time.

"There's rain coming in on the wind." He sniffed as he gave the alpaca a parting pat on the head. "We should go. I have one more thing to show you."

"I can't imagine what." She looked out over the land, her hair whipping about her face in the breeze, and breathed in the scene. The hills of Aurora, Ohio, morphing from green to dull gold, the small lake with the charming stone footbridge—even the corner of the back garden, scene of her horror, where the oaks held onto their shredded leaves to the last. "I think I love Wolfe's Gate."

He placed his hand softly against her back, and they retraced their path to the house. Scarlett's heart was in high gear as she wondered about his surprise. There'd only been one thing missing from the past two days: the touch of those skillful hands on her body.

She was almost completely well now. The only evidence that anything had gone wrong was the fast-healing scar on her leg and a slight limp. She wanted—needed—to feel him inside her again, gentle, rough, beast-like—any way she could have him. As soon as possible.

"Right back here."

They'd passed the main body of the house and were heading toward the rear of the largest of the guest cottages. And he'd been right. The sun had lost its battle with the clouds, and three drops of water pecked her in the face. "You're being very mysterious, Mr. Wolfe. Very quiet today. News about Jacob?"

"No." She could see the change in his posture, the darkening of his eyes at the sound of the name. "But word gets around. He can't hide forever."

"And this mood of yours—does it have something to do with all the people I've seen arriving? They can't be much of a bother. They don't seem to stay long. Are they coming to pay homage of some kind? What's going on?"

Following the small, circular driveway, he led her toward the back door. "I think this will explain."

She nearly did a little dance of joy, weak leg and all. He wanted privacy, wanted to be alone with her! This largest of the cottages would do nicely. Any place they could...

Rounding the jutting corner, she stopped, frozen in place. "I... I don't understand." Her body seemed to shrivel inside the bulky jacket, and her stomach cramped, as if someone had dealt her a blow. "My car? You wanted to show me my car?"

He was silent, a part of the gathering storm, hands shoved deep into the pockets of his long black raincoat.

Red walked stiffly over to the little Miata. It had only been a few days, but she hardly recognized it. Especially with the two small, buff-leather suitcases packed neatly inside the open trunk. "Gray?" Did that small, pinched voice belong to her? "What's going on?"

"You'll need clothes." His voice was detached, distant behind her. "I remembered you said you didn't have any. Thought it was the least I could do for you, after your—well, your unfortunate experience here."

"The least you could do for me?" She couldn't seem to grasp the cold, hard reality of this. "You think this is the least you could do for me?"

"Scarlett—"

"You want me to leave." With a supreme effort, she turned and walked back to him. Standing mere inches away, she turned her face up to examine his. "Is this your subtle way of getting rid of me, Wolfe?"

He shrugged, peering up at the darkening clouds. "It's been fun, Red, but it really is time for you to go. I warned you again and again. I told you this was not a game. I told you to run."

"Run? You *want* me to run?!" She stared at him, refusing to look away until his eyes met hers. Hard bits of water struck her face, just enough to be punishing. "Come on, Grayson. I've been shown the door before—but nobody ever packed my *bags* for me. What is this? What are you doing?"

"My people..." He stopped, nearly laughed. "Some of my people are not fond of people of mixed heritage. They want to keep the lineage pure. As their leader, I have to consider their feelings in choosing an Alpha female."

She gaped at him, astonished. "You weren't worried about my heritage when you were screwing me in the backyard for all to see. Come on, Wolfe. You're not the type to care what other people think of you. Try again."

He stared back at her, the dark clouds mirrored in his eyes. "Wolfmen have a taste for the females of your species. You're like a delicacy for us, something exotic, alluring. But we easily tire of it, and feel the need for fresh meat." The wind blew his hair back from the hard lines of his face. "Nature of the beast, y'know."

"No. No, I don't know." She looked for some tell, some sign of the lie she knew it had to be, and found none. Barely managing to keep the tears out of her eyes, she couldn't keep the heartbreak out of her voice. "You can't mean this. Grayson, these past three days—"

"Scarlett. There's a storm brewing, and this is becoming tiresome." He reached for her arm and gently squeezed. "I've done all I can to make up for things. The sex was good, but I've had better, and will have in the future. It's time for you to go. If you insist on staying here…"

She could hardly speak, couldn't begin to understand. "My God. It's true, after all. You aren't quite human, are you?"

"If you insist on staying here," he continued briskly, "you'll be considered available to any man-wolf who wants you. Only the Alpha female is entitled to my protection." He leaned forward, whispering in the wind. "I can arrange that for you, if you want to stay in one of the cottages. Maybe you'd like that. A parade of rough, hungry men, one after another, just dying to get between your legs, hmmm? Maybe you'll even let me watch sometimes…"

She was in the car before she knew it, before a steady patter of rain began to thump against the hood. She didn't remember tearing out of the driveway or hitting the gravel road. She only remembered that the trunk was still open when she saw it waving at her in her rear view mirror, along with the pale, tear-stained face she barely recognized as her own.

Red stopped in the middle of the road and, resisting the urge to toss the luggage out, slammed the trunk closed. The first rumble of thunder rolled overhead, and she quickly continued, keeping her eyes on the path, unblinking, barely breathing. She'd be fine once she got to her grandmother's house. She'd find another job, a real lover, and make a new life. She'd keep going. Keep running, if necessary.

She floored the gas pedal, taking the curves at breakneck speed. If she could get to safety without wrecking the little red car, she might even manage to outrun this particular storm.

Chapter Twelve

"Scarlett. Man to see you."

Startled out of her stupor, Red scrambled to a sitting position, knocking the tiny television she'd been watching to the floor. Lounging in her bedroom with the door wide open, she hadn't even heard Lucas' approach. Her body immediately tensed beneath the shorts and ratty old T-shirt she wore. The luggage had been tossed into her closet when she arrived yesterday. It was still packed. "Gray."

She said the name without thinking, and felt like crying when Lucas shook his head. Relief. That's what it was she was feeling. Relief...

"Nope. It's not Mr. Wolfe. Some ass-wipe in a new suit who thinks he's too good to wait at the door. I put him in the living room. He says his name is Jacob."

He was smiling and relaxed, supremely confident of himself in a white linen suit and large gold jewelry. His huge black umbrella was making a puddle on Lucas' refinished hardwood floors, startling her. For once, she'd nearly forgotten it was raining.

Rising as she entered, he flashed a huge smile, bowing slightly. "Scarlett. Lovely as ever."

"Jacob. You look like a California pimp who made a wrong turn. What are you doing here? And watch your step," she added, nodding. "My cousin's just beyond that door."

"You've got the wrong impression of me, Red. I don't want trouble. I've come to make you an offer."

She gave a short laugh, crossing her arms defensively. "You've got nothing I want. I thought I made that clear when you tried to force yourself on me before."

"That was a mistake," he admitted, tugging at his cuffs. "I played my hand too quickly. But it's your own fault, you know." He took a few careful steps toward her, locking his hands behind his back. "The males of my species have a certain weakness for human females. I couldn't resist. And I'll wager that, after I left, Gray couldn't resist either."

She would not allow him the pleasure of seeing that he'd struck a chord. Tapping an impatient foot, she sighed. "Get on with it, Jacob. What do you want?"

"Simple. I want Gray's woman. I want revenge for being cast out from the pack for wanting Gray's woman. And I want the position as Alpha male. I deserve it. Nobody else has the backbone to take on that job if something..." He smiled brightly, and she thought his canines looked unusually long. "If something should happen to Gray."

Red shook her head, amazed. She had to give him credit for having balls. She remembered them well, and the pounding they took behind Disa's backside. "You're insane. What makes you think I'd do anything to help you?"

"Because I can make it worth your while." He leaned in, tall and lithe, his voice lowering to a seductive level. "I can give you pleasure. Make you feel excitement like you've never known. You haven't forgotten the little garden party. I know it. Disa was always useful enough—but *you*...you I would *enjoy*."

She watched him wet his lips, watched his eyes roam her body. Oddly, there was a slight quaver in her voice as she spoke. "I can get laid anywhere, Jacob."

"It won't be the same, and you know it. I've heard stories about Gray's sexual prowess, but I can—"

"Stories? From whom?"

"Disa." He ran a light finger up her bare arm. She shuddered, but did not resist. "Surprised? Gray has sampled most of the females in the pack. But he seems to have an aversion toward the human ladies. Unlike me. I love a fresh, tender cunt. Especially the darker meat." He smirked.

She was having trouble thinking clearly, trouble seeing beyond the image of Gray with Disa. Bitch. "I don't..."

"And there are others. Wolves outside our pack, other creatures. Creatures who prefer the night. They'd kill for a chance to have you, Scarlett."

She bit her lip when his hand strayed to her hip, cupping her left cheek. And still she did not move.

"Think of the pleasure, Scarlett. Think of getting revenge against the man who used you, then spit you out. Money? No problem. Power, connections, influence—I can get them all for you." His fingers played with the hem of her shorts. "Anything you want, Scarlett. What d'ya say?"

She considered the nauseating idea of being just one of Gray's "samplings." She remembered the way he'd literally tossed her to the curb, the cold gleam in his eyes as he offered to loan her out to his friends. "What do I say?"

With two firm fingers, she removed his hand from her backside. "I say you're a bottom-feeder without the backbone to fight like a man for what you want. And I'd say you'd better leave, before I have my cousin throw you out."

"You realize, of course, that my request is a polite formality. I can just take what I want." He leered at her, minute traces of hair seeping slowly through his jaw to form a beard. With a jolt of fear, she realized he was beginning to change. "I could snap your cousin in two without a second thought."

"Well, think on this."

Scarlett made a half-turn, nearly falling backward in surprise. There was Lucas, one hand tucked casually in the bib of his overalls, the other pointing a shiny .38 caliber pistol at Jacob. "Now, I don't know who you are, mister, but I heard enough to know my cousin wants you to leave. I think you'd better oblige."

Jacob turned on him, his face darkening, bone-white teeth framing a vicious snarl.

Lucas bent his thumb, cocking the pistol as Jacob went still. "I stand corrected. I not only don't know who you are, I don't know *what* you are. But I'll wager that even you can't outrun a bullet." He sniffed nonchalantly. "What say we give it a look-see, hmmm?"

* * *

As the strobing light of the movie flickered behind her, Alana set a small porcelain tray in the empty seat. "I've brought you something to eat."

The angular face did not turn away from the huge flat screen. "I didn't ask for it, don't need it. Take it away."

Alana took one step back and bowed her head. Waiting. He could kill her for disobeying, and no one would ever ask why.

She held her ground. "You haven't eaten since yesterday, Wolfe. You need food. I brought you a nice, fresh steak."

"I don't need to be told what it is," he snapped. "I can smell the blood. Take it away!"

"Grayson." She spoke his Christian name gently. "You have a house full of guests. Obligations. You're the leader of these people, and you can't let yourself go this way. You must feed."

"Later, then." His growl was more threatening than that of the Wolfman on the screen. "Leave it, and I'll have it later."

"I may not be here later. I..." Taking a deep breath, she steeled herself for his retort. "I ask permission to leave the pack."

The movie sizzled to a stop as the lights immediately flared. "Leave?" He looked tired, his eyes wide and shadowed, his skin nearly bloodless. He looked like he'd been sitting in the darkness for a very long time. "Of course you can't leave. I forbid it!"

"Please don't." Of course she knew he wouldn't let her leave without explanation. Not with her pride intact. "I need to leave. I'll find another pack somewhere. Or I'll blend in with the humans, live alone. But I can't stay here."

"Alana." He reached for her hand and she skittered away. She couldn't bear a sympathetic touch right now. She would shatter into tiny little pieces. "I can't let you go. You mean more to the pack than anyone. Why this sudden urge to leave?"

"Will doesn't want me." With truth came relief and the bitter taste of regret on her tongue. "He cares for me, finds me entertaining. Comforting. But there's nothing else in his heart. It's not enough for me, shouldn't be enough for anyone. I want someone who really wants me. The way you want your Scarlett."

His eyes became a vacant stare. "We won't talk about that. But you—"

"I'm beginning to think she was right, your lady. Sometimes running away is the right thing to do. Sometimes there are no answers, no solutions. I can't make Will care for me more than he does. And every time I lie with him, all I can think of is wanting more—more of his body, his mind, his affection. I can't change him. But I can live another life, a different life, without him. I can *run*. Just as you're doing here, in the darkness, by escaping into your movie."

With a violent kick, Gray loosened the chair in front of him from its moorings, sending it tumbling over itself. "You'd be wise to attend to your own business, and leave mine alone. If you want to leave, you have my permission to do so. Pack and make your arrangements."

If she stayed one moment longer, she was sure she'd cry. And that would be the most humiliating thing of all. Without another word, she moved quickly toward the exit, not surprised when the room with the lone wolf darkened again and the movie resumed play.

Chapter Thirteen

"Here's to you, Lucas. I didn't know ya had it in you."

"Didja see him take off outta here? I swear, if the man had a tail, it would've been tucked between his legs when he left."

Red laughed and sucked juice out of her can of beer at the irony of his statement. She didn't even like beer. But it didn't matter. He wanted to share it with her, and she was grateful to him for the low-key rescue—and for making her smile. "Well, I'm just glad you were here."

"Friend of Mr. Wolfe's, hmmm? Always thought there was something strange about that bunch that hung around there. And Mr. Wolfe is impressive enough; but if you ask me, there's something wrong about a man keeping sheep."

She spewed beer on the floor, choking until she could manage to laugh it out. "They're not sheep, Lucas. They're alpacas."

He shrugged, chugging away. "Same difference. From what I heard when I moved here, Wolfe just sorta swooped in, bought up everything he could, and dished out money for whatever he wanted. I have more respect for a man who does a little hands-on hard work once in a while. Gets himself dirty, works with tools. Like this." He held up a large instrument, caressing its curves like those of a woman. "Porter Nail Gun, series 415. It'll be a helluva help come time to put up the deck I'm planning. Runs on batteries for up to four hours."

His words barely registered. She could only see Gray, flexing and perspiring, working on the field near the house, goading her to run, to run... "What?"

Lucas shrugged, blushed, looking embarrassed. "You're a million miles away. Just talkin' about my equipment here. Having the right tools to do a job is important in every aspect of life, y'know."

He was a sweetheart of a man, but talking about power tools just didn't do it for her. "I suppose," she muttered vaguely.

"Having this nail gun has gone a long way toward fixing this house up the way I want." He carefully placed it on the small end table by the sofa. In one smooth move, he picked up the gun that also lay there, pointing it straight at her, a broad grin splitting his face. "And this particular tool will go even farther in getting me *everything* I want."

Chapter Fourteen

Scarlett shuddered into stillness, the beer can poised at her lips. "Lucas?" The faint grumbling sounds of approaching thunder could be heard in the distance, and the rain gleefully increased in strength. "Lucas, is this some kind of joke?"

"I don't find it especially funny. But I'm afraid it *is* necessary."

"I—I don't understand." Had she been repeating those three words over and over in the past two days? Had she become so dense she couldn't see the truth behind anything? "What are you doing?"

"Please put the can down, Scarlett. It's bad enough that your little feral friend got my floor all wet. Beer can leave a nasty, sticky residue I'd rather not have to clean up."

Moving very slowly, she carefully placed the can on his coffee table, returning to a stiff sitting position opposite him. His voice was as plain and folksy as ever, his smile comfortably bland. But he held the gun with a sturdy hand, and there was a strange light in his eyes she'd never seen before.

"You're probably wondering why we've gathered here today like this."

The last time she'd heard such words was at an old-fashioned church revival. Her whole world was becoming one surreal nightmare. She gulped away the lump of fear in her throat as the rain beat harder against the roof. "Yes?"

"Well, see, this is all very simple—and unfortunate. I sorta got to like you, Scarlett, in our brief time together. But other than your mother, you're nearest next-of-kin to the old lady. You could claim this house. And after I went to so much trouble to kill dear grandma, I can't have you traipse through here and take it away from me. I need a place to call home. Don't you think I've made a nice little nest of it?"

The room was growing dim as the sky over the cabin darkened to indigo. "You?" She blinked hard, as if seeing him more clearly would help her understand better. "*You* killed my grandmother?"

"As I said—I needed a place. A few of us, outcasts one and all, crossed over from Canada when Lake Erie froze over last winter. No passports or birth certificates necessary. The old woman was so glad to have company, she gladly accepted me as some bullshit 'distant relative.'"

"You said it was a heart attack." Trying to force back tears, she clasped her hands to keep them from shaking as badly as her voice. "You *shot* an innocent old woman?!"

"No, actually I didn't. I'm a practical man, honey, as I'm sure you've noticed. Waste not, want not?" He winked as the burgeoning thunder made the house tremble. "I must say, she was a bit tough and stringy. But there was something of the taste of your blood in hers, Red."

She leaned forward, covering her mouth in horror. "Oh, my God…"

"But yours was a good deal tangier, your flesh a lot more supple. Fresh. And the fact that I could smell your just-used sex was…" He closed his eyes, sucking in air through his nose. "Irresistible."

"*You're one of them.*"

She whispered the words as lightning brought daylight to the room, then left it in deeper darkness than before. His eyes became an antique gold, and these eyes she *remembered*. She'd seen them in the garden that night, glittering the color of the moon as she waited for Gray. She'd been so afraid she hadn't remembered that Gray's eyes were blue, even after he changed. The eyes of the wolf who attacked her were the color of envy. The color of hate. "Lucas, this isn't necessary. I don't want the house. You can have it. Just let me leave, and—"

"And take a chance on you coming back to claim it later?" He shook his head, tucking the gun inside his overalls. "I'm afraid I can't do that. And I'm sorry for it. But I try to be a fair man whenever possible. I'll allow you one phone call, before you 'go'—to anybody 'cept the police, of course."

He laughed quietly, retrieving his beer. "Isn't there anybody you'd like to say goodbye to, Scarlett Grier?"

Chapter Fifteen

Gray watched the film fade to black, his tired eyes drifting shut.

He hadn't slept for three days. Even for a creature with his constitution, it was a bit much. He'd watched the film again and again, thinking it might distract him, entertain him, give him some insight into who he was. What the hell he was.

At last, he'd had enough. He pushed the button to close the screen's draperies and put the lights on dim, allowing his eyes time to adjust. The platter of meat had turned cold in the seat beside him, swimming in its own blood.

It wasn't enough that he'd tasted her, mingled her blood with his, that he would carry that bit of her until the end of his days. He couldn't get her out of his mind. Moist, ready lips, eyes that inherently bore a challenge…and the sex of her. The scent, the wetness, the way her body clung to his, never seeming to get enough.

He'd barely had a chance to taste her. He wasn't sure now that he was ready to throw it all away before knowing…

Yes. He could admit it now. He wasn't sure he was ready to throw it all away before knowing whether they might have a chance.

Suddenly, he was hungry. He rose, stretching, invigorated, and headed for the kitchen. He'd satisfy that hunger first. It'd give him time to think about how to satisfy the other.

Alana was sitting at the bottom of the spiral staircase, the telephone pasted to her ear and a small suitcase beside her. She'd been with the pack almost since the beginning. She'd been friend, confidante, caretaker, comforter. She was, he thought grimly, probably more important to the family than *he* was in his current state.

Will could be as big a fool as he pleased, but Gray was not going to let her get away.

He snatched the phone away from her and pointed a stern finger. "You can't leave."

Alana's hand remained fixed, as if she still held the phone, her eyes widening. "But Grayson…"

"We'll figure something out." He spoke quickly, giving her no chance to argue. "You'll just have to give the relationship more time, or have a long talk with Will about expectations, or find another Beta within the family who suits your needs. If necessary, I have the authority to *insist* that he marry you."

"You can't!" she cried. "Oh, *please* don't do that!"

"Then tell me you'll stay. Tell me you won't throw away your whole future because the present looks dim." He slowed his barrage of words, his heart softening at her distress. "Tell me you won't be the fool I've been. Tell me what I want to hear."

"All right. I will." Pursing her lips, she pointed at his hand. "Your Scarlett is on the phone. She wants to talk to you."

* * *

"Now, you will behave yourself, won't you? I'm allowing you this final goodbye, but remember—there are lots of ways to die."

Red put the phone to her ear. There was a voice shouting over the line. She could hardly hear it over the deafening thunder, and the fear-swollen pulse of her heart in her ears. Opening her mouth to speak, she choked, her throat dry as her eyes filled with tears. She couldn't get the words out.

"Last chance," Lucas whispered, holding the gun to her temple. "I'm getting impatient. And *hungry.*"

Locking her fingers tightly around the cell phone, she squeezed her eyes closed, shutting out the image of the smiling thing beside her, and forcing sound through her tight throat. "Gray?"

"Scarlett? Scarlett, where are you? I was just thinking about—"

"Please don't talk. Just listen." They were croaking noises rather than words. She could only pray he'd be able to understand. *Really* understand. "I wanted you to know that I'm leaving. I won't be a bother for you anymore. But I had to tell you what I thought of you before I left."

"Red." His voice was split by static, the reception giving way to the storm. "Let me tell you—"

"Has anybody ever told you what an arrogant sonofabitch you really are?" Her voice grew steadier, stronger. "Did you think you had to dismiss me, like I was gonna become some kind of fucking *burden* to you?? All I ever asked you for was one night's shelter from a storm, and a good lay. Most men wouldn't find that to be a chore. But then, I forget—you're not really a *man,* are you?"

The line was silent, but he was there. She could hear him breathing.

"You and your group of fucking freaks," she continued vehemently. "You and your 'master race.' Hell, you came and went so fast in the garden, I had to finger-fuck myself to finish getting off! That's really what you keep those foul-smelling mutant sheep of yours for, isn't it? Because a real woman wouldn't *have* you!"

The voice was that dangerous, hoarse whisper that had sent chills through her before. "Now wait just a minute—"

"I haven't got time for the bullshit, Wolfe. Just wanted you to know that you and your friends can go to goddamn Halloween hell. You're a fucking asshole, and I can't get away from this place fast enough."

She clicked off, letting the phone she could no longer hold crash noisily to the floor before burying her face in her hands.

"My, my, cousin." Lucas laughed, kicking the phone away as he waved the pistol in the air. "Harsh words for a final goodbye. Perfect. I'm sure whatever your message was, he'll pick up on it."

"I…" She felt dizzy, short of breath. "I don't know what you mean."

"You're a bright girl, Scarlett. I'm sure there was something about that conversation meant to alert Grayson to your predicament. Something to get him to come to your rescue. And he is, after all, the one I've wanted all along."

Her eyes went wide with the horror of realization. "You used me. Used me to lure him here. It's the position you want, just like Jacob. You want to be the Alpha."

"And your lover's death will assure me of that." Putting the gun aside, he loomed over her. His smile disappeared as his mouth lengthened into a short snout, and silver-tipped hair began to sprout over his hands, face, and neck. "And I'll be ready when he gets here." The laugh became a snarl as he hunched over, baring sharp, deadly fangs.

* * *

Gray held onto the phone long after it was dead. He was not an easy man to stun, but she'd managed it. So much anger and bitterness! He couldn't blame her—he'd deliberately provoked it. But there was something wrong about that conversation, something he couldn't quite get a fix on... "Alana? I know I never pay attention, but you keep track of the people around us, yes? In case they start becoming suspicious, and we have to move on?"

"Yes. Why?"

"What do you know about a neighbor, a Mrs. Elise Walker?"

"Old Mrs. Walker?" She shrugged. "Lived about fifteen miles south of here. She had a couple of acres of her own, I think. I remember reading something about it in the paper. Body found by the authorities after her mail began piling up. Seems she'd fallen or fainted somewhere in the woods near her house. By the time the wildlife had finished with her, there wasn't much left."

Heart attack as she slept...

Distractedly handing the phone back to her, he felt the prickling sensation that always preceded the change, or the urge to do so. No reason, he assured himself. There was no reason for the rush of adrenalin, the urge to run. "And this so-called distant cousin of hers. Who is this guy? What do you know about him?"

"Oh, you mean Lupas..." She stopped, snickering at her own slip of the tongue. "I mean, Lucas Sterling. Quiet, laid-back, basically boring. He's been doing a lot of renovating on the old Walker house, and...Grayson? Are you okay? You've turned positively ashen!"

He slowly swiveled, turning to stare at her. "What did you say?"

"I said he's been doing a lot of renovating on—"

"No, no. *Lupas.* You said lupas?"

"I meant Lucas, of course. One-track mind, and—"

"It isn't much of a stretch, is it?" He frowned, and began pacing the hallway with a vengeance. "Not much of a stretch to think of 'sterling' and 'silver,' either. She said it was a silver wolf that attacked her. What're the odds of the words being so similar?" He was prancing now, bursting to get free of the confining walls.

"That's really reaching, Grayson."

"She just told me off pretty well, Alana. Called me every name imaginable. And had every right to—so dammit, what's bothering me?" Pounding a flattened hand against the far wall, he focused, thinking, trying to be logical as his arms bulged and furred and his blood began to boil in his veins. "She was upset, more upset than when she got here..."

I never do that...

He barely heard Alana's vague words, voicing concern. He heard Scarlett, clear as the day she'd arrived.

I never curse like that, unless I'm afraid—or in trouble...

"That's it!" Punching a hole through the wall without flinching, he turned to face Alana. He dropped to all fours, felt his fangs forming behind his elongating snout, his haunches tensed, ready to charge. "Where's Will?"

"Will?" She looked frightened. "You can't believe he'd... I don't know. I haven't seen him in a couple of hours."

"I may be wrong." He spoke with some difficulty, so advanced in the change that his words were barely more than curt, growling noises. "It might be him, might be Jacob. But I know where she is. Her grandmother's house. She's like us. She would've chosen a familiar, comfortable place to lick her wounds."

"Scarlett?" Alana stood, tensed, as if ready to join him. "Is she in trouble? What—"

"*Mine.*" He glared at her, kicking his shoes away as he exploded through the seams of his clothes. He felt the fur on his back bristling, and turned to bark the only word he could still manage. "*Stay!*"

Bounding toward the door, he crashed through the wood with the blunt force of his shoulder. Exulting in the freedom of flight and the rush of violent purpose, he raced toward the shortcut through the woods at top speed.

Chapter Sixteen

"You look a little dazed, cousin. This really isn't that hard to understand." Lucas ran a furry hand up her bare calf, admiring the scar that was his handiwork. "I was cast out of my pack. Considered incorrigible. I need a home, others to rule. Taking Grayson Wolfe's position will do very nicely."

Red sat shivering on the couch, hugging herself. The storm had grown violent, and she started every time the lightning flared, every time the thunder rattled the old windows. And every time he touched her, which he seemed to do with more frequency as time went by. "Why didn't you kill me in the first place? Why all the pretense?"

"I knew Gray would be taken with you. Any man would. And I needed to lure him from the safety of his compound, from the followers who'd protect him." He chuckled as he removed the elastic band from her ponytail, loosening her hair and stroking it as he would a pet. "He's a clever man. He'll figure your message out. I expect him any moment. And I don't blame him one bit."

Easing cautiously away from his hand, she studied him. It was incredible. He controlled every aspect of the metamorphosis, allowing the silver fur to grow on any part of his body at any given moment, then willing it away without effort. In one instant he was taller, bulkier; a moment later, he was uncommonly common Lucas.

"You could always stay, Scarlett. I think you'd enjoy being an Alpha female." He smoothed her hair behind her left ear and ran a long, dog-like tongue up her throat, tasting her as she winced. "And I know I'd enjoy you."

"Are you saying you'll let me live if I cooperate? Help you kill Gray?"

"Grayson Wolfe is dead either way. It's just a matter of how much you want to live." His hand slithered down her throat and chest to circle her left nipple. "What's your life worth, Red?"

She'd reached her breaking point. Swatting his hand away, she lunged at him, her fingers forming claws, aiming for his eyes.

He was faster. Deadlier. His open hand grabbed her throat in a vise, cutting off her breath and lifting her to her feet. "I hear panting."

Scarlett gagged, choking, tugging uselessly at his wrist, pounding his arm with her fists. "Just below the bellowing of the thunder and above the rush of the rain. I hear him breathing, circling the house."

He dragged her struggling body over to the stairway and climbed halfway up. With a sigh of contentment, he sat down and seated her between his legs on the lower step.

The room was growing dim, everything becoming a shadowy shade of gray as she felt herself weakening, slowly losing consciousness.

Lucas loosened his grip slightly, allowing her one deep, torturous breath before locking his hand around her neck again. "Guess we'll never know your decision, eh, cuz? But don't check out just yet. Your lover's run a long way to save you. Help me greet him properly before you die."

* * *

Gray slowly stood erect in the pouring rain, willing his wolf-form away with some difficulty. He was having trouble with the metamorphosis. He knew why. He was still furious, still thirsty for his enemy's death.

He'd checked the exterior of the cabin. The front door was ajar, the rear door wide open. He was being invited in. Scarlett was there. He'd detected her scent. The other was new to him, neither Will nor Jacob.

And he'd decided to face his enemy as a man.

Taking short, careful steps, he peered around the frame of the back door. The cabin was as dark as the sky, and he took a moment to separate all of the various smells. Beeswax. Motor oil. Freshly-hewn wood.

Fear.

"Come in, Mr. Wolfe."

Gray hesitated. Focused. The urge to drop to all fours and risk a frontal attack was nearly overwhelming.

"Let me put it this way," the voice continued pleasantly. "Come in, Mr. Wolfe, or I will certainly kill your lady before you get a chance to say goodbye."

Quickly rounding the corner, Gray stood in the center of the doorway. Scarlett's wide, frightened eyes shone in the darkness, with the metallic gleam of a gun angled at her head. And there was no way to reach her without coming straight up the stairway. Well planned, well conceived.

The young man whose hand encircled her neck was no more human than he was. He detected the scent of an enemy wolf, and began to salivate. "Let her go. I'm the one you want."

"An old-school gentleman to the last. Don't do that." His grip tightened as Gray took one step forward, stopping at the excruciating sound of Red choking. "You know I could break her neck before you take your next breath. I want you right there. In your true form, please. There's no satisfaction in killing a mere man."

Scarlett was pulling at his arm, raking away skin with her nails, to no avail. Every cell in Gray's body screamed for the change, for the chance to attack.

Lucas smiled softly, reading his expression. "*I* am the one in control now, Wolfe. I can maintain this intelligent form because I remain unemotional. Unaffected. But *you*—she's your Achilles heel, isn't she? Let's see." Moving his hand, he turned her head sideways. She immediately went still. "I'll give you five seconds to affect the change, or I'll snap her neck like a twig. One...two..."

Grayson gave in to the hatred, the hunger for the death of his enemy. He was on all fours, fully furred and baring his teeth faster than he'd ever been in his life. He felt his pupils narrow, concentrate. There was only Lucas, the gun, and the girl, and the growl that rose like bile in his throat.

"That's it!" Lucas aimed and, with a gleeful smile, fired his weapon.

With the instincts of the wolf, hunted since the beginning of time, Gray skittered aside, ignoring the splintering of the doorjamb as the bullet hit.

Resisting the urge to retreat to the safety of the woods, he trotted a zig-zag pattern before the door. The girl was the important thing. Even his feral brain retained that memory— and the fact that the weapon held only so much death. Once the enemy needed to pause to reload, he was vulnerable. *His.*

Another bullet whizzed by, this one catching the tip of his right ear. Good. Pain. It helped inflame him. Saliva dripped from his tongue as he ran a wider area now, braking, turning abruptly, twisting, keeping his gaze on the wolf-man at all times.

The black eye of the muzzle trailed him, the forefinger tightening. The girl made a sudden move. Slipping her chin lower into the palm that held her prisoner, she bit hard into the skin that webbed the thumb and trigger finger, drawing blood.

With a yelp, Lucas shoved her down the stairs, and she cried out. The sound broke Gray's concentration. Pushing off with his hind legs, he lunged forward.

An explosion struck him down in mid-air. His body contorted, a searing burst of pain hitting his flank, sending him head-over-heels before slamming him against the floor.

He dimly heard an exultant howl, and Scarlett's anguished scream before both became a part of the thunder and the vortex that rushed him mercilessly into darkness.

* * *

"Up, bitch."

Lucas grabbed a fistful of hair, dragging her to her feet. He was eager to end it now. He could smell Wolfe's blood soaking into his silver fur.

It smelled like victory.

"Let's wrap this up, shall we, cuz?" Fed up with her resistance, he pulled her to the quivering body of the animal before throwing her down beside it. "You've only got a few minutes left. Anybody *else* you'd like to call?"

She didn't seem to appreciate his humor. Sobbing uncontrollably, she leaned over the animal, tenderly touching the limp head. "Gray...oh, God, Gray..."

"C'mon, Wolfe. Get it over with." He kicked the sonofabitch in the back, noting the lack of response with satisfaction. Eyes closed. Breathing shallow, becoming more irregular. Just a few seconds more would tell the tale. Moving the gun back and forth between them, he felt his own excitement mounting—and with it, the urge to induce the change himself. "What's it gonna be, bud? Checking out as a man, or a wolf? I need to call the authorities soon. So I need to know if I should tell them how you showed up here naked and strangled my cousin to death, or display the wolf I shot after it ripped her throat open." He grinned, imagining the Sheriff's surprise. "I vote for the latter, but it's your call, man."

The massive head moved. He was sure of it, even as she wrapped her arms around the thick neck, her face pressed against his. And before he could move in, wrench them apart, pump another bullet into the body, he heard the creature whisper a single word.

"*Run.*"

She was up and off before Lucas could take careful aim. Taking a lesson from her lover, she veered right, pivoted, then left, heading for the door. He aimed there, at the narrow space she'd have to pass through. It didn't matter, he assured himself—he could tell the Sheriff that Gray killed her, one way or...

The gun bobbled in his hand as he felt fangs pierce his skin, and he fell, staring into the frigid blue eyes of Grayson Wolfe. Not so dead after all, and smarter than he'd thought. Still unable to rise, he'd grabbed the meat of the calf and was worrying Lucas' lower leg with a vengeance born of hatred. Distracting him, allowing the girl time to escape. Stirring his blood to incite the metamorphosis.

Slamming the butt of the gun against the side of the animal's head, Lucas limped a few steps away as the beast released him and fell back to the floor. Hand shaking, he took aim for the last time. "As much as I'd like to finish this the old-fashioned way, beast-to-beast, it'd be too hard to explain the evidence of *two* wolves, Grayson."

Dripping sweat and charged with adrenalin, he raised his shoulders against the icy thrill at the base of his neck. They froze there, bunched beneath his ears, as the rest of his body seemed to go cold and rigid. With a superhuman effort, he turned halfway around to see Scarlett's face and the weapon in her hand, both gilded by a blinding flash of lightning. It was the last thing he saw before he stiffened and fell with the crashing thunder.

Chapter Seventeen

"Grayson Wolfe."

She pillowed his head in her lap, softly calling his name. "Come back."

There was a flash of blue beneath the furred eyelids for only a moment before they wearily closed again.

"Grayson Wolfe." She raised her voice, beginning to panic as his tongue lolled from the side of his mouth. "I won't let you leave me now."

Scarlett began to weep and, bending closer, kissed the wolf's muzzle, his eyes, the fearful wound upon his head. "Grayson Wolfe. I think I've fallen in love with you."

She held her breath. Waiting. Dying inside. If she was too late, if he couldn't hear her chant, if it was some old wives' tale, some ridiculous legend, like that of the werewolf...

The fur began to shorten, inch by inch, drawing back into the flesh until rough skin began to emerge. First his face, his neck, then his hands and feet became human with agonizing slowness.

Her heart bursting with excitement, Scarlett began to shout words of encouragement, cheering him on as the storm battered the cabin, until the magnificent body of her lover, lying limp on his side, was completely formed.

"Wolfe?" His hip was still bleeding, and the gash on his head sent a thin stream of blood down his cheek. "Gray, can you hear me? Oh, please—"

"It was…"

Straining every bone in her body, she nearly flattened herself to put her ear to his lips. "Gray? You spoke! Do it again, damn you!"

A ruddy flush of color began to creep into his cheeks. "It was really the storm that drove you back in here, right, weather-lady?"

Burying her face in his neck, she cried again as she laughed hysterically. "What storm?" she blubbered.

"I told you to run. You were a fool to come back. How…" He stopped, swallowed, his voice barely audible. "How did you manage to…what did you use? You had no weapon…"

Scarlett sat up shakily. The light of life was back in his eyes. That was all that mattered. "Maybe I'm tired of running. Or maybe I need to brush up on my fairytales. I'm too thick-headed to allow myself to be rescued. I certainly couldn't leave you here to die. I circled the house. Came back in from the front. He never even heard me. Must be some of that tainted blood I received lately." Shakily sitting up, she vigorously wiped her wet face. "And I did find a weapon," she proudly announced, attempting a smile. "The good ol' Porter Series 415 came in handy after all. You might say I nailed him. Right at the base of the skull."

Gray closed his eyes, groaning. "Fragile my ass."

"Speaking of your ass," she said briskly, "shouldn't we be getting you to a doctor, a hospital?"

"No. No, no doctors. Call Will. Tell him what's happened, have him come and get me. And tell him—" He paused, wincing in pain. "Tell him I'm sorry for being such a bastard. And Alana, tell him to have Alana waiting. She'll take care of me."

"You're just looking for an excuse to get felt up. No." Red tenderly smoothed the wet black hair from his face. "She'll show *me* how to take care of you."

"Scarlett, it's not necessary. There are hundreds of potions, centuries of knowledge involved, and—"

"Then I'll have to stay until I learn everything. Or until I'm ready to run again." She touched the gash on his head. Miraculously, it had already stopped bleeding and developed a thin pink skin. "Does the hip hurt awfully?"

"Stings a bit."

Meaning it hurt like hell. Gently kissing his dry lips, she teased him with her tongue. "Want me to lick it for you?"

The corner of his mouth lifted in a weak smile. "Ask me that in a day or two."

Carefully leaving him, Scarlett made the phone call to Will. Gingerly skirting the body of the dead man, she quickly returned to her position on the floor. "He's on his way."

"Red, I have to be honest with you. There's nothing easy about this life. It means secrets, and hiding, and subterfuge, and moving on at a moment's notice, and—"

"Let's not get ahead of ourselves, Wolfe." She smiled at the sound of the thunder. It seemed so insignificant now. Linking her fingers through his, Scarlett pressed the pentagrams in their palms together. "I didn't ask for forever. But I wouldn't mind another romp in the moonlight, or front seats in your home theater as long as I stay. As for the rest..." She shrugged, laughing. "I'll worry about that tomorrow."

Wolfe relaxed into her lap, rubbing his cheek against the silky skin of her thigh. "Lady, you've watched too damn many old movies..."

Raine Weaver

Raine Weaver loves the art of creation.

Having dabbled in music, photography, and painting, she's found pleasure in them all.

But writing was always her truest love.

When life didn't seem to go the way it should, she could make up stories that ended the way she wanted. Create her own worlds.

After all-that was the way things should be.

Now living in her own little cottage on her own piece of land, complete with a wide assortment of four-legged creatures, she writes, paints, and plans her future.

And she's SURE she was meant to be a top-selling novelist, writing at home in her jammies, still creating her own reality.

After all-that is the way things should be.

Visit Raine on the Web at www.raineweaver.com, or email her at raine@raineweaver.com.

ALL HALLOW'S MOON

Jeigh Lynn

Dedication

To my sister-in-law, Jeanne, for being my test reader and for always being so supportive. Special thanks to: Andre, Brenda, Lori, Olivia, Lesley, Laura, and the great crew at Loose Id.

Author's Note

All Hallow's Moon is part of the *Moon* series. It takes place before *Latin Moon,* but can be read in any order, with or without having read *Latin Moon* and *A Lover's Moon.* I hope you enjoy Dash and Jill's story, as well as the glimpse into some of the other characters' pasts.

Chapter One

Devon "Dash" Rigotti pulled into the drive and cut the engine. God, it was good to be home, even if it was only for a weekend. Although his apartment was only a four-hour drive away, it was still too far for his peace of mind, and *any* break from vet school was a welcome one. He loved the classes, but it was hard work; not to mention it was tough being away from his family, whom he loved very much.

Coming home every full moon and during vacation breaks just wasn't enough. He missed fishing with his dad, playing with his little sister, eating his mom's cooking, and roughhousing with his brother and cousins. These past two years had been the first time he'd spent away from them since he could remember, even before... He sighed and shook his head. In another couple of years, when he got his diploma, it would all be worth it. He couldn't wait; he'd wanted to be a veterinarian since he was seven, just as his brother had always wanted to be a doctor.

Was his brother home yet? He looked at his watch—3:50 p.m. Nope, Alex was still at school. Getting out of the car, he went to the rear door to get his things out.

As he opened the door and leaned in to get his bag from the back seat, a high-pitched squealing sound pierced the air. Before he knew what hit him, he was attacked from behind. Some sort of wild animal latched onto his legs, then clawed its way up his back. He caught a glimpse of brown fur as he fell onto the seat, the rabid beast clinging to his neck. Pushing himself up and catching his breath, he managed to turn over. The shrieking creature turned with him, wiggling onto his chest, then caught his face in its grimy little paws. "Didja bring me anything, Dash? Huh? Huh? Didja, didja?"

Dash grinned up into his little sister's big brown eyes. He'd spoiled her the past year by bringing her candy and the occasional toy from the campus bookstore. He chuckled, wishing he could bottle up the six-year-old's energy and take it with him. "No, Marisa, I didn't, but if you will let me up and let me go inside for a few minutes, I'll take you to get ice cream."

She cocked her brown faux-fur-covered head in contemplation. Then she grinned. Which was rather charming since her two front teeth were missing. "Umm... Okay, I guess that'd be all right." She scooted off him and back onto the drive.

The little pest was dressed in some sort of brown, furred Halloween monstrosity. There were two floppy pieces of material on the top. He assumed they were supposed to be ears, but they'd been cut into triangles and had stuffing hanging from the sides. He laughed. He had no idea what she was supposed to be or how to ask without hurting her feelings.

Oh, well, she was cute anyway, missing teeth and all. And even now, it was obvious that Marisa was going to be a beauty one day. It was a day he and Alex were dreading. Their dad was none too pleased with the prospect, either. They were going to have to beat the boys off with a stick! Or maybe tooth and claw.

He slid out of the car and grabbed his bag. Locking the door, he turned to Marisa and ruffled her fur-covered head. "Who all's home, squirt?"

"Just me and Mom. Alex won't be here for another hour, and Daddy is at the restaurant until five o'clock. How come you didn't bring me nuthfin'?"

Dash chuckled. "I'm broke, kid! I'm up to my eyeballs in student loans. I spent my last dime filling up the gas tank to get home." He pushed the front door open and walked in after Marisa.

She stopped just inside the door and turned to look up at him. "Really? You can have what's in my piggy bank if ya need it."

Damn, if that just didn't beat all. He nearly got choked up. He set his bag down and picked her up, then kissed her nose. "No, squirt, I don't need your piggy bank, but thank you."

She wrapped her little arms around his neck and kissed his cheek. "If you change your mind, just tell me."

"Sure thing. Why don't you go play, while I talk to Mom and get settled in; then we'll go get ice cream." He squeezed her in a big hug, then placed her on her feet.

"Okay. Mom is in the kitchen. Call me when you get ready to go!" She took off up the stairs.

What in the world? Dash tilted his head and stared after his sister. On the butt of her costume was a tail—a half-circle sewn onto the actual costume. On that tail were four strips of fur, also with stuffing hanging out the sides, safety-pinned in a line. The tail hung to the back of her knees. He shook his head in bemusement and went into the kitchen.

His mom was frosting a pumpkin-shaped cake. She glanced up and smiled. Putting the knife down, she rushed around the bar. "Hi, honey! Happy Halloween! How was the drive home? Are you tired? Are you hungry?"

He picked her up and swung her around in a circle as he kissed her cheek. "Happy Halloween to you, too, Mom. The drive was fine. I ate on the way, and I'll take a nap later. God, it's good to be home." Setting her on her feet, he eased around the counter, hoping she wouldn't notice what he was doing. "So, what are you going to be for tonight's party?"

"Your father is going as Count Dracula, and I'm going as the bride of Frankenstein. What are you going to be?"

He shrugged and nonchalantly stuck his finger in the cake. "I'll have to see what I can throw together." When she didn't smack him for stealing frosting, he got braver and stuck his finger in his mouth. Ummm, that was good. Homemade was always the best. "Speaking of costumes. What in the heck is Marisa supposed to be?"

Claire sighed and stepped around the bar. She picked up the knife and fixed the spot he'd just stolen the frosting from. "Marisa called *Tía* Sarah and found out that the twins and Julian were going as werewolves. So, naturally, she wanted to copy the twins. I told her no. When we went to pick out a costume, she found an adorable teddy bear one—"

He reached out toward the cake again.

She slapped his hand. "Stay out of the cake, Dash!"

He sighed, rubbing his hand.

"Anyway, I thought she'd given up on the werewolf idea, so I bought it for her. Not five minutes after we got it home, she came down asking for safety pins. I asked what for, and she said that she had to make some costume alterations. Well, come to find out, her alterations had to be done because werewolves have pointy ears and long tails."

Dash laughed. The kid was cute, no two ways about it! "Poor Rome, Rand, and Julian. Being thirteen sucks enough without a six-year-old following you around."

His mom grinned and looked up from fixing the cake. "Tell me about it; I've already gotten two calls today. One from Julian, complaining about her copying them. The other from Rand, telling me he knew she was going to dog their every step and the least I could do is sew up the seams so she doesn't look so ragged. They both saw her at school today."

He grinned and shook his head. "She still moving to California so she can be a movie star and marry the twins?"

"So she says."

He chuckled.

"I don't know what I'm going to do with her; she's such a handful. Your father thinks everything she does is funny. He lets her get away with murder. So does Alex."

Brushing her hair back, he leaned in and kissed her cheek. "So do I. I'm taking her for ice cream; you want anything?"

She grinned and shook her head. "Nah, you two go. I've got to finish this cake and start on the cookies. Just don't let her eat too much. One scoop is plenty."

Nodding, he stepped back. Then as fast as he could, he swiped a finger toward the cake again, stealing another bite of frosting.

She groaned, then laughed. "Get out of here!"

Damn! Alex had stolen his parking spot while he and Marisa had been at the ice cream parlor. He pulled into his dad's spot with a chuckle.

Marisa giggled next to him. "Um! You're in Daddy's spot. He's gonna gripe about that, you know."

"Yup, I know."

"You are so bad, Dash!"

He nodded. "Yup, I know that, too." Turning the car off, he opened the door and got out, then walked around to her side of the car and opened the door for her.

Marisa grinned and handed him her ice cream cone. She undid her seatbelt and slid out. "Shame on you."

He returned her mischievous grin. "I know, but what can ya do?"

She shrugged. Then with one last smile, she grabbed her ice cream and took off for the house. At the front door, she turned. "Thanks for the ice cream, Dash." Jerking the door open, she ran inside and almost plowed right into Alex, who was on his way out.

"Watch it, squirt!" Alex shook his head and smiled at Dash. "Hey, bro! How was the drive up?"

"It sucked!"

Alex laughed. "Yeah, I bet. That's why I decided to go to school here."

"Yeah, well, if there had been a vet school here, I would have stayed, too." As Alex drew near, an intriguing scent wafted across his nose. Dash leaned toward his brother as he stepped closer. Alex obviously intended to give him a hug, but Dash stopped him by leaning forward and putting his nose to Alex's shirt. His cock stirred. *What the hell?* "What is that smell?"

Alex stepped back, his eyebrows raised. "What smell? What are you doing? Get your nose off me."

Dash couldn't help it; he leaned further in, inhaling deeply, taking the wonderful aroma into his lungs. Again his cock paid attention. Damn! He was getting hard from sniffing his brother's shirt. What the hell had Alex been doing while wearing that thing? "Man, what did you do? You smell freakin' wonderful."

Alex backed up further, holding his hand out. "Back off. You're freaking me out. I come to welcome you home, and you sniff me." He dipped his head down and took in a breath near his shoulder, then shrugged. "I don't smell anything unusual. What the fuck?"

"Dude! You smell different. What is it?" He took another step toward Alex.

Alex frowned and retreated. "I don't know. I didn't do anything that I don't normally do. I went to classes. I met Jill for a late lunch. Is it pizza? Do you smell pizza?" Alex bent his head and sniffed himself again.

No, it wasn't pizza. Dash shook his head.

"I went to my last class; then afterward I walked Jill to her car. I made sure she was coming to the party tonight. Gave her directions to the cabin and hugged her bye. Then I got in my car and came home. That's it, so stop with the sniffing, wolf boy!"

"Wolf boy?" Dash grinned. "I'm no boy, but I guess the wolf part fits. Who's Jill?" He moved closer to Alex.

"Come on, you know Jill. She's probably my best friend...well, my best friend that isn't related, anyway. We double date occasionally. You've heard me talk about her." Alex stepped back again. "Would you stop stalking me, damn it?"

Dash hadn't realized that that was what he was doing until Alex mentioned it. He stopped walking. "Jill? Your buddy Jill? The one whose apartment you crash at before finals? The one you don't want to *do?* That Jill?"

Alex nodded. "Yes, that Jill."

"Okay, I've never understood how you can have female friends you don't want to bang, but I've dismissed that as a defect in your personality. Still, how in the hell could you not want to do her, if she smells that good?"

Alex threw his hands up and groaned. Turning away, he stepped up on the porch and opened the front door.

Dash followed him. He couldn't resist the temptation. He leaned forward and put his nose to the shirt again, inhaling deeply.

Alex groaned and stepped out of reach. "Stop it!" he hissed.

"I can't help it! Tell me about Jill."

They walked into the kitchen, where their mom was taking a batch of cookies out of the oven. She looked up and smiled. "Hi, babies!"

"Hi, Mom," they answered in unison.

Dash reached over and snagged a cookie off the cookie sheet. "Oh, oh, ah, hot!" He tossed the cookie back and forth from hand to hand, then looked up at Alex. "Well? Tell me about Jill." He had a hard-on from her scent alone; the least Alex could do was give him a mental picture of her.

Their mom looked up and frowned. "Stay out of the cookies, Dash. Alex's friend? Why do you want to know about Jill? She's a sweetheart. And smart, too."

"Because Alex smells like her."

She scrunched up her face. "What?"

Alex sighed. "He keeps sniffing my shirt. He says I smell different, and the only thing I can come up with is that Jill hugged me before I left this afternoon."

Dash walked over to the table where Alex had taken a seat, unable to fight the allure of that scent. He sat down next to Alex and took a deep breath. His gums began to sting. *Shit!* His teeth were lengthening, just like his cock had. He stuffed the cookie in his mouth, hoping no one would notice. He had to meet this Jill. "Did you say she was coming to the party?" he asked with a mouth full of cookie.

"Yeah, why?" Alex turned to look at him. "Holy shit! Your eyes changed."

Dash blinked. Well, son of a gun, so they had—everything was monochrome. "What's she look like?" Drawn to her essence, he leaned over and rubbed his face on Alex's shoulder.

Alex shot out of the chair. "That's it! You are totally weirding me out!" He pulled his shirt over his head and threw it at Dash.

Dash caught it and pulled it to his face, taking a big whiff. He looked up as Alex stormed out of the room. Claire was standing there with a puzzled look on her face, studying him. "What's she like, Mom?"

She grinned, turned back, and grabbed a cookie off the plate. Taking a seat across the table, she slid the cookie to him. "She tall, about five-nine, I'd say. Slender, with long, light brown hair that goes to the top of her butt. She's pretty, but in an understated way. She isn't one to fuss with a bunch of makeup, but then, she doesn't need it. The few times we've met her, she's been very polite and soft-spoken. Jill seems very bright, and she appears to have a good head on her shoulders. Your father and I like her very much."

At six-three, Dash was tall, too, so the first thought that popped into his head was that he wouldn't have to stoop over to kiss her. The image of a tall, willowy brunette with natural beauty crept into his mind. His stomach tightened and his cock jumped. He loved long hair on a woman—loved the way it felt against his skin. Damn! If he didn't quit, he'd embarrass himself in front of his mother! His overactive imagination and Jill's fragrance were going to do him in.

He stood up, dropping Alex's shirt to hang in front of him to conceal his now straining erection. "Thanks, Mom." He started to walk out of the kitchen, then remembered the cookie. He snatched it off the table. "Thanks for the cookie, too."

"Dash, wait. Do you think she could be—"

"I'm going to take a nap. See you in a few hours, Mom!" With that, he bounded out of the kitchen and up the stairs to his room, cramming the cookie in his mouth as he went. Eating with lengthened canines in human form was no easy feat, but he was never one to turn down sweets...especially during a crisis.

He stepped into his room, closing and locking the door behind him. Crossing to the bathroom door that joined his room to his brother's, he locked that door, too. He was in no mood to answer questions regarding his behavior. Heck, *he* couldn't figure out what was going on, much less explain it.

He adjusted his engorged cock and sat down on the edge of the bed. He should have gotten another cookie; to his way of thinking, this certainly qualified as an emergency. Why did her scent affect *him* this way? Alex seemed to be oblivious to her sweet aroma.

Flopping backward onto the bed, he closed his eyes and dropped the shirt over his face. Inhaling Jill's lingering scent, he tried to decipher what made it different from other women. Why was it special? If it had this big an effect on him now, how would he react when he met her in person? His stomach clenched at the thought of seeing her face to face, and an ache began in his balls. He reached down and unfastened his pants, trying to relieve the pressure.

What would Jill be like? Would she be as attracted to him as he already was to her? He freed his cock from his pants. *Ah, yeah! Much better.* Did she have long legs? Mom had said she was tall. There was nothing like having long, sexy legs wrapped around you when you fucked. Dash groaned as the ache in his balls intensified. This line of thinking wasn't helping the situation any. He was no closer to figuring out what was going on, and he was well on the way to a case of blue balls.

Good Lord, how long had it been since he'd last had sex? Two weeks? Three? Too damned long! And it had been with Cindy, who had long hair and had loved it when he'd wrapped it in his fist and pulled it while he was taking her from behind. Would Jill like her hair tugged?

A drop of precome hit his stomach. "Oh, the hell with it." Dash pushed his pants to his knees. He sat up, moved to lean against the headboard, and took his cock in hand. Grabbing the shirt from where it had fallen off his face, he draped it across the headboard next to him so that Jill's fragrance filled his senses. He squeezed his cock and began to move his hand. He watched as another pearly drop slipped from the fat head. Closing his eyes, he dropped his head back and continued to stroke himself. His other hand slid down to tug at his balls. He hadn't been this turned on in quite some time, yet he'd barely even started and he was already about to explode.

Pumping faster he took another deep breath. His balls tightened and pulled into his body. He continued to stroke, setting a steady rhythm. Within seconds he was coming, spewing semen onto his hand and stomach. He let out a groan and relaxed. Then a thought occurred to him. Was Jill his mate?

Chapter Two

Jill Parker glanced down at the dashboard clock. Fantastic! She was on a little country dirt road, alone, lost, and late. To make matters worse, she could hear thunder rumbling in the distance. She hated being late...even for a silly Halloween party. Why had she even agreed to come? Parties were not her thing and never had been.

She looked for any indication of where she was. The route she traveled seemed to go on forever. If she could just get out of this maze of winding roads, maybe she could backtrack and find her way to the party. Unfortunately, not only was the road not paved, but it didn't have any signs, either, and there were trees on both sides, making it impossible to find any sort of landmark. Not that they would help her, as she wouldn't recognize them anyway. Why hadn't she taken Alex up on his offer to travel with him to the party? It wasn't like her laundry wasn't still going to be there tomorrow. Better yet, why hadn't she just stayed home and watched some Halloween specials?

Lightning lit up the sky, and the first big drops of rain splattered onto her windshield. The wind seemed to pick up suddenly, making a whistling sound. The trees swayed, throwing leaves around as they moved. Jill shuddered and turned up the radio.

She finally came to a crossroad. Stopping, she reached for the map Alex had drawn her. Turning on the dome light, she tried to decipher the map. There were two crossroads before she was supposed to turn right onto the third crossroad. Well, she hadn't seen any other roads until now—did this mean she was on the right track? She turned off the light, tossed the map onto the passenger seat, and continued driving. The rain was really coming down. In fact, it was blowing horizontal in her headlights.

Her visibility was limited, so she slowed down. Something darted out in front of her. She slammed on the brakes, trying to stop. The car slid. A...dog?...looked up and seemed to make eye contact just as her car hit him and came to an abrupt stop. *Shit!* Jill took a deep breath and tried to calm down. The car had almost been stopped when she'd struck the animal, but she hadn't seen it run off again. Fortunately, she hadn't felt it under her tires, either. She couldn't stand the thought of killing someone's beloved pet.

Jill opened the car door and scrambled out, immediately becoming drenched. She cautiously walked around the front of the car. Who knew how the wounded animal would react—assuming it was still there, of course.

As she drew around the hood, she heard a soft whimper. On the ground in front of her car lay a huge black...dog? Maybe it was a wolf. Jill stepped back.

It whimpered and stared into her eyes; it didn't look vicious or wild.

Jill took a cautious step toward it, then crouched down and held her hand up. When the animal didn't growl or look away, she got braver and moved her hand closer. "Hi, there, fella. Are you nice? Are you going to try and bite my hand off if I look you over?"

The dog cocked his head and stretched his head toward her hand. It's long pink tongue snaked out and brushed her knuckles. She drew closer and he began bathing her hand in kisses.

"Ahh, you *are* someone's pet, aren't you?" She brushed her hands over his fur, checking for any injuries, and all the while he covered her in kisses—on her hands, her face, anywhere he could reach.

She pressed gently on his stomach—yep, he was a boy dog—to see if he would protest. He didn't seem to, so she moved to his legs. When she examined his left hind leg, he pulled it toward his body with a whimper, trying to keep it away from her.

"Oh, I'm so sorry. Poor baby, let's get you out of this rain and see if we can get you into the car, big fella. We're getting soaked, and we look like a couple of drowned rats."

As if he understood her, he slowly got to his feet, then limped to her car door, avoiding any weight on his injured leg.

Jill stood there her mouth hanging open, astonished. This was one smart dog!

His bark spurred her into action. They were soaked, and the wind was making it especially chilly. She opened the back door for him, then slid into the front. She cranked the heater up and looked around for something to dry herself with. She found a towel she used in the summer to keep her leather seats from sticking to her legs and burning her. As she was drying her hair, it started raining inside the car. *What the—?*

Jill turned in time to see the dog finish shaking the last of the water from his body. "Oh! Bad boy! No! Stop that!"

He stopped and lay down on the back seat. She could have sworn he smiled at her. She sighed and dried off the rest of herself and the now drenched car. *Great!* The car smelled like wet dog! Jill shook her head and put the car in drive. "You know, I had a towel. You could have waited. I'd have dried you off."

He whined.

"Yeah, well, I was trying to save what was left of my costume, but I'd have gotten to you eventually. You didn't need to saturate everything."

Jill drove for what seemed an eternity, without finding another crossroad. The rain was getting worse, if that was possible, and she was pretty sure she saw small pieces of hail in her headlights. Her tires were not getting much traction and began to spin on the muddy lane. If she didn't get off this road soon, she was going to get stuck. She needed to get to the party. Alex might know whom the dog belonged to, and together maybe they could patch him up. His injuries didn't look serious, but she hadn't been able to check very thoroughly in all the rain and wind. "Damn! I'm never going to find this stupid party!"

A loud bark came from the backseat. Jill screamed and swerved, but she quickly regained control of the car. Her heart was pounding in her chest at the scare his deep bark had given her.

The dog jumped into the front seat, whining when he landed on his hind leg.

"Damn it! Bad boy! Do that again, and you can walk home without my help."

He pressed his nose to the passenger window and barked again.

She jumped, and her still-hammering heart beat faster. "Stop it! I've got to get us off this damned road. We need to get to Alex's party. If we get there, he can help me take a look at you, and maybe he can help me get you back to your family."

Again he barked, but remained otherwise still. She glanced in the direction he was staring. There seemed to be a building. Was that where the party was? There weren't any lights. She slowed down. "What is it, boy? What are you trying to tell me?"

Bang, bang, bang! Large chunks of hail bounced off her car. Jill started. The small hail had suddenly turned into a barrage of large pieces.

The dog barked again, still facing the structure.

"All right, you win, boy. We need to get out of this weather." She turned the car onto the dirt drive, hoping and praying that she wouldn't get stuck in the mud. Pulling in front of the little building, she stopped and looked at her new companion. "Well, what now?"

He barked and pawed at the door.

Maybe he lived here. The place looked unoccupied, but it also looked well kept. It was obvious that someone had been here recently.

How were they going to get in there? More to the point, what if they did get in? They'd be trespassing. Well, she would;

she kind of doubted they'd charge a dog with breaking and entering. She sighed. *Well, hell!*

She grabbed her purse and opened the door, then stepped out into the rain. The dog limped across the front seat and out the driver's side. She locked up the car and raced up to the small porch as the dog limped along behind her. Jill reached for the door and tried the knob, but it was locked. The dog looked up at her and barked again. He put his head against the door and pushed. A section of door opened up. Of course. A doggy door. Maybe he really did live here.

Once he was inside, he stuck his head out and barked at Jill once more, then pulled his head inside again. Jill took a deep breath and blew it out. Lightning struck nearby and thunder boomed. She tossed her purse through door and scrambled in. As soon as she cleared the door, she got licked in the face. "Bleck! Would you stop that?"

She stood up and looked around, trying to find a light switch in the dark. Lightning lit up the room long enough for her to find it. After a minute, her eyes adjusted to the light. The place was indeed well kept, even if it was small and unoccupied. There was a bed, a couch, a little kitchenette with a small refrigerator, and an oven and a sink. There were two doors, presumably a closet and a bathroom. Jill looked at her new friend. He'd lain down with his head resting on his front paws and was watching her every move. "Well, now what?"

He cocked his head.

She chuckled and picked her purse up, then set it down on the couch. It was cold, and she was soaked to the bone. She decided that exploring the place was her first order of business. She went to the first of the two doors—it was an empty closet. She moved on to the next door—the bathroom, just as she'd suspected. Finding a towel, she returned to the main room and dried her hair and her body as best as she could. For the moment, there was nothing she could do about her wet clothes.

She was freezing. There were logs in the fireplace, so she decided to light a fire. She'd deal with the consequences of getting caught later. On the mantel were fireplace matches and on the hearth were newspapers, so she built her fire while the dog watched. As she stirred up the flames and got them going, she wondered what she was going to do if someone caught her here. It was pretty clear that the small cabin was some sort of hunting cabin or other type of weekend retreat, so the odds of someone coming were not very high. But how had the dog ended up here? Obviously, he was someone's pet, and he knew about the little cabin and even the doggy door. Had he gotten left behind from their last hunting expedition, or were the owners somewhere nearby?

She sat down in front of the fire with the dog and tried to get warm. "Well, pal, how are you doing? Can I look at your leg now?"

She touched his leg and began to examine it. This time he didn't cry out or try to pull away. That was odd; he didn't act like it was bothering him any longer. He licked her hand as she let go of him. She grinned; he certainly was a sweet dog. She loved animals and had had several growing up, but there was no time for them now while she was going through medical school. She'd get a dog or maybe a cat after she graduated and finished her residency. After that she should have some semblance of a normal life. Maybe then she'd get married, too.

She sat and watched the fire, listened to the storm outside, and petted her new friend. Her stomach grumbled, reminding her that she hadn't eaten. No way was she going to steal food as well as trespass; she'd have to make do with some of the crackers in her purse. Good thing she always carried snacks! Medical school and rotations were so hectic that she had to snag a bite to eat whenever and wherever she could.

Jill got her purse and brought it over in front of the fire. "Well, boy, let's see what we have here." She pulled out a package of peanut butter crackers, a package of peanut butter cookies, and a box of animal crackers. "What do you think? Peanut butter crackers first? Yeah, that's what I think, too." She tore open the wrapper and offered him a cracker, then took one for herself. They finished off those and started on the animal crackers, then finally devoured the cookies.

Jill was lying by the fire, listening to the hail hit the roof, when the dog started to convulse. "Oh, no! What's wrong, boy?" She sat up quickly and looked him over; she had no idea what to do for him. Her heart sank. Had she caused this by hitting him with the car? Were the cookies poison to his system or something? No, canines were very closely related to humans; they had very similar physiologies. It wasn't the food.

His fur was shrinking.

Jill's eyes widened in horror. His fur wasn't the only thing disappearing—his snout was, too, and so was his tail.

She backed up, unable to keep from staring as his limbs lengthened. She blinked several times and shook her head to clear it. She couldn't be seeing what she was seeing.

His body continued to contort until there was a man in his place. A very naked man, with shoulder-length, dark-brown hair and tan skin. He raised his head, and she sucked in a breath at the sheer beauty of his face.

Even though he was lying on the floor, he appeared tall. He pushed himself up on one elbow; then his big brown eyes looked into hers. He held out his hand toward her. "Jill?"

Jill backed herself against the front door.

"Jill?"

She stared wide-eyed, then threw her head back and screamed at the top of her lungs.

Chapter Three

Dash blinked, letting his eyes adjust. He could hear the pounding of rain on the roof and the rumble of thunder. How had he gotten here, and how had he come to be with Jill?

The last thing he remembered was going for a run before the party. He'd ridden out to the cabin with Alex, and then after setting up the decorations and food, he'd bailed for a run in the woods. Now here he was in one of the small cottages provided for shelter on pack land, with a screaming, hysterical woman.

There was no doubt that this was Jill. Her scent matched the one on Alex's shirt. Almost immediately, it became obvious why her scent had affected him so thoroughly—she was his mate. He didn't know how he knew it, but he did, just as Dad had told him he would. Somewhere deep inside, he felt an attachment to this woman that wasn't from her scent alone. She was everything he'd imagined and more. Blood rushed to his cock, making the already hard member twitch; he'd gotten hard within seconds of changing back.

She must have been out in the storm, since she looked pretty bedraggled, albeit a beautiful mess. Her long, wet hair was pulled into a ponytail on the top of her head, and she was dressed in some sort of pale blue genie costume, which had almost dried, clinging to her and showing off her every curve, making his mouth water. The blouse adhered to her generous breasts and showed off her slim, bare waist. Her long, toned legs were visible through the sheer fabric covering—or, rather, hugging—them...

His mother was wrong; there was nothing understated about Jill's looks. Her features were very sensual, and as far as he was concerned, she was one of the sexiest women he'd ever seen. The need to claim her was almost unbearable, despite her continued screaming.

God, he wished he had his brother's power to retain human thoughts in wolf form. Maybe he could get Jill to fill in the blanks, if he could snap her out of her hysteria. At least she hadn't run. That was a definite bonus.

He spoke in a calm, non-threatening manner. "I won't hurt you. Please stop screaming; you're hurting my ears. I need to know what happened."

The shrill noise ceased, but the look in Jill's eyes and her scent said that she was far from calm. Gulping down a deep breath, she seemed to gain some semblance of control. "What are you?"

It was pretty clear that she wasn't going to come closer, so he dropped his hand. "I'm a werewolf."

She blinked. "There are no such things as werewolves. They are make-believe. And I should know; I'm almost a doctor."

"Well, doc, I hate to burst your bubble, but there *are* werewolves. And I should know, because not only am I one, but I'm almost a vet."

Her mouth dropped open. "Who are you?"

"Name's Devon Rigotti. Is that what you wanted to know?"

She nodded, looking shocked. "Why have I never heard about werewolves being real? Are there vampires, too?"

Dash chuckled. Her scent and heart rate showed she was still rattled, but you'd never know by her demeanor. She was going to make a hell of a doctor, if this was her normal way of dealing with things. "Not that I know of, but anything is possible. I imagine that if there are vampires, they guard their secret as well as we wolves do."

She took a deep breath. "Okay, that makes sense. The medical and scientific community would want to test you to death...so to speak. I guess I'd keep my identity a secret, too. Do you eat people?"

Dash grinned. "Only beautiful women, and only if they ask."

She gasped, then glared at him. "Are you always this frank?"

"Yup. I've been accused of being blunt a time or two." Waggling his eyebrows, he leered at her.

She snorted. "Hmm. Are you hurt? How's your leg?"

"It's fine. Why do you ask? What happened? How'd we get here? More to the point, where'd you come from? Not that I'm complaining about waiting out a storm with you."

She took another deep breath and let it out. She must have decided he was harmless, because she took a step forward. "Don't you remember? You ran out in front of me, and I couldn't stop. I clipped you with my car."

Dash frowned. "I can't really remember what happens after I shift back. I know who I am, and what I'm doing for the most part, but things become fuzzy when I try to recall more than that. I guess you could say I pretty much become a wolf, and my memories don't always carry over with the change. But I can still comprehend the nuances in people's speech and hand gestures...stuff that any normal canine would recognize. So it isn't like I'm stupid or anything, just not human."

"Well, then, how do you know you don't attack people when you're a wolf?"

"I can usually remember a hunt. And most of the time my brother and cousins are with me."

"So? If werewolves can't remember everything when they are wolves, maybe they're attacking people, too. Besides, how'd you become a werewolf anyway? Did one attack you?" She paused. "Hey, wait a minute! There isn't a full moon tonight—how come you were a wolf?"

Dash chuckled and motioned her forward. "Come sit down by the fire and get warm."

Jill hesitated, but apparently her curiosity got the better of her, because she stepped up to the back of the couch and looked down at him. Suddenly, her eyes widened, then shot up to his face. "I am not going to sit and talk to you while you are naked."

"I thought you were almost a doctor? Doctors talk to naked people all the time."

Color rushed to her face and she cleared her throat. "I am, and no, we don't. We wait till a patient is clothed before we talk to them. I assure you, even if I do talk to naked people, they are not...aroused!"

She was too cute, and the blush was becoming on her. Which was a good thing. She was going to be blushing a lot, if the sight of his erection was what triggered it. He grinned and looked around for something to cover himself with. Spotting a quilt folded over the back of the couch, he leaned forward and snagged it, draped it over his lap, then raised a brow at her.

She came around to the front of the couch and sat down on the end farthest away from him.

"Okay, what did you ask? Oh, yeah, the full moon. I can change at any time—it doesn't have to be on a full moon—but I do have to change on the full moon. My body leaves me no choice. As for my brother and cousins, they are a lot stronger than I am. They retain human thought processes in wolf form, and they remember everything after they shift. An attack can change someone into a werewolf, but that isn't what happened to me. I have a gene that makes me a werewolf. Does that answer your questions?"

She nodded. "I think so." She cocked her head. "Are you sure you're all right? I mean, you were limping, and you didn't like it when I touched your leg."

"Maybe you just didn't touch the right one, darlin'." Dash held up his hands in surrender as she glared at him again. "Okay, okay. I'm fine. I don't feel anything. We heal amazingly fast. If it wasn't healed before, then it probably healed during my change."

She looked thoughtful. "Hmm, interesting. You know, maybe you should let scientists study you. There must be something in your immune system that helps you heal so fast. Think of how it could help others…uh, humans."

Dash shook his head. "No way! Would you want people poking you with needles and doing who knows what and watching your every move?"

"Actually, I feel like they do that now. Medical school can be a little—" A loud clap of thunder rattled the windows. Jill started. "Eep!" The lights flickered, then went out completely. "Well, great! I'm trapped in a tiny and dark cabin with a werewolf, who might or might not eat people."

He chuckled. "I already told you under what conditions I eat people. Did I seem vicious to you when I was in wolf form earlier?" He didn't wait for her to answer, but he saw resignation in her face. Holding the quilt securely around his waist, he got up and walked over to stand in front of her. She was shivering, and he suspected that it wasn't all due to nerves. She'd lost the stench of fear, but she still had a good case of anxiety. He reached for her. "Come on, I know you're freezing. Get over here by the fire while I find another blanket.

She stared at him for a minute, bit her lip, then placed her hand in his. She allowed him to pull her to her feet and lead her toward the fire.

He pushed her down, went to the bed, and pulled the comforter off of it. "All right, Jill…strip. You can't stay in those damp clothes."

"What?! I'm not taking off my clothes. I don't know you, and I don't know where the hell I am. Anyone could come in here at any moment."

"Do you really think anyone is going to be out in the storm? Besides, this place belongs to my pack." He handed her the comforter. "Go to the bathroom, wrap yourself up in this, and come back in front of the fire."

She shook her head stubbornly. "Nope. I still don't know you. No way am I getting naked with you."

Dash sighed and sat down next to her. "I'll make you a deal. I'll tell you everything you could possibly want to know about me, and werewolves in general, if you go get out of those clothes. You saved me earlier tonight; now let me save you. You are going to catch a chill." Not to mention it'd be much more difficult to make love with her clothes on. Of course, he could work around that, but it'd be easier if she were naked. And he was definitely going to make love to her. She was his mate—how could he not? He gave her a gentle, coaxing grin, trying not to let his thoughts show on his face.

She scrunched up her nose. He could tell he'd caught her attention and her curiosity was more than obvious. She wanted to know about werewolves. He suspected that was the reason for her apparent easy acceptance of his nature.

With open reluctance, she took the heavy blanket and stood up. "Okay."

Jill pulled the blanket tight around her and stepped out of the bathroom. What a night! *Werewolves! Who'd have ever thought?* This was without a doubt the weirdest night of her life. Why did such a gorgeous man have to be...non-human?

Devon was lying on his side, watching the fire. She couldn't help but stop and stare. He was so handsome, and he looked as Italian as his last name sounded. It also appeared that he didn't have a care in the world. The man was truly comfortable in his own skin. His tanned limbs were exposed, hanging out of the quilt that only covered his groin area. The firelight glinted off his dark-brown hair, making it appear almost golden, and cast shadows on his square, masculine jaw, accenting his sensuality.

The small dimple in his chin added an air of sophistication, but something told her it was an illusion. Her gut said that in bed the man would be as wild as his wolf nature. Devon simply screamed sex.

The memory of the view she'd gotten earlier made her tingle in all the right places. His body was as nice as his face. There was hair on his legs and arms, just enough to add to his masculinity, and he had long, athletic legs, slim hips, and washboard abs. His chest was nicely defined, with just a bit of hair. It thinned out and trailed down his stomach, narrowing into a strip below his navel. And his cock! Oh, Lord, she felt her face heat just thinking about it. From the quick glances she'd stolen, she knew he was long and thick—really thick.

Jill swallowed. She had to get her raging libido under control. This man was not her type, and it had nothing to do with him being a werewolf. In fact, that was the least of it. He might be a predator, but she sensed no malice from him. And she was good at reading people. Truthfully, the whole werewolf thing made him even more appealing. She was dying to run some tests on him. The thought of what it might mean to the medical community if she could duplicate his healing ability was exciting. The problem was, if she was reading him right, he was a player. No one looked that blatantly sexual without having tons of experience. And she was not a one-night stand kind of girl.

"I love your hair. I had no idea it was so long."

Jill reached up and touched her damp hair. She'd taken it down in the bathroom and used her fingers as a comb. It *was* long—too long, actually; it fell past her butt. She shrugged. "It needs to be trimmed."

He sat up, shaking his head. "No, it doesn't. It's beautiful." He patted the spot next to him. "Come have a seat, and I'll answer your questions."

She hesitated. The look he was giving her said that wasn't all he'd do for her if she let him. And, boy, was she tempted. More tempted than she'd ever been, but she wasn't about to have a casual fling with a stranger. She'd never done so, and she wasn't going to start now.

He must have read her mind, because he sighed and said, "I'll keep my hands to myself."

Now, why was that almost disappointing? She sat down. "Okay, tell me all about being a werewolf."

They talked for hours. She never would have guessed how much they shared in common. He told her about being a werewolf and about vet school; she told him all about her experiences in med school. Just as she'd always wanted to be a doctor, he'd always wanted to be a veterinarian. He loved animals, but like her, he was petless at the moment because of the demands of school. He talked briefly about his family and how he really missed them when he was away at school.. He also mentioned that he was adopted and had a brother and a sister, but mostly he talked of his parents and how they loved him and treated him like he was their own flesh and blood.

They eventually ended up looking at each other, lying on the floor on their stomachs, with pillows off the bed. Her feet were pointing toward the kitchen, his toward the bed.

Jill gazed into his warm brown eyes and felt her belly flutter in response as he talked. His voice was deep and smooth...as sexy as the rest of him.

Suddenly he stopped talking , reached out, and brushed his fingers across her cheek.

She swallowed hard, fighting the urge to lean into his hand.

"Did I mention that werewolves, like real wolves, mate for life?"

Jill shook her head, mesmerized by the sweep of his lashes as he glanced at her lips, then back into her eyes.

"Well, we do." His voice was low, almost a whisper. "And when we find our mates, we know. Instantly." He leaned forward and brushed his lips across hers.

She closed her eyes and sighed.

His tongue traced her lips and she shivered. He pulled back just enough that he wasn't touching her. But he was so close she could feel his breath on her, feel the heat from his lips.

So much for no one-nighters; she was helpless to resist him. She had never wanted a man so bad in her life. The stormy night, the cozy fire, his smooth, deep voice—it was just too overwhelming...too perfect. Just this once...

As she inched forward, he whispered against her lips. "You're my mate, Jill."

Chapter Four

"What?" she whispered. She appeared to be in a daze.

The woman obviously overanalyzed everything. No way was Dash going to allow her to think at a time like this. Her arousal was flooding his nostrils, and it was the sweetest fragrance he'd ever smelled. She was his, and he was going to claim her. He felt a growl bubbling up in his chest, but suppressed it. The last thing he wanted to do was scare her.

He leaned forward, pressing his mouth to hers, sliding his tongue across her lips and in between. God, she tasted good. He caressed her teeth, then boldly plunged further inside. At first, she didn't respond, but gradually her tongue tentatively sought out his. He sucked her bottom lip into his mouth, teasing it with small love bites.

She moaned.

It was like music to his ears...or, rather, his body. His cock, which had been impossibly hard since he'd first caught her scent during his change, now ached. His balls drew tighter against his body, and his stomach clenched. Damn, she was going to be the death of him.

"Come here, darlin'." He came to his knees, pulling her up with him. He didn't give her any time to protest the loss of her blanket; he immediately slanted his mouth over hers and kissed her again.

Her breasts pressed against his chest, and he cupped her butt in his hands, molding her against his body. Jill's hands wrapped around his back, holding him softly. When he groaned his approval, she melted into him. Pulling back slightly, Dash nipped her lips. He opened his eyes and met hers. Together they knelt there, staring at one another for several seconds.

She gasped. "Your eyes...they're...they look like they did when you were a wolf."

"It's okay. I promise. I'd never hurt you." He dipped his head and caught her bottom lip between his teeth again, then drew back to look at her, asking her with his eyes to trust him.

She hesitated for only a second before he read the capitulation in her eyes...the hunger.

Dash trailed kisses down her neck, nipping the skin with his teeth as he went. His canines lengthened, and he did his best to hide them from her. She'd been caught off guard by his eyes; no way was he going to distract her and give her a chance to worry about his teeth. He caught one full breast in his hand and lowered his mouth to it. He glanced up into her eyes as he sucked her nipple. She watched as he lavished attention on her breast, her hands tangling in his hair, then cradling his face. All the while, she stared into his eyes. Dash couldn't help himself; the urge to bite her, to mark her as his, was overwhelming. Catching the hard peak of her nipple between his teeth, he tugged. She gasped, but didn't pull away.

Growling low in his throat, he let go of her breast and reached for the other one. He flicked the hard pebble with his tongue before he sucked it into his mouth with rhythmic pulls. And he kept his eyes on her, gauging her reactions.

Jill closed her eyes and arched her neck. She held his head to her breast, sighing in time with each hard tug of his mouth. His cock twitched at her uninhibited response, and he felt the first few drops of precome slip down his shaft. "Oh, darlin', you're making me crazy. I want to be inside you so bad."

Jill's whole body tingled at his words. She could feel the wetness growing between her legs. She needed him inside her so desperately, she was about to beg for it, when his hand slid down and cupped her. He slid a finger along her crease, gathering moisture.

He moaned. "You are so fucking wet. The smell of your pussy is killing me. I've got to taste you." Abruptly, he dropped to all fours in front of her. He leaned forward, burying his nose in her pussy, inhaling deeply. It was such an animalistic act, unbelievably and utterly erotic. Jill watched as his tongue snaked out and flicked through her damp folds. The contact sent chills racing up her spine. She felt incredible.

Devon got back up to his knees and moved to the end of the coffee table, shoving it out of the way. It screeched loudly against the wood floor. He looked over his shoulder at her and held out his hand. "Come here, Jill."

She took his hand and allowed him to pull her to him. When she reached his side, he picked her up and set her on the couch, then pulled her hips to the edge of the cushion as he bent forward to kiss her belly. He gently pushed her knees wide and leaned back over her. She reclined against the couch back and watched as he kissed his way down her abdomen. His dark hair tickled her legs as he slid down, scraping her hipbones with his teeth as he went. Jill squirmed and giggled. She tried to close her legs so she could get leverage to move away, but he was firmly wedged between them.

His head shot up, his glittery gold eyes meeting hers. He held her gaze, his wolf eyes twinkling with mischief as he lowered his head and nipped her hipbone. Again she tried to squirm away.

Devon grinned and cocked one eyebrow. "Ticklish?"

She tried to hold in a giggle and shook her head.

"I don't believe you." He dipped his head, covered her hip with his mouth, and sucked lightly.

It was too much. Jill started laughing and tried to jerk out of his hold.

Devon chuckled and held her tight. "Oh, no, you don't, darlin'. I've got you right where I want you." He nibbled her hips for several minutes, snickering at her laughter and evasive tactics.

She managed to wiggle her way back up the couch. She took a deep breath, then noticed that the tickling had stopped. She glanced down to find him eye-level with her pussy.

His hands loosened their grip on her hips and slid to her center. His thumbs parted her labia, and his gaze zeroed in on her. His nostrils flared and his eyes closed. Slowly, he lowered his head and licked her. His tongue traced down one side, then up the other, before stabbing into her wet core. Jill shivered with pleasure. The moist heat of his mouth made her inner muscles spasm.

The wet sounds of his lapping drowned out the rain and wind, making them accompanying background noise. It was the most erotic thing she'd ever heard. The flickering firelight played over his brown hair and tan shoulders, gilding them. The moment was almost dreamlike. She couldn't help but watch him. He was so incredibly sexy.

Between his fingers, he lightly pinched the skin covering her clit and pushed it up, exposing the hard little pink nub beneath. Staring into her eyes, he flicked his tongue across it.

She gasped. Her stomach muscles jerked. He oh-so-gently scraped his teeth over the sensitive flesh before sucking it into his mouth. Jill could feel her wetness combined with his saliva dripping down her perineum. Her vaginal muscles spasmed, and her back arched as he continued to suckle her clit. She closed her eyes and whimpered, reveling in the intense pleasure.

She was on the verge of orgasm when a finger slid up and down her crack, gathering the moisture from her pussy. The digit caressed her anus, rubbing back and forth. It was a strange sensation, but not unpleasant. It felt good. He pressed against her anus, and she snapped her eyes open.

He lifted his head slightly. "Shh, relax."

The soft puff of air against her exposed clit as he spoke had her panting. She nodded and squeezed her eyes shut. She was willing to do anything to get him to cover her clit with his mouth again.

When he did just that, she exploded. Her pussy squeezed tight, her legs tensed, and she arched upward. His finger pressed into her anus. In helpless wonder, she pushed closer to his invading finger. It should have hurt, but it didn't. She had no time to puzzle over it. Her whole body tingled; everything intensified. She cried out and came harder than she ever had before. It was so wonderful she could barely breathe.

Dash watched as she pressed against him in complete abandon and lost herself in her orgasm. She was the most beautiful thing he'd ever seen. His cock ached to be inside her. He could actually feel the drops of semen running down his shaft. If he didn't fuck her soon, he was going to lose the chance and come. He groaned at the thought. How awkward would that be for his first time with his mate? Well, it would certainly be something they'd always remember.

He thrust his finger in and out of her rear in a slow, steady rhythm as she rode out her climax; then he pulled it out, released her clit with a growl, and sank his teeth lightly into her upper thigh. He couldn't wait any longer.

He raised himself up, grabbed his cock, and plunged into her wet, spasming cunt. "Ahh!"

Jill sucked in a deep breath, and her eyes shot wide open. "Devvvon!"

His own breath caught at the tight grip on his cock. As he gripped her hips, his fingernails, as well as the hair on the backs of his hands, started to grow. Within seconds he had a full set of claws.

Jill stiffened under him. "Dev?"

"It's all right. Ignore it. I'm not going to change, I promise."

"Are you sure?"

"Trust me."

She looked deeply into his eyes, nodded, and seemed to relax.

He hooked his arms under her knees and thrust steadily into her. Her breasts bounced with each hard plunge of his hips. Before long they were both grunting and moaning. Sweat covered them both, and the wet slap of their bodies grew louder in the small cabin. Her eyes stared into his as he drove into her. He was so close to climax, he ached with trying to hold it off. When he could no longer stand it, he bent over her, sucked the flesh of her breast, and pinned her in place. He came with a low growl and felt her clench around him.

"Oh, Devon! Oh, yes! Ahhhh!"

He lay in a sweaty, sprawling heap on Jill's chest for several minutes. Finally, he let go of her breast and looked smugly at the mark he'd made. He grinned in satisfaction and glanced at her beloved face. Her eyes were closed. She had a fulfilled smile on her pretty lips.

Pulling her up against him, he slid down to the ground and flopped ungracefully onto his back. Her legs tangled with his, and she sighed her contentment.

Suddenly, her head popped up and her eyes opened wide. "Oh, my God!" She pushed herself up from his chest, causing his cock to slide from her moist heat. She sat astride him, a look of complete terror on her face. "Oh...my...God!" She dropped her head into her hands, shaking it back and forth.

Dash sat up and reached for her. "What is it?"

"We didn't use anything."

He tried desperately not to grin at the horrified look on her face, but failed miserably. "Is that all?"

She gasped and pushed his hands away from her. "What do you mean, is that all?"

"I mean it's not a big deal. What are you worried about, pregnancy or disease?"

"Both!"

"You aren't in heat...er, ovulating. I'd smell it if you were, and werewolves don't carry diseases. So stop worrying."

She seemed to relax slightly. Then her head dropped and started shaking again. When she looked back up, her eyes were glittering with tears. *Great!* He grabbed her and pulled her into his arms without giving her time to protest. "Ah, darlin', don't cry; it's ok."

She took a deep breath as she looked up at him and blinked, clearing the tears from her eyes. "I've never done anything so irresponsible in my entire life. How could I be so stupid?"

"It wasn't stupidity; it was lust. And like I said, there's nothing to worry about." He bent and kissed her forehead. "Besides, I think I'd be really disappointed if you were actually able to think about something like that during the heat of passion—talk about a blow to the ego."

She grinned halfheartedly, but he knew that was as good as he was going to get. She wasn't going to forgive herself anytime soon. It was obvious that as far as she was concerned, she'd had a major lapse in judgment. And really, if had it been with anyone else but him—her mate—this would have been a mistake. He was just going to have to make her forget about it. He mentally patted his own back. He was certain he could make her forget about their lack of condoms.

Dash dipped his head and took her lips. It didn't take long for her to return his fervor. Soon, they were making love again in front of the fire.

Chapter Five

Dash glanced down at his sleeping mate and sighed with bliss. She was beautiful, and she looked so peaceful and...well, innocent lying in his arms. Who would have ever thought that giving up one's freedom would feel so good? The thought of just one woman for the rest of his life wasn't at all scary. In fact, it was wonderful. He had no idea how they were going to work out their living arrangements, since they were both in school, but they'd figure it out. No way was he giving up his mate, not even for a year. If he had to commute back home every weekend, well, then, he would. But he'd rather see her every day.

He bent and kissed her nose before he slid his arm out from under her head. As much as he wanted to stay here with Jill, he knew he needed to let his family know he was all right. Tossing the blanket off his legs, he sat up and looked around. He had no idea what time it was, but the rain had stopped sometime during the night and the sun was shining brightly through the windows. He was pretty sure his parents were still at the cabin;

they'd planned on staying the night after the party. He just hoped they hadn't stayed up all night waiting for him. Dash flinched at the thought and stood up. The only way he was going to find out was to go to the main cabin. Oh, well, if he was going get an ass-chewing, then so be it. He was too happy to let it bother him.

He thought about leaving Jill a note, but she was sleeping so deeply and he figured he'd be back soon, so she'd never miss him. The thought of being away from her for even a moment was unbearable. Hell, they hadn't even had sex this morning. Not that it hadn't crossed his mind, but the thought of his family worrying about him nipped that in the bud. He was nothing if not a good son.

Over and over in his head, he concentrated on the main cabin. Once he shifted, he knew his other half would try to take over, so it was going to take some effort to keep on his course. He didn't want to get sidetracked and become caught up in being a wolf, then miss half the day, which could happen quite easily. He shifted and let himself out the doggy door.

Trotting through the woods, he reached his destination in no time. He went through the doggy door in the back of the cabin. The scent of breakfast assailed him, but he knew he had to stay focused or he'd forget his purpose. His wolf mind could so easily overcome his human one; then he'd be eating breakfast as a canine and forget all about changing and getting back to Jill. So he trotted up the stairs to his room. He heard Alex say, "Dash is home," as he began to shift into human form.

He barely got to his closet and into some jeans before his father came storming in. "Where in the hell have you been? We've been worried sick! I sent your brother and your cousins out looking for you in the direction you said you were going, and they couldn't find hide or hair of you. Your mother was convinced that someone was using your fur as a rug."

He tried not to grin at the image. They were on private property, and there had been no hunters around these parts for years. "Sorry. Would you believe that I got hit by a car?"

"No! Don't jack with me, son."

"I'm not! I really did get hit by a car. I spent the night at the small cabin at the west end of the property."

His dad raised one black brow. "Really?"

He nodded. "Really. And you're going to love this—my mate was the one driving."

Diego nearly doubled over with laughter. He was laughing so hard his face turned red.

Alex had come up the stairs to see what their dad was carrying on about and now stood behind him in the doorway with a complete look of amazement on his face. "What the heck did you do to him? Geez, does he need CPR? He's turning colors."

Dash rolled his eyes. "I got hit by a car last night."

"Are you ok?" With a look of astonishment, Alex glanced down at their father, who was now bent over and hanging on to the doorframe for balance. "He's laughing about you getting hit by a car?"

"Yeah, by my mate."

Alex chuckled.

Dash grinned and shook his head, then looked back at their father. After about another minute of his guffawing, Dash was beginning to lose his patience. "DAD! It's not *that* funny!"

While Diego tried his best to rein in his laughter, Alex asked, "So where is this bad-driving maniac of a mate? Did you bring her back with you?"

Digging into his closet for a shirt, Dash took a deep breath and wondered how Alex would take the news. Only one way to find out. "I left her asleep in the small cabin to the west. Your friend Jill is my mate."

There was a brief silence. "Really?"

Dash stepped back out of the closet with a T-shirt in hand. "Yeah." He pulled it over his head and looked up at Alex, who was smiling. He noticed he'd gotten his father's undivided attention, as well. "You okay with that?"

Alex grinned. "Yep. She'll keep you in line; that's for sure. Although I kinda feel sorry for her."

His dad was smiling, too, only he was shaking his head. Dash directed his stare at him and frowned. "What?"

Diego continued to shake his head, and his smile widened. "Nothing. I was just thinking what a contrast the two of you make. Jill is so quiet and reserved. You are going to drive her up the wall." He gave a quick nod of emphasis, then turned and headed out the door. "Congratulations, son. I'll go tell your mother."

The brothers both turned to watch him go. Dash went to his dresser to find some socks and sat down on the edge of his bed to put them on.

"So, does she know?"

He looked up at his brother. "That we're wolves?"

"Yup."

Nodding his head, he pulled the other sock on and went to grab his shoes. "Well, she knows that I am. She doesn't know that I'm your brother."

"Why not?"

Dash came back to the bed and started putting on his hiking boots. "Didn't have time. I had a lot more on my mind than claiming your sorry ass as kin."

It got real quiet. He tied his shoe, then looked up. Alex was leaning on the doorjamb with a look of shock on his face.

"Geez! I was joking! I didn't really mean you were a sorry ass. I—"

Alex shook his head. "No, it's not that. Did you, uh...umm...you didn't, uh—"

"Fuck?"

Alex nodded.

Dash smiled. "Oh, yeah!"

Alex's eyes widened even more. "Really?"

He beamed. "Oh, yeah, really. What, you want details?" He stood up, ready to go downstairs and round up some breakfast for his mate and himself.

Alex scoffed. "Grow up! No, I don't want details. It's just that I don't think Jill has ever had sex before. She's never really said so, but I'm pretty sure she's a virgin. In all the years I've known her, she's never gone home with a man or had one back to her apartment unless it was me or another classmate, and that's to study together or just crash."

Dash dropped back onto the bed with a thud. His mouth hung open. "Are you sure?"

"Pretty sure. I guess it wasn't obvious."

"Hell, no, it wasn't obvious. Damn... She should have told me."

"Would it have made a difference?"

Dash looked at him. "Well, no, but I feel like I should have known." He should have, shouldn't he? A person only lost their virginity once, and while he was glad she'd lost hers with him, and he knew for a fact that she'd enjoyed herself, he could have slowed things down a bit. What if he'd hurt her, for crying out loud? He was going to have to have a discussion with her about keeping such important details from him.

"Don't tell her I told you. Maybe she didn't want you to know."

Dash scoffed. "What? Of course I'm going to tell her. She can't keep things like this from me! The woman is obviously going to have to be put in her place."

Alex laughed.

"What?"

Alex waved his hands. "Oh, no, if you haven't figured out by now that she's going to be the one calling the shots, I'm not going to burst your bubble." He turned quickly and walked out of the room.

What was that about? Certainly he was going to be the "boss" in his and Jill's relationship. Just who did Alex think he was? Busybody brothers. "Think they know everything."

He left his room, closed his bedroom door, and went downstairs to get breakfast.

His brother, parents, and little sister sat at the table, along with his cousin Brent. As he entered the kitchen area, Brent looked up and smiled. "So you found your mate? Or, uh, should I say, she found you?"

Dash rolled his eyes. "Yeah, yeah! She hit me with a car. So what? Yours got you snake-bit."

Brent got a faraway look on his face, and for a minute, Dash was sorry for reminding him of his lost mate, Rhett. But then Brent grinned. "Yes, she did. But at least she got bit, too." Everyone smiled at the memory, except Marisa, who was too young to remember Rhett. Her family took turns telling her the story.

Dash, Brent, Alex, and their other cousin, Adrian, had been around seven when they'd gone on a camping trip with their fathers and Michael, Rhett's father. Rhett, five, had stowed away in the back floorboards of Dash's uncle Emilio's car. To this day, Dash swore Emilio and Michael had known; how could they not? They would have smelled her.

After they'd gotten to the campsite, Rhett had popped out of the car—to the boys' disgust. No one had wanted to turn around and take her back, so she'd gotten to tag along on the fathers/sons outing. The boys had taken off together on an adventure, but unbeknownst to them, the hellion had followed. When they'd gotten back to camp, his uncle Emilio had asked where she was. After learning that she'd followed them, Brent had panicked and run off looking for her.

Dash and Adrian had just caught up to Brent when he'd found her. She was limping and had proclaimed herself to have been snake-bit. When the three boys had questioned her about the snake, she'd proudly shoved it into Brent's hand, saying, "This is the snake that bit me." The snake had then bit Brent. Fortunately, when Brent dropped the snake, Dash and Adrian had jumped back and avoided getting bitten, too.

"Yeah, but if I remember correctly, that wasn't a good thing at the time. 'Cause you had to share a hospital room with her."

"Tell me about it. She talked all damned night! Who'd have thought a five-year-old could talk that much?"

Everyone looked at Marisa. She looked up from her pancakes. "What?"

They all laughed. Then Dash went about gathering food to take back to the cabin. "Mom, do we have a picnic basket?"

As he returned to the cabin, Dash wondered how Jill would act when she saw him again. Would she regret their evening together? If she had been a virgin like Alex assumed her to be, she might. Why had she never had sex? Was she "waiting for the right guy"?

He grinned. Yeah, she'd better believe he was the right guy. In fact, he was the *only* guy! She was *his* from here on out. As Dash approached the cabin, he put a little extra spring in his step. He couldn't wait to make plans and start their future together.

He walked through the woods into the clearing where the cabin sat. The car was gone. Where was it? He rushed into the cabin, hoping that she'd just moved the car to the back, but he knew the truth—she'd left without saying goodbye. Had she even left a note? Maybe she'd had some sort of appointment this morning.

He looked everywhere in the cabin. There was no note. The blankets and pillows had been replaced on the bed. Everything had been straightened up like nothing had happened. He could still smell her and the scent of their lovemaking.

He wandered back to the main cabin at a much slower pace than he'd left it. Disappointment kept him from eating as he went; in fact, he was no longer hungry. Why would she just leave, after the night they'd shared? As far as he knew, she didn't know he was Alex's brother. She didn't even know how to contact him. His shoulders slumped at the thought.

As soon as he stepped into the main cabin, four sets of eyes zeroed in on him.

"Well, that was fast. Where's Jill?" Alex asked.

"She left me."

Chapter Six

Jill yawned and pulled into her apartment complex. She was still shocked at her own behavior. Not that she really regretted it, but...well, she just couldn't believe she'd done it. And *it.* She'd never have thought herself capable of losing control like that in a million years. She just wasn't a one-night-stand kind of girl, any way you sliced it.

What had she been thinking? Well, that was easy. She hadn't been thinking, not really. She'd let him overwhelm her senses and good judgment. He was just too incredible to be true. The man obviously had no problems getting women.

Okay, the werewolf thing was a little strange. But still. And his animalistic behavior had been very appealing. Were all men so raw and uninhibited in bed? Or on the floor, rather? She got butterflies in her belly just thinking about the night before.

She got out of the car and stiffly climbed the stairs to her apartment. She was dying to get out of the stupid, ruined genie costume and take a shower. Her stomach growled as she opened the door and went inside. Food or shower? It was a tough

decision, but she felt icky from the rain and
fluids. She was a little on the sore sid
activities, too, so she decided on the shov
bound to relieve at least some of her aches
was going to help the ache in her heart, but,
away quick enough. She hoped. *Like there is any way someone
like him would have stayed with a nerd like you!*

Jill scoffed at herself and stripped out of the now hideous
see-through costume. She stopped in front of the bathroom
mirror and took a long, thorough look at her body. She didn't
think she was an unattractive woman. She had a nice figure,
decent breasts, long legs. Guys liked long legs, didn't they? And
she—What in the...?

Jill looked down at her right breast. She had a hickey! Her
face heated at the sight. It was such a primal thing. Her pussy
clenched as she remembered how wild he'd been. Her nipples
hardened at the memory of his mouth on them. Groaning at her
own reaction to what amounted to a bruise, she grinned and
even chuckled. Well, one thing was certain—who'd ever
believe that she, the stick in the mud, would have a hickey?

Touching it lightly, she smiled some more. She had had the
best night of her life. Then she frowned. Why couldn't he be
more sedate? Less of a smartass? She was almost positive he was
a party animal. He just had that look, and oh, was she good at
spotting them. She'd been pretty good at avoiding that type ever
since her ex-best friend from second grade to high school had
gotten involved with a player and ruined their friendship.

She shook her head and stepped into the shower. She still
remembered Kristin's face when Jill had told her that John was
cheating on her. Kristin hadn't listened to a word she'd said
after that. She'd just started yelling, accusing Jill of being

when that had been the farthest thing from the truth. only had the pig tried to seduce *her*, but one night Jill had caught him red-handed in a bar, necking with not one but two women. But Kristin hadn't wanted to hear it, hadn't believed her, and she'd married him anyway. The last Jill had heard, Kristin and her two kids were back at home with her parents, waiting for the divorce to be final. *You can't save everyone, Jill.*

If nothing else, the experience had taught her two very important things. One, to stay away from guys like John. And two, men made much better best friends than women. Alex was a much better companion than Kristin had ever been. And he'd never accuse her of being jealous and catty. Heck, she really wanted to talk to Alex now. Maybe he could help her make heads or tails of her situation.

Jill's stomach growled again. She finished up her shower, got out, and dried off. She needed to get a bite to eat. Wrapping the towel around her, she went to the kitchen and made a peanut butter and jelly sandwich. Grabbing a soda, she returned to her living room and sat down on the couch.

Devon was like no one else she'd ever met. Heck, he was a werewolf! Even if he was a lothario, he still seemed like a nice person. Was it possible that he wasn't what he seemed in other areas, too? Surprisingly, he'd genuinely seemed to like her. He hadn't acted like he was just trying to pass the time by getting laid. Could she trust him? What would it be like to have and be with a man like that?

She flipped through channels as she ate and thought back on her night. Which was a mistake because her already over-sensitized body was not cooling down any. It was strung like a bow, begging for sexual release. Her body yearned for it and wouldn't take no for an answer. Geez, one night of sex had turned her into a nymphomaniac! Damn that man!

She shook her head and turned off the TV. It didn't matter; she'd left and… Heck, he'd left first—how was she to know he'd even intended to come back? More than likely he was as happy to go and get away from her as she was him. Okay, so she wasn't all that happy about getting away from him, but she knew it was for the best.

Going into the bedroom, Jill tossed her towel aside, trying to ignore her idiotic hormones and thoughts of Devon. Maybe she could catch up on the sleep she'd lost last night. Thank goodness it was the weekend. She pulled the covers back on her bed and climbed in.

Yet, tired as she was, she couldn't quit playing the "what if" game. There was just something about Devon that she couldn't let go of. Sure, technically, he'd been her first, but that wasn't it. She was a grown woman, and she could separate sex from love. Just because she hadn't done it before didn't mean she was like the sappy girls she'd hung out with in high school who fell in love with everyone they'd slept with. Sex was nice—she could feel herself getting wetter thinking about it—but she could make do with a vibrator, just like she'd done so far. It would last until she finished school and her residency; then she'd find a boyfriend.

She'd always been a very goal-orientated person. Her life was planned out, and she seldom deviated from her plans, so that was another big minus in the Devon column. He seemed to be a "fly by the seat of his pants" kind of guy, a "take things as they come" sort. She couldn't be like that! Everything had to be planned down to the smallest detail, then double-checked. There was a time and a place for everything, after all. Oh, sure, she'd wandered off the path last night, but that was a minor, insignificant thing. Really. Unless she ended up pregnant or diseased.

But she had no reason to think he'd lied about not carrying STDs; he'd offered the explanation without hesitation, and he'd been very frank about being a werewolf. So pregnancy loomed as a much bigger threat in her mind. However, based on what Devon had said about being able to smell if she were in heat... Her face warmed. Besides, according to her own calculations, it was just as unlikely. Not impossible, of course, but the timing wasn't right. Still, she couldn't believe she'd taken a huge risk like that! She was not a risk-taker, so she should just put Devon out of her mind. He could be classed as a definite risk—and not just to her sanity, but to her heart.

Jill had almost convinced herself that she had done the right thing by leaving, when the phone rang. She started, then grabbed the phone. "Hello?"

"Jill, it's Alex. Are you okay?"

"Yeah, I'm fine. I'm sorry, Alex. I tried to come to the party, I really did, but I got lost...honest."

Alex chuckled into the phone. "I know how you hate parties, but I do believe you. I just wanted to make sure everything is okay."

"Yes, everything is fine." Except she couldn't get one damned man out of her mind!

"Uh, ok, then. I'll see you, Monday?"

"Yeah, see you then. Bye, Alex."

"Bye, Jill."

She hung up and let out a sigh. Maybe if she got rid of the sexual tension, she could block Devon from her memory. Sitting up on her bed, she opened her nightstand drawer and grabbed her vibrator. She held it up and inspected it. It wasn't as big as Devon, but it had never let her down.

Jill grinned and reached in the drawer for the lube. She opened the cap to the lube, smearing a little on the toy and herself. She set the bottle aside and slid back down into the bed.

Closing her eyes, she tried to imagine Devon naked and above her. She slowly slid the vibrator inside. Oh, yes! That felt good. She pulled it out, then pushed in again. Her pussy clenched around it, and she set up a steady rhythm. Dev felt so good inside of her. His cock made her feel so full. Jill moaned and rolled onto her stomach.

She slipped the vibrator out of her greedy pussy and turned it on low. Pulling her knees beneath her, she put the toy against her clit. Ah! Almost as good as Dev licking her pussy. She moved her hips in a slow grind, mashing the toy against her clit. Pumping her hips up and down, she slid her clit across the vibrating wand as she pictured Devon under her. Her inner muscles throbbed, and she could feel herself growing wetter, the moisture dripping from her pussy.

He'd sucked on her nipples last night. One of her hands crept up and pinched one hard nub. She pulled and tugged, trying to simulate his hot mouth, while her hips continued to move. Letting go for a moment, she stuck her fingers in her mouth, then returned them to her nipple. The wetness felt even better, and as she moved her fingers around and tugged on the tip, she felt a shudder deep inside. She needed to be filled.

She rolled over...he had rolled her over and pulled her legs up over his arms, watching himself slide in and out of her. She pulled the vibrator away from her clit, spreading her legs wide, then plunged it into her pussy with one hand while fondling her clit with the other. Rubbing in a circular motion over the stiff little nub, she moaned loudly.

Her knees bent, her feet planted firmly on the bed for leverage, she tightly pressed the vibrator inside her and moved her hips. She rubbed her clit faster, pinching it in her fingers as she pumped up and down. It almost felt like it had when Devon had sucked on it. That dark head between her thighs had been a thing of beauty, and he'd watched her response as he nibbled and cherished her clit. His dark eyes had turned golden and practically glowed. He hadn't seemed able to keep from making little grunts of satisfaction in the back of his throat.

She continued to rub her clit and thrust even faster. Her stomach tensed, her body preparing for the ecstasy. She was so close to coming. Her inner walls grasped the toy hard, then convulsed around it. Her clit throbbed in pleasure. A picture of Devon as he came flooded her mind. He'd thrown that glorious mane of dark brown hair back, and his eyes had squeezed shut as he groaned and screamed her name.

"Devvvon!" Jill's eyes flew open as her orgasm peaked. Breathing raggedly, she stared up at the white ceiling. Gradually, she relaxed, her hips still slowly rocking back and forth. Finally, she slipped the vibrator out and turned it off. She suddenly felt so empty. It just wasn't the same as Devon, but at least she was sated enough to catch some sleep.

She put the toy on her nightstand and closed her eyes. She was almost asleep when his words from the night before came back to her. "...Werewolves, like real wolves, mate for life... You're my mate, Jill."

Jill sat up abruptly, her eyes wide. Was that true? What if it was? Did she want to take a chance? She covered her face with her hands and flopped back on the bed. "Oh, my God! What have I done?"

Chapter Seven

Their parents left the cleaning and locking-up to Dash and Alex, so the brothers rode back home together. As soon as they got on the road, Alex had called Jill at her apartment. She hadn't even mentioned him, just apologized to Alex for not showing up at the party. Talk about a huge letdown.

Alex had reassured him that he'd talk to her on Monday and asked him to let it alone for now. He didn't want to do that. What he really wanted to do was talk to her, make her understand that she was his and there was nothing she could do about it.

He sighed and closed his eyes, deciding to rest.

"Look at the bright side… You found your mate. And you got laid."

He chuckled. "Yeah, there is that. It was really nice."

"Yeah?"

"Yeah. But I'm not telling you about it." His eyes popped open. *That* was surprising. He *didn't* want to brag about it. He looked at Alex. "I actually don't want to tell you about her. What's with that?"

Alex shrugged. "I guess because she's your mate and you don't want other men thinking about her that way."

Dash let out a little growl at the thought. "*You* don't think of her that way, do you?"

Chuckling, Alex shook his head. "No, she's my friend. That's it, I swear."

"Good. You know, it's still weird that I don't want to tell you about it."

"Nah, it's not. Maybe you're just maturing."

He shook his head. "Nope, you are way more mature than me, always have been, and you still talk about your sexual conquests."

Alex snorted. "I don't have sexual conquests. I can't even remember the last time I got laid."

"That's just sad, bro."

"Well, hell, I have enough to worry about, what with getting my ass through school. When is the last time you had sex...last night excluded, of course. Because, believe it or not, I don't want to know; Jill's probably my *best* friend."

It was good to know that the thought of an intimate relationship with Jill didn't appeal to his brother. "Three weeks ago. Her name was Cindy." He grimaced. Somehow the memory just wasn't all that pleasant anymore. Thinking about it seemed somehow disrespectful to Jill. "Ugh! I just don't even wanna talk about it."

"That bad?"

"No. Actually it was pretty good. But I feel... I don't know...dirty. Like thinking about her is somehow being unfaithful to Jill. It's just—" Dash slapped his hand over his mouth and glanced at his brother.

Alex stared back, wide-eyed and grinning.

"Oh, no! Oh, no! Don't you dare repeat that! You'll ruin my reputation."

Alex's grin turned into a full-fledged smile. "Oh, yeah! This is good! So tell me…what's it worth to you? What will you do to keep me quiet?"

Dash laughed and shook his head. "I'll kick your ass; then I'll deny it. Maybe I'll tell the guys how long it's been since you had any."

Alex laughed. "Not that you *could* kick my ass, but, okay, I guess I'd better keep it to myself."

"Of course, I could just tell everyone that you didn't lose your virginity until you were nineteen."

"Hey! You were eighteen. It's not like that's much better!"

"I was seventeen."

"If I remember correctly, it was two days before your eighteenth birthday. So you were eighteen!"

"Seventeen."

Alex scoffed. "Whatever. You had the same parenting and lectures on responsibility as I did, so shut up!"

"Yeah, well, at least I actually have a sex life *now*. You can't remember the last time you had a piece of ass."

Alex was quiet for several minutes, so Dash closed his eyes and dropped his head against the seat again.

"Two months."

Dash opened his eyes and turned his head toward Alex. "What?"

"It was two months ago. That was the last time I had sex. It was after a party Jill and I went to on a double date. The guy she was with was a real jerk, just wouldn't take Jill seriously when she said no. She—"

"What?!" Dash sat up straight, narrowing his eyes.

"Chill…let me finish. She busted his nose. I punched him in the gut and threatened to beat his ass. He took off like a shot."

Dash rubbed his nose and smiled at the thought of Jill holding her own against some guy. She hadn't tried to bust *his* nose. He relaxed and let Alex finish his story.

"Anyway, we ended up leaving early, and after I dropped Jill off, my date…uh, Kara, asked me to go home with her. It was okay, but not all that memorable. She was nice, but way too clingy… You know, I envy you that."

"What? Jill isn't clingy. Look how fast she ran."

"No, the fact that you've found your mate. You don't have to worry about clingy women anymore. You don't have to deal with them wanting to marry you and have your babies."

Dash snorted. "Nope. Don't even have to worry about that from my mate, apparently."

"Give her time, bro. This is new to her. I'll talk to her Monday. She's probably a little freaked that she let you get so close. Jill doesn't have a lot of friends; she keeps to herself, and she has a one-track mind…to get through med school. She studies hard and makes great grades. It doesn't leave a lot of time for socializing, as you well know. From what I can tell, she's always been a bit of a bookworm. She'd rather curl up with a good book than party. I would imagine your carefree attitude is a little frightening to her."

"I'm not really as carefree as I pretend to be, and you know it."

"Yeah, I know it. But most people see you as you want them to. And you...well, let's face it; you take things as they come. Nothing gets you down for long."

"What's the point of that? If I can't change it, then I can't change it. It doesn't do any good to worry over it and get all depressed. Life is too short. Besides, Mom always tells me not to borrow trouble."

"She tells me that, too, but I worry more than you. I can't help it. My point is, you take things in stride, and you don't let much depress you. If something doesn't work for you, you just find another way and carry on. You don't shirk your responsibilities, but that easygoing personality of yours leads people to think you don't take life seriously. "

"But I do!"

"I know, and after Jill gets to know you better, she'll know, too."

"I want to call her."

"Of course you do, but I really think you should let it go for a bit. At least a week. Let me talk to her first."

Dash sighed and closed his eyes again. He must have fallen asleep, because the next thing he knew the car had stopped and Alex was shaking him awake.

"Wake up, sleeping beauty. We're home."

He blinked his eyes open. They were sitting in the driveway. He got out and followed Alex into the house.

His parents were lying on the couch together, watching TV. He smiled at the picture they made. With any luck, that would be him and Jill in a couple of years.

After dinner, Dash found himself on the back porch with his dad. When he opened the door, his father nearly fell out of his chair. Dash raised his brows. What the hell was he doing?

His dad met his eyes, then straightened up. He took a swallow of beer and nodded his head toward the lounger next to him.

Dash took a seat and sat silently for a few minutes. He was staring out over the pool when a bottle was thrust in front of him.

"Here. Have a beer. Looks like you could use one."

He grabbed the bottle, twisted the cap off, and glanced over at Diego, who was in the process of taking a drink of his own beer. "Thanks. What are you doing out here?" He took a swig.

"Hiding from your mom. She wants me to clean the kitchen."

Dash chuckled. Aha. "She's already cleaned it."

"Oh. Well, she wanted me to go to the mall with her after the kitchen was cleaned. And I *really* don't want to do *that.*"

Dash shook his head and grinned. "Hate to break it to you, but she knows where you are. She told me where to find you."

"Damn! That woman knows everything." His dad sighed and took a drink. "Well, did she say anything about me?"

"Nope. Just told me where you were."

"Good, maybe she's given up on the mall idea."

"Nope. But she and Marisa just left, so you're safe." Dash took another drink, then began peeling the label off the bottle.

"Whew! That was close. So, what's troubling you, son?"

"Nothing…everything…Jill."

"Ah."

Dash smoothed the label out and, thanks to the condensation, stuck it on his forehead. Then he lay back in the chair and relaxed.

Diego looked over at him, shrugged, and began to peel his own beer label. "Well, look on the bright side. You know how to find her again. It's not like she's going very far."

"Yeah, I know. But why in the world did she just take off? Why didn't she wait for me to get back?"

"Don't know. Women are strange. Take your mother, for example."

Dash closed his eyes and propped his beer bottle on his chest. "Mom isn't strange. Well, if she is, it's because she's had to put up with us. My birth mother, maybe, but not Mom."

"Well, I was thinking about Claire, but Vanessa is a good example, too. Your birth mother was so convinced that she'd have a werewolf mate that when she met your father—who was human—she didn't even consider marrying him. When she finally decided maybe she wasn't going to find a mate among the were males, he'd already married and moved back to Italy."

"Vanessa knew my biological father?"

"Sure she did."

Dash snorted. "Well, of course she *knew* him, at least a little. But...did you know him?"

"Well, I met him a few times. He seemed like a nice enough fellow, but he only spoke Italian. So, it wasn't like I could really converse with him, ya know? He was an old family friend of your mother's parents. I don't think he knew about your grandfather being a werewolf, though."

"Hmm. So, what happened to him?"

"He and his new wife died in a car accident in Rome a few days before you were born."

"Did she regret it? Vanessa, I mean. Did she regret not trying to build a relationship with him?"

"I don't know. In a way, I think she might have. You'd have to ask your mom. Vanessa talked to Claire about those sorts of things. She only came to me when it had something to do with you."

"You've always been my father…"

"Yup. I was even there when you were born. Claire was the first one to get to hold you."

Dash opened his eyes and turned his head toward his dad. "Really? You never told me that. I remember staying with you and Mom…a lot. Actually, I barely remember Vanessa. My childhood memories are of you and Mom and Alex. Why was I always with the two of you and not her?"

"She was really young, Devon, only sixteen when you were born."

He turned his head back and closed his eyes. "Why?"

"Why what?"

"Why did you raise some teenage girl's child?" He heard his dad sit up and felt his stare, but Dash kept his eyes closed.

"It wasn't like that, son. She was young and a little on the foolish side, but she did try. And she loved you enough to know she couldn't take care of you on her own. Her parents had just died, and she had no family here in the U.S.—"

He shook his head. "No, no, no… I don't mean it like that. I mean… I don't feel any ill will toward her. Hell, I even honored her by keeping her last name, when all I ever wanted to be was a Hernandez."

"Son, you *are* a Hernandez! Claire and I couldn't love you more if you were our biological child. You know that, don't you?"

He smiled. He did know it. He'd never felt second-best to Alex and Marisa. His parents had never treated him like he wasn't their flesh and blood.

The sound of the chair creaking told him Diego was lying back down on his chair. "If you must know, I…we couldn't help ourselves. After you were born and the nurse brought you in…Claire was holding you, resting you on her stomach—she was pregnant with Alex then—and Alex immediately protested by kicking." He chuckled. "I took you to keep you from getting beat up. And I…you…you looked up at me and…"

It got really quiet for several minutes. Dash peeked at his dad. "And?"

Diego cleared his throat. "And it's just really hard to explain. You'll understand when you have a kid of your own."

"But I wasn't your kid."

"Oh, yes, you were. From that very moment on, you were mine."

Dash was silent for several minutes while he digested that. He felt tears spring to his eyes. He squeezed them shut and smiled. Finally, he asked, "What about Mom—why is she strange?"

Dad chuckled. "She wouldn't marry me until she got pregnant."

Dash's eyes opened wide. "What?! Are you saying that she was pregnant with Alex before you got married?"

"Yup! Wouldn't believe that wolves and human had compatible DNA. I asked her to marry me, and she said not until after she knew she could have children. She just wouldn't take my word for it that my mother was human. Sheesh! She wanted to make sure she could have kids. Then, after the fact, she bitched at me for months. Said she didn't mean *now*. Like, how in the hell was I supposed to know she didn't mean right then?"

"What are you two still doing out here?"

Dash jumped at his mom's voice, making his beer fall over. "Shit! That's cold!" He sat up abruptly and fell out of the chair.

Diego looked down, then burst into laughter.

Claire closed the back door as quietly as she'd opened it and came to stand in front of him. "Are you okay, honey?"

Dash brushed beer off his shirt. "Yeah, I'm okay. Next time, will you make some noise before you sneak up on us? Geez, you 'bout gave me a heart attack."

"Sorry. We just got back; the mall was closed already." She sighed and sat down in Diego's lap. "So, what are you two talking about?"

His dad leaned forward and nipped her neck. She shrugged him off and stared at Dash expectantly.

"We were talking about women."

"Ahhh. Jill?"

"Well, not exactly, but in a roundabout way…yeah."

"Umm. Do you know what I think?"

Dash could hear the smile in his dad's voice as he mumbled, "No, but I'm sure you're going to tell him."

"Yes, I am. Quit biting me, Diego—"

"I'm not biting; I'm nibbling. There's a difference."

She groaned. "As I was saying, I think you should give her some space and let her come to you."

"What?!" he and his father asked in unison.

"Haven't you ever heard the saying: if you love something, set it free—"

Diego snorted. "Love doesn't really play into it. They just met."

"Well, she's his mate; of course he loves her."

"He just met her!"

"So?"

"So!"

Dash grinned, wondering if he should step in. Something told him that Dad was about to put his foot in his mouth. Yeah, what the hell! He'd hate to see the old man sleep on the couch. He cleared his throat.

Both of them looked at him.

He grinned. "I wouldn't exactly call it love, Mom. I mean, it's pretty obvious that it will be, and, well, I can already tell that I like her...a lot. But, well...like Dad said, I just met her."

Diego was nodding his agreement. His mom made a little humph noise.

"So you're telling me that you don't care whether you have a relationship with her or not?"

He practically growled. "No! That's not what I'm saying at all. I'm *going* to have a relationship with her. There's no question about that. She's *mine!*"

"Uh-huh. That's what I thought. As I was saying, I think you need to let her come to you. Let her feel like she has some control over the situation. Because I know you men! You're all aggressive and overbearing. And you try to walk all over your mates."

"I do not!"

"No, we don't!"

He and his dad protested simultaneously. Claire held up her hands. "Look, all I'm saying is, I think you should let her come to you. If you try and bulldoze her, she's going to resist. She's a strong woman, and she likes to be in control. I can tell that just by the few times I've met her. And if I know you as well as I think I do, she *will* come to you. After all, you are *my* son, so how could she resist you?"

Dash groaned and dropped his head in his hands. "That's the problem, Mom! She can't come to me; she doesn't know how to reach me."

His mother chuckled. "Well, then, I guess it's a good thing that your brother knows both of you, isn't it?" With that, she stood up, kissed Diego on the lips, and walked back into the house.

They both watched her go.

His dad was the first one to break the silence. "Well, I for one think you should get her address from Alex and go over there first thing in the morning."

The back door opened again, and the porch light came on. Alex stood silhouetted in the doorway. "I agree with Mom. Jill likes to call the shots. It will just scare her off if you go chasing after her. Hell, the whole werewolf thing would be enough to make me reluctant...I mean, if I didn't know already." He ran a hand through his hair. "Look, I'll let her know who you are...to me, and tell her how to get in contact with you. I'm sure she will. It seems to me that the whole mate thing works both ways. The women might not *know* like we do, but they seem to have the same instant attraction...or so I've gathered."

Dash glanced over at their dad to see how he was taking Alex's support of Claire's idea and noticed for the first time the beer label that was stuck to Diego's head, too.

He laughed and looked back at his brother. Alex smiled, then shook his head.

Diego motioned to Alex. "Join us."

Alex shook his head. "No way! I have a rule about conversing with drunks by large bodies of water."

Dash looked at Diego. Diego looked at him. They smiled at each other, then jumped up and ran toward Alex.

Alex's eyes widened, and he spun around in the doorway. He was too late. His dad grabbed his left arm and his brother grabbed his right.

As Alex flew through the air toward the pool, Dash yelled, "We aren't drunk!"

The next thing Dash knew, he was in the cold water right alongside Alex. He came up spitting water to find their father with his hands on his knees, laughing his ass off.

Chapter Eight

Jill closed the door to her apartment and dropped her backpack on the floor. What a day! A septicemic patient, a case of ruptured appendix, some motor vehicle accidents, and Devon! She couldn't get him out of her mind. The more she thought about it, the more she was afraid she'd really screwed up by not finding a way to contact him. The what-ifs just kept popping up.

And then there were the inconvenient sexual fantasies. It was really hard to concentrate on a clinical lecture when her whole body was begging for his touch. It would figure that after one night with him, she was already a sex addict. And sadly, she had a sneaking suspicion that no other man would ever measure up to Devon.

On top of all that, there was the whole werewolf thing. Someone really should study him. She was excited just thinking of the possibilities and what it could mean in the medical world. Not that she wanted him kept in a cage and stuck with needles constantly, but...

Jill ran her hands down her face and leaned against the door. She had a pediatric exam tomorrow. She needed to get some food and start studying. *Damn Devon!* And where was Alex? He was supposed to come over and study with her.

Men! Who needed them? Okay, that really wasn't fair. Alex hadn't done anything wrong. He wasn't even late, and she'd just gotten home herself.

Knock, knock, knock.

"Ack!" She jumped away from the door. Deep, masculine chuckling came from the other side.

"Damn it, Alex! That wasn't funny." She opened the door and looked up into his smiling face. "I just got in and was leaning on the door when you scared the crap out of me."

"Sorry." He didn't sound at all repentant as he came in and set a duffel bag and his backpack next to hers. He handed her a small white sack.

Jill took an eager whiff. Hamburgers and fries. Yum! "Oh, you're forgiven."

He chuckled again and shut the door. "You got sodas?"

"Yes, and I think there's some ice cream for dessert. Maybe I can scrounge up some stuff to make us a sundae." She took the bag of food to the kitchen and got out two cans of soda from the refrigerator.

When she came back to the living room with two trays stacked with their assorted food items, Alex was on the couch, flipping through channels. Seeing her, he turned off the TV, set aside the remote, and got up to help her.

"Thanks."

"No problem." He sat back down and unwrapped his burger. "So, how was your day?"

Jill sighed, then sat down in the chair cater-cornered to the sofa where Alex was sitting. "Okay, I guess."

Alex took a bite of hamburger and studied her as he chewed. When he finished, he took a swig of his drink and set it down. "Well, that doesn't sound okay. You wanna talk?"

Did she? Heck, if anyone could make sense of this thing with Devon, it was probably Alex. He might not date a lot, but he still had more experience at it than she did, so she nodded as she ate a fry.

While she chewed, she tried to figure out where to start. She couldn't tell him about the werewolf part, of course—he'd think she'd lost it—but maybe he could help her anyway. Was it possible that he knew Devon and how to get in touch with him?

NO! She needed to get Devon out of her head. Maybe talking to Alex would get Devon off her mind "I met this guy on the way to your Halloween par—Why are you smiling and nodding your head?"

"You met my brother."

She blinked. What? "No, your brother's name is Dash, and his last name is Hernandez. This guy said his name was—"

"Devon Rigotti?"

Whoa! Jill blinked again. "Uh, yeah."

Alex looked awkward. "Dash is...uh...Devon is Dash. What I mean is, Dash is Dev's nickname. Our dad gave it to him on account of Dev is always *dashing* about."

"*What?*"

Alex grimaced, nodding his head as he took another bite of his meal.

She slumped back in her chair and took a minute to absorb the unexpected news. Good God above, she'd slept with her best friend's brother. Alex and his brother were really close, so he probably knew every tiny detail. She felt the blood rush to her face and hoped that Alex didn't notice. "But why isn't his last name Hernandez? How could I not know he's your brother?"

"Dash said he told you that he's adopted."

"Yes…he did." Jill sat up. "How come you never mentioned that your brother was adopted?"

He shrugged. "It never came up. To be honest, I've known him my whole life and never think of him that way. He's always been…well…he's just always been my brother. The only time it ever comes up is when someone notes the difference in our last names."

"Why doesn't he have the same last name, if he was adopted?"

He brought his hand to his mouth, burped, then shrugged again. "Excuse me. It's kind of a long story. He pretty much lived with us ever since I can remember. He used to share my room and stuff, because his mother was very young, not to mention very sick—" He shook his head.

"I don't know… Anyway, when she died of leukemia when we were about eight or so, not much changed really. He got his own room, and then at sixteen or so, Dad gave him the decision to choose whether to keep Rigotti or go by Hernandez. I think he was used to the name and that's why he didn't change it. It must have hurt our dad's feelings, but he seemed to understand."

Geez, talk about feeling left in the dark. She didn't know whether to be relieved that she now knew where to find Devon, or to be pissed because he hadn't told her who he was. Okay, he had told her who he was, just not that he was Alex's brother.

She tried to think of anything that would have made her guess who he was. Jill groaned.

"He knew my name!" He'd known her name, and she hadn't told him. "Why, that low-down, dirty dog. He knew who I was the whole time, didn't he?" *Dog? Wolf!* Her eyes widened. "Oh, my God!" Did Alex know? Jill clamped a hand over her mouth and met Alex's eyes.

"I know what you're thinking. Yes, I'm one, too."

She gasped. "Really?" This was absolutely unreal. She'd known him for three years now, and she'd never suspected. How many other closet werewolves did she know? Were his whole family werewolves, too? Devon hadn't mentioned his mother or sister when they'd talked about shifting, only his brother, father, and cousins.

She stood up and walked around Alex, studying him. How could she not have known *all* this time?

"Really. It's a genetic trait in my father's family, just as it was in Dash's birth mother's family."

"Show me."

"Right now?"

She nodded. She really needed to know she wasn't imagining everything. It just seemed so incredible. The whole thing seemed surreal.

He sighed and got up, then walked behind the couch, pulling his shirt over his head as he went. "Okay, you're not going to freak out and scream or anything, are you?"

Jill shook her head and watched as Alex stripped. She couldn't decide whether to be shocked, be embarrassed, or just admire the view, so she just stared and tried to remain clinical and objective.

Alex shucked off his pants and boxers, then stood completely naked.

Wow! Okay, so much for being the cool, professional doctor. The man was gorgeous! Was she blushing? God, she hoped not.

Alex's chuckle snapped her head up to meet his eyes. "Jill, you're pink."

"Shit! I was trying to remain analytical. But, dang, Alex, it's a little weird, you know. It's not like I have men stripping in my living room all the time. Especially not my best friend."

He smiled, and his eyes seemed to grow warmer. "You're my best friend, too...well, aside from Dash and my cousins, but they don't really count; they're kin, after all."

She grinned and shook her head. "Okay, this is very touching and all, but will you get on with it? As I said, much as I'd like to sit here and admire the scenery, you're my best friend and...it's strange!"

He laughed and held up a hand. "Point taken. Here goes— Oh, wait. Do you want me to come around so you can see? I'll end up on all fours before I'm completely shifted."

Jill nodded. Her mind was already revved up and focused on the upcoming change. She was going to witness something not very many people knew about, and she wanted to see his every move and take in all the details. She knew without a doubt that he'd never allow her to videotape him. More's the pity.

Alex stood there for several seconds with his eyes closed, breathing deeply. Suddenly, his mouth dropped open and fangs became visible. His hands flexed, and his nails began to grow. When his eyes snapped open, Jill took in a startled breath. Instead of a warm brown, they were now amber...and the whites of his eyes had shrunk. They had that reflective quality that dogs' eyes had.

The hair on his arms grew longer, and soon the rest of his body hair followed, including that on his head. As he dropped to his knees, his nose became longer and his face narrower, until she was staring at a canine head.

She watched in fascinated horror. The process was almost the reverse of what she had seen when Devon had changed to human. It was absolutely unbelievable and amazing! And it definitely called for more research. As she watched his arms and legs contort, she wondered if Alex would let her do tests on him.

His wolf form finally stood before her, waiting and watching. He cocked his head in apparent question, much as she'd seen Dev do.

Jill smiled and approached him slowly. She wasn't scared of him, but she was cautious. Who knew what he could remember? Did he still know who she was? Dev had said that he couldn't retain human thought processes, but that his brother could. Did that mean this wolf was essentially still Alex in his thoughts and memories?

"Alex?"

The wolf head bobbed once. "Can I come closer? Can I touch you?"

His head bobbed again, and he walked toward her outstretched hand.

She dropped to her knees as he met her in the center of the room. She immediately started examining him, looking closely at his ears, his back, his legs. Holding his muzzle in her hand, she turned his head side to side, then looked him over from head to tail and every place in between. She got back up. "Wow! This is awesome! Can I get my stethoscope?"

He sighed and flopped down on his stomach, but dipped his head once.

When she returned, he stood up and allowed her to listen to his heart and lungs. When he even took a few deep breaths for her like a human patient would do, Jill giggled. "I don't suppose you'd let me draw blood, would you?"

Alex shook his canine head and began to shift back. She stood and watched as he reverted to his usual form the way Devon had done, only faster. Within a few seconds, Alex pushed himself up with his hands and knees to his full six-foot-four height, then walked back behind the couch.

"Well?" He asked as he pulled his boxers back on.

"That is... WOW! Alex, that is so freaking incredible!" Her mind raced with more questions. "Do you retain your thoughts? I mean, of course you do, but are you *you* in that form? How come you changed back faster than Dev...er, Dash? Have you or Dash done any testing on yourselves? What is—"

Alex pulled his shirt over his head, laughing. "Whoa! Wait a minute. Slow down! I should have known you'd see this as yet another puzzle that has to be solved. Can we finish eating first?"

She nodded and went back to her chair. Taking a bite of her cold hamburger, she chewed quickly and waited impatiently.

With a huge smile on his face, Alex shook his head and resumed his seat. "Take a drink. Have a few fries. I'm not going anywhere. I'm crashing here, remember?"

She grinned and did as he suggested, still eating quickly and wishing that Alex would do the same. She had tons of questions.

Heck, she'd forgotten all about her problems with Dev…Dash. She sighed and slouched in her chair.

Devon! She still had to figure out what to do about him. With her newfound knowledge that he was Alex's brother, Devon was even more appealing. Oh, sure, he was in trouble for not telling her who he really was, but before she had ever met him, she'd already had a bit of a crush on him from Alex's descriptions.

She sat back and let the memories of Alex's countless stories about him and Devon sink in. She reconciled those tales with the man she'd met and knew that Dev was every bit the honest, friendly man she'd thought him to be. She also knew he was indeed a bit of a wild man. And now he was so much more.

"Yoo-hoo! Earth to Jill! Where'd you go? Why the sudden silence?"

"Dash."

"Ah! Is there anything I can help with?"

"Yeah, I think so. Finish eating and we'll talk. If you don't mind, that is."

"Not at all. We'll talk until you've got it figured out. Of course, we do still need to study. But, hell, we've pulled all-nighters before. I don't see why we can't do it again."

Jill grinned. Yes, they had stayed up all night before exams countless times. And after the exams, they had both crashed at her apartment, which was much closer to school than his home, and usually stayed there until Alex's mom called, looking for him around dinner time. "Thanks, Alex."

They finished eating in silence, Jill once more lost in her thoughts of Devon, and Alex apparently lost in his meal. After they'd both finished, Alex cleaned up, insisting that she relax in the living room. While he was in the kitchen, she took the time to gather her thoughts, formulate more questions.

Alex joined her on the sofa a few minutes later. "First off, yes, I'm me in wolf form. I have no problem remembering who, what, when, where, and why. Dash, like some of the other wolves, has more of a problem. When he's a wolf, he has to keep reminding himself what he's doing because he gets too caught up in the freedom of being one. On the night of a full moon, he completely loses his human thoughts...the change just overwhelms him. Once he shifts back, he usually doesn't remember anything from that night. However, I remember, as do my cousins." He brushed a hand through his hair. "Dash's genes aren't expressed quite as strongly as ours are. That's also why I can change back and forth faster than he can. He and I haven't done any research ourselves. We know things from our father and other pack members, but we've never done much beyond that because, to be honest, we never thought to do so. This is just who we are. Wolves don't get sick, and we heal very quickly when injured."

She shook her head. "No, not like that. I mean research to find out how things work? What makes you change? To help humans! Alex, if you don't get sick and you heal so quickly, maybe something intrinsic about you can be duplicated and be beneficial for humans!"

A teasing smile spread across his face. "And put myself out of a job?" Then he became very serious. "Actually, Jill, I've never thought of it. Shallow of me, I know, but it never crossed my mind. Maybe we can look into it together, but for right now, what else do you want to know? Or do you want to talk about Dash?"

Jill thought for a minute. She had tons of questions still. But the most important one was about Dash—and her. "Tell me about mates. Dash said I'm his and that wolves mate for life. What did he mean?"

Alex grinned. "So he *did* tell you?"

She nodded.

"We do mate for life—one mate, our soul mate." Alex forestalled her protest. "I know it sounds like romantic bullshit, but it's true. We all have a mate, and we know them by instinct, but I don't know much more than that. I haven't found my mate yet, so everything I know is hearsay, but my father, my grandfather, my uncle...all the mated male wolves I know have said it's true. I clearly see it with my dad. He loves my mom, and he's very...er...hmm, how do I put this? He seems very possessive where she's concerned, but they're also the best of friends." He chuckled. "They're also forever embarrassing us by kissing and touching and that sort of stuff, but mating goes far beyond that. It's like there's a deeper connection, a more primal one. He needs her. It's—"

"I know." And oddly, she did. She could see that connection Alex spoke of whenever she saw Diego and Claire together. "I've seen how your parents look at each other. It's obvious to anyone who meets them. I've always envied you that they're so much in love. It's almost like they can see what the other is thinking. The first time I met them, and they started speaking for each other..." She smiled at the memory. "It was...well, it was really cool! My parents were never like that. They got along okay, but they weren't anything like yours."

Alex's eyes twinkled. "Yeah. They are something, aren't they?"

"Yes, they are. It would be nice to have a marriage like that."

"You will."

She blinked. Would she? "I don't know, Alex. I just...well, I have to get through school and internship before I can even think about getting into a relationship. And Dev—Dash—he's so different from me. He's so...so...he's... Well, he's used to going out and having a good time. And—oh, hell! He just doesn't seem the type to want a commitment!"

Alex had started to shake his head before she'd even finished. "You should have seen him when he came back from the cabin and you were gone. He was crushed. Jill, he's playful and he kids around, but you have to understand—things just seem to fall into a logical place for Dash. He can't change the circumstances of his birth, and he wouldn't try even if he could. His philosophy is that things are meant to be this way. He sees his life from the point of view that he was meant to be a Hernandez. In that, he's a lot like our dad; he deals with life as it comes. But that doesn't mean he isn't responsible. Hell, he's in vet school! C'mon, Jill, you know how hard it is to get in; it's even harder than admission to med school. And he's on the *A* honor roll! He takes his responsibilities very seriously; he just does it with good humor."

Jill let Alex's words soak in. She'd known how smart and how family-oriented Dash was from Alex's tales through the years. And he was right; someone who wasn't responsible and goal-oriented would never even get into veterinary school, much less be on the *A* honor roll. But after meeting him, it was a little overwhelming.

Plain and simple, she was scared. She had not expected to have such strong feelings for anyone, much less someone she'd just met. A relationship had always been an afterthought—after college, after med school, after internship. She sighed.

"As your best friend, I'm going to give you some unsolicited advice. And I want you to know I have your best interests at heart."

"I know you do. But you're also biased. He's your brother."

Alex chuckled. "Yeah, but this is sound advice."

"All right, let's have it then."

"Stop thinking! You don't have to dissect everything. Just this once, ignore your overdeveloped brain and go with your heart!"

Chapter Nine

Tuesday afternoon, Dash was lying on the couch, watching TV and waiting for Alex to call. He'd finished his last class and gone straight to his apartment. While he knew that Alex and Jill had a major exam today, that should have been over hours ago, and he was quickly running out of patience. Why hadn't Alex called? He was supposed to have talked to Jill.

He sat up, rubbed his face, and took a deep breath. "That's it!" He couldn't wait any longer. Against his better judgment, he'd waited three whole days. He had vowed to wait until the weekend, but he just couldn't do it. He was going home, and he was going to talk to his mate. Alex would give him directions to Jill's apartment whether he liked it or not, and he was determined that he and Jill were going to come to an agreement. There was no way she was getting away from him.

He turned the TV off, stood up, and tossed the remote onto the couch. Grabbing his keys off the counter, he headed for the door. He flung it open, stepped out, and ran right into someone.

"Oww!"

"Jill!" Dash quickly grabbed her arm to steady her and stepped back. His mouth dropped open. What was she doing here? "Are you all right?"

She blinked up at him. "Hi."

He stood there for several seconds, unable to believe that she was really there on his doorstep. She'd come to him. He smiled and pulled her into his arms.

"Oof! Devon, I—"

His mouth dropped to hers, and he took advantage of her surprise by thrusting his tongue in. She tasted so good! His body responded immediately, his cock filling with blood so fast, he'd swear it was making him lightheaded. God, he'd missed her.

She moaned softly and returned his ardor as he maneuvered them into the apartment. He shoved the door closed, then backed her against it, pinning her body with his. He knew his eyes had changed already because they were unfocused, making him blink several times to clear his vision. His gums began to itch, and he broke their kiss for fear of hurting her when his teeth lengthened. Staring down into her flushed face, he caught a whiff of her arousal, and his canines extended abruptly.

She dropped her purse off her shoulder and blinked up at him. She'd noticed his teeth. A slow smile spread across her face, and then she reached up and caressed his cheek. Pulling his head toward hers, Jill licked his lips.

He lost it. Groaning low in his throat, he ground his erection into her hip and devoured her mouth. He kissed her until he could barely breathe; then he made his way down her neck.

Her hands slid into his hair, holding him tight. She was panting as hard as he was, and her heart was pounding. He stopped nibbling long enough to grab the hem of her shirt and whisk it over her head.

"Ahhh. Dash."

Her lust-filled voice was music to his ears. His lips greedily moved down her chest while he unhooked her bra. When her beautiful breasts tumbled free of their confinement, he sucked one already tight nipple into his mouth and started working on undoing her jeans.

By the time Dash had her pants off and her panties around her ankles, Jill had lost what little restraint she'd had. She'd planned on talking to him before she made love to him, but that kiss had really fired her blood. She had to have him. *Right now.* Her body had been screaming for his since they'd first met. In the past three nights, she'd been strung so tightly that she'd had to take matters into her own hands several times. She'd even masturbated in the shower while Alex was asleep on the couch, for heaven's sake!

Jill got to work on his pants. He gasped, but didn't try to stop her eager fingers as she unsnapped his jeans. She had to see that glorious cock. She had to make sure she hadn't dreamed it.

"Here, let me help." Dash pulled his shirt off.

"Go sit on the couch. We have to get your shoes off."

Dash practically ran to the couch and sat down. He immediately pulled off one shoe, then the other. By the time Jill stepped out of her panties and made it to the couch in front of him, he had his pants down around his feet. He stood up, and his gorgeous cock bobbed with every move he made.

When she stepped in front of him, he dropped to his knees. His eyes gave her body such a thorough inspection, she could practically feel him touching her. Her belly contracted at the possessiveness she read in his gaze. No way was she going to let him take control of the situation. If he did, she'd get caught up and let his lust sweep her away, just as she had at the cottage.

She sank to her knees in front of him, running her hands over his shoulders. His body was amazing. She'd always thought Alex was sexy, but he had nothing on his brother. Dash was perfection, as far as she was concerned. She wanted so badly to taste him, to take him in her mouth. Even though she'd never done it before, he made her want to.

He reached for her, but she caught his hands and shook her head. "No, please. Please let me..." He groaned a sound of surrender and closed his eyes in consent.

Jill's hands shook with excitement. She trailed her hands across the thick muscles of his chest, through the soft hair there. He had just the right amount of both, not too much, but enough to make him appear very masculine. His stomach was well defined and tanned. His naturally dark skin was beautiful, but he had bathing-suit lines, proving that he'd been in the sun. His stomach quivered as her fingers trailed down the path of hair leading to his cock. She was completely fascinated. She leaned over and dragged her tongue across his skin and was rewarded with a whimper.

His fingers combed gently through her hair, and the head of his cock nudged her chin. It was so warm. She pulled back slightly, studying him. The darker color of his cock contrasted with the paler skin on his hips. It stood out from a nest of brown curls, thick and veiny. He was quite a bit thicker than her vibrator and maybe a bit longer, too. No wonder she'd felt so full, so stretched.

As she watched, a pearly bead of precome gathered on the tip. She leaned forward and flicked her tongue across the head, tasting him.

He sucked in a breath. His fingers tightened in her hair. "Ahh, Jill...suck it. Put your mouth on me."

She glanced up into his already amber wolf eyes, suddenly unsure of herself. "I've never done this before. I'm not really sure what to do."

He smiled tenderly at her and dragged his hand across her cheek. "Anything you want, darlin'...do anything you want."

It was all the encouragement she needed. He didn't expect her to be a siren. She knew she could improvise; she'd read plenty of erotic romances and sex manuals, and it wasn't like she didn't know the male physiology and anatomy.

She flicked her tongue across the round tip several times before licking down one side, then up the other. His hands tensed in her hair, boosting her confidence. She angled her head to the side and covered his shaft with her mouth, sucking tentatively, then licking. The texture was so unique; it was like a soft caress to her lips. He was firm, yet his skin felt as soft as rose petals there. When her mouth closed over the head of his cock, he hissed, making her feel ten feet tall. She reached for his testicles, wanting to know if they were as smooth as the rest of him. She might not know exactly what she was doing, but it was clear she wasn't the only one enjoying her explorations.

As she set a steady rhythm with her mouth, she continued to play with his testicles, rolling them around in her hand, squeezing gently. Her hand slid under him, to his perineum, then up to stroke his butt. She raked her nails down his cheeks lightly. He seemed to like it, so she got bolder, remembering what he'd done to her and something she'd read in an erotic romance novel.

Coating her index finger with saliva, Jill slid her finger over his anus.

He tensed, his hands stilling in her hair. "Jill?"

"Shh, trust me."

Dash didn't know what to think. She'd already admitted she didn't know what she was doing, and now she wanted him to trust her? It actually felt pretty good, but...well, he just didn't know how far she was going to go, and he didn't think he really wanted to find out. Sure, women seemed to enjoy it, but...

Her slick finger smoothed across his perineum again, then back across his anus. "Ahhh..." It really did feel pretty good. And, oh, Lord, what was she doing with her throat?

As she got halfway down his shaft, she made swallowing motions with her throat. If she'd just go a little further down... "Jill, darlin', try to take more."

She did. The head of his cock lodged in the back of her throat, making her gag a little, just as she slid her finger inside of him.

He gasped at the sudden invasion. Dash knew he should protest, but just as he was about to, she did something wonderful—she touched his prostate, making him shiver. God, her inquisitive nature was going to kill him. Was she always going to be up to trying new things? On him? That was a scary, yet somehow arousing, thought.

She did it again, slid against that spot. Ahhh. His cock slid out of her mouth, and her gaze met his. His fingers tightened in her hair as she continued to stroke his prostate. His cock jerked, drawing her attention. She licked away a drop of ejaculate, then looked back up at him, a knowing grin on her lips. His balls drew up tighter. He was so close. Who would have thought he'd enjoy this so much? His stomach and his legs tensed; he was so close. "Jill," was all he could manage before he climaxed.

She must have understood, because her mouth covered him. She kept his cock in her mouth, sucking as he came.

"Oh, fuck! Oh, yeah! Oh, darlin'! Yessss..."

When Dash stopped seeing stars and his body finally relaxed, he looked down to see his mate grinning widely at him. Her knowing smirk was too much; the little wench needed to be taken down a few notches. He growled, then took her to the floor.

Pushing her legs open, he buried his face in her pussy and inhaled her intoxicating scent, making her giggle. Dash's senses were flooded with the sweet smell of her. He pulled back to look. God, she was beautiful, so plump and slick with arousal. If he were still seeing in color, he knew she'd be a beautiful pink.

The little nub at the top of her sex was erect and begging for attention. He locked gazes with her and bent slowly, making her anticipate his touch. When he finally took her hard clit into his mouth and suckled, she shrieked. Her legs tensed under his palms, and her hips lifted toward him.

Oh, yeah, he had her right where he wanted her. She tasted so good, he could do this for hours. He dropped his attention to the tiny, seeping entrance below, thrusting his tongue in.

She began to pant and squirm, trying to get closer. He held her open and at his mercy, fucking her with his tongue. Her heavy breathing and restless movements were arousing him all over again. He could feel his cock hardening against his stomach and the hairs on his arms beginning to grow. Before her, he had never had such a hard time keeping his wolf nature in check. She made him want to bite and growl and rut in her like the animal he was.

"Devon…"

He growled against her and moved back up to her clit, nipping it.

"Oh, God! Devon, please…"

How could he resist such pretty begging? He found her snug, saturated little hole with his finger as he sucked her clit in rhythmic pulls. He hooked his fingers toward her stomach, searching for her G-spot.

She screamed and flooded his hand with her orgasm. Dash had never been more turned on in his life. He barely registered the claws on his hands as he raised himself and thrust into her hot, spasming sheath. In seconds, he was screaming out his release with her.

Jill grinned against his shoulder. She'd watched his hands, eyes, and teeth go back to normal as he lay panting next to her in the aftermath of their lovemaking. It really was exciting knowing that he lost all control with her and that he had trusted her with such a monumental secret. But she'd also noticed that he'd tried to hide his teeth from her and wondered why. Did he think she couldn't accept that part of him? She'd have to set him straight, and maybe while she was at it, she could talk him into allowing her to do some testing on him. But at the moment she had more important things to discuss…like their relationship.

She chuckled. She'd come to talk to him, and they'd barely even said hello to each other. Actually, *he* hadn't said hello. Still, sex as a welcome had been pretty damn good.

Dash raised his eyebrows and looked down at her with a smile on his handsome face. "What?"

"You haven't even said hello to me."

His smile widened. "Hello, darlin'." His head dropped back to the carpet, and he closed his eyes.

She scooted up and stared at him. He was so handsome as he lay there naked, appearing completely relaxed. Actually he looked...half asleep? She reached over and nudged him. "Dash?"

His eyes popped open. "Huh?"

She shook her head, then gave him a quick peck on the lips. "I came here to talk."

"Okay, you talk; I'll listen." He closed his eyes again.

Jill chuckled, then straddled his waist, leaning down to lie on his chest and gaze at him. "Oh, no, you don't! I want your undivided attention."

He smiled, but didn't open his eyes. "Remind me the next time we do that to do you first. After I come, I want to sleep. I feel like someone shot me with a tranquilizer dart. And you...you are like a damned hummingbird. Where the hell did you get all this energy, wench? I know darn well that you came."

She groaned. "Dash—" Warning was clear in her tone of voice.

His eyes snapped open, and he sighed, obviously resigned to talking. "All right, darlin', what is there to talk about? I think your coming here pretty much says it all. Well, except for when the wedding is."

Jill sat up. "Wedding? What wedding?"

His face paled and became blank as he sat up, too. "*Our* wedding."

"Dash, we can't get married. We just met."

"We're mates."

She nodded. "I know. Alex explained it to me, but we still can't get married. Not now. We both have to finish school."

"Why do you have to be so damned practical?"

She blinked. "Because I am."

He grinned. "And it's really admirable—in most cases. But not in this one. There is no reason why we shouldn't get married. Come on, throw me a bone, darlin'." His smile faded. "Don't you want to marry me?"

"Give me some time…please? This is really new to me. I've never been in a serious relationship before."

A pause, then a huge smile spread across his face, and he looked at her with such warmth and possession that she felt cherished. Finally, he smiled and pulled her down for a quick kiss. His hand made its way to the back of her head as he hugged her tight. "As long as you realize that I'm never letting you go."

Jill sighed and snuggled against his chest. That sounded just fine to her. As long as he realized that it went both ways.

After a few minutes of silence, she asked, "Well, did you like it?"

"Ummm. Like what?"

"You know what." She trailed her finger across his cheek, then lay her hand on his rump.

He grinned, eyes shut, and leaned in to her caress. "Where in the world did you learn that?"

She chuckled. She knew he was trying to keep from answering the question. He didn't want to admit that he had liked her massaging his prostate. "I like to read. Don't try and change the subject; just answer the question. Did you like it?"

He groaned and blinked his eyes open. "Yeah, I liked it. It was kind of obvious, don't you think?" Abruptly, he sat straight up again, tumbling her off his chest. "Don't you dare tell anyone about that!"

Jill was startled by his unexpected movement. Then she smiled. "I hadn't planned on it."

He squinted at her, studying her for several seconds, then relaxed and lay back down. He pulled her against him and kissed her forehead.

Jill grinned, trying her best not to laugh outright. "Besides, who would I tell—my best friend?"

His face drained of all color when it sank in who her best friend was. His eyes widened in panic.

She couldn't hold it back any longer and burst into laughter. She laughed so hard, tears sprang to her eyes.

Dash watched her with a look of abject horror on his face.

Finally, when she quit cackling and wiped the tears from her cheeks, she leaned down and kissed him. "Don't worry, there are some things that a girl just doesn't tell...even to her best friend."

"Not funny, Jill!" he growled. He tried to look stern, but pretty soon he was grinning and laughing, too.

Chapter Ten

Halloween... One year later

Jill looked up at the sky as she walked to her car. Thankfully, there wasn't a cloud in sight to mar the perfect night. It was nothing like last Halloween. She knew exactly what she was doing this year, and she knew exactly where she was going.

Opening the car door, she tossed her purse inside and got in. Tonight was going to be a good night. Somehow the prospect of a costume party didn't bother her anymore. She was getting somewhat used to socializing, thanks to Dash. He was a people-magnet, easy to talk to and fun to be around. People loved him. Wherever they went, someone was stopping him to talk. The man knew everyone, or so it seemed.

She drove to the cabin and thought about the past year. What a great twelve months it had been. Not only was she able to manage school and a relationship, but she was actually able to get a little sleep on occasion, as well. Jill grinned. Okay, so who was she kidding? She was tired most of the time, but it was worth it. She was still making great grades, and now she was having regular and great sex, too.

Dash had turned out to be the perfect man...perfect for her, anyway. He was nothing like the player she'd initially thought he appeared to be. He took his life and everyone he loved very seriously, and he tried to make himself and his loved ones full of joy. It was his biggest flaw, really. He wanted everyone to be happy, and he tended to brood when someone he cared about wasn't; then, after the brooding stopped, he'd demand that they be happy. She chuckled and shook her head. He still pretended that he called the shots. Not just with her, but with his whole family. And they all loved him, too, so they let him keep pretending.

Despite their tight schedules, she saw Dash almost every weekend. She'd either drive up to his place, or he'd come home and stay with her, and sometimes they'd actually go out and do something date-like. Lately, he'd been pressuring her like clockwork to get married; he'd even started looking for apartments midway between their homes. She'd finally decided that she was going to put him out of his misery...and her, too, for that matter. Jill grinned, imagining his reaction tonight.

Dash glanced at the door, then back to his watch. Where was she? If she didn't hurry up, he was going to lose his mind. He'd been waiting all afternoon to see her. When he'd driven down, he'd stopped off at her apartment, but she'd shooed him off, saying she had things to do before the party tonight. He'd used his time wisely, though. He'd gone out to the small cabin where they'd first met. It was stocked and ready. He planned on whisking her away as soon as she got here. He hadn't even bothered with a costume. He wasn't going to be at the party long enough to warrant one.

Just thinking about the night to come was making his cock hard. He grinned and shifted from foot to foot, trying to relieve a little pressure off his straining member. He wasn't having much luck, but at least his jeans were loose enough to not make it too noticeable.

Alex walked by in his scrubs, with a beer in hand. Then stopped and backed up. "What are you doing? Aren't you going to get into costume?"

Dash gave him a once-over, then raised a mocking brow. "Isn't that kind of like the pot calling the kettle black? Where is *your* costume?"

Alex frowned. "This *is* my costume. I'm dressed as a doctor."

He snorted. "How original."

Alex chuckled. "No, not really; just lazy."

Before he could respond with a good come-back, Dash caught her scent and then saw her walk in the door. He inhaled deeply, causing his already straining erection to twitch. He turned away from Alex and found Jill right inside the entrance, talking to his cousin Adrian, who was also a med student, but attending the medical school in Fort Worth instead of the Jill and Alex's school at Temple. Too many years of shared schooling between Alex and Adrian had proven that they'd likely spend more energy bickering and crowing over grades and exams than focusing on becoming great physicians. Dash shook his head in amusement.

Jill looked adorable dressed in a brown bodysuit. A tight bodysuit. He felt like the breath had been knocked out of him. That skin-hugging costume showed off her long legs and tight ass to perfection. She had a lengthy tail sewn onto the back of her suit that swished around the backs of her knees. What was she supposed to be? Her long hair hung loose down her back and curled above her tailbone, and she had on a headband with small, floppy ears. She turned around, and he noticed a black nose and whiskers painted onto her face. A puppy? Her sensual body ruined the illusion of cuteness, but it was obvious she hadn't tried to look sexy.

She caught sight of him finally, and a huge grin split her face.

His gums started to sting, and his eyesight went blurry. Shit! He glanced around the room. And noticed something that he hadn't earlier—There was no one but family at the party. No other pack members, no friends, just family.

Suddenly, it got eerily quiet. What the heck was going on? Jill made her way to him. He looked around at the room's occupants to find them staring at him. He got antsy.

Jill kissed him on the chin, bringing his attention to her. "What's going on?"

She grinned and got down on one knee.

He grinned back. "Uh, darlin', what are you doing?"

"I guess you've noticed that the only people here are family. Alex was sure you wouldn't realize until I got here, and by the look on your face, he was right."

Dash nodded and looked around nervously, then back down to her.

"Well, the reason for that is…we thought we'd make it an engagement party. Will you marry me, Devon?"

His mouth dropped open. His stomach tightened. He smiled and reached for her. He'd been trying to get her to marry him for the past year, and now *she* was proposing to him?

Before he could help her to her feet, she shook her head and handed him...a dog bone? Dash looked down at the rawhide bone, tied with a perky ribbon, in his hand. Then he remembered the first time he'd proposed to her, how he'd told her to throw him a bone, and he laughed. He grabbed Jill and pulled her into his arms. He was never going to let her go. His mouth slanted over hers, and he kissed her so fiercely that he forgot where he was until applause broke around them.

He leaned back and looked into her beloved face.

"Well, is that a yes?"

Dash shook his head in amusement. "Of course it's a yes, you impossible wench! I love you, Jill."

"I love you, too, Dash. Does this mean that I can start some studies on you?"

He growled. "No, it does not! But you know what...?"

"What?"

He bent down and whispered in her ear. "If you're real good, later I'll give you a bone, too."

Jeigh Lynn

Jeigh Lynn lives with, her real life hero, her husband and their two rowdy sons. She is an ex-dance instructor and dancer of over twenty-five years. She lays claim to several National and Regional Dance Competition trophies, including Showstoppers, Stars of Tomorrow and Star Power. She was also featured twice on a variety show for the BBC. Currently, Jeigh is a stay at home mom and a writer, not to mention an avid reader of Romance and Mystery. When she's not fetching Kool-Aid and swapping out video games, she can usually be found enjoying the decadence of chocolate, in between her workouts and writing. Her hobbies include, gardening, practicing her marksmanship, art, typing email to her critique partners and, of course, reading.

Visit Jeigh on the Web at www.jeighlynn.com.

Check out these titles

NOW AVAILABLE in Print from Loose Id®

THE SYNDICATE: VOLUMES 1 AND 2

Jules Jones & Alex Woolgrave

STRENGTH IN NUMBERS

Rachel Bo

VIRTUAL MURDER

Jennifer Macaire

VOICES CARRY

Melissa Schroeder

THE TIN STAR

J. L. Langley

AVAILABLE FROM YOUR FAVORITE BOOKSELLER!

Publisher's Note: All titles published in print by Loose Id® have
been previously released in e-book format.

Printed in the United States
82370LV00005B/37-42

9 781596 323339